RIVERS
RUN
TOGETHER

Also by James Sherburne

HACEY MILLER

THE WAY TO FORT PILLOW

STAND LIKE MEN

RIVERS RUN TOGETHER

James Sherburne

1974   HOUGHTON MIFFLIN COMPANY BOSTON

FIRST PRINTING   W

Library of Congress Cataloging in Publication Data
Sherburne, James, 1925–
    Rivers run together.
    I. Title.
PZ4.S5498Ri [PS3569.H399]   813'.5'4   74-6242
ISBN 0-395-19425-3

Printed in the United States of America

To Nancy, my wife and friend

In fire, chaos, shadows,
In hurricanes beyond foretelling of probabilities,
In the shove and whirl of unforeseen combustions
The people, yes, the people,
Move eternally in the elements of surprise . . .

Carl Sandburg, *The People, Yes*

CONTENTS

RIVERS

RUN

TOGETHER

CITYSCAPE
Moler the Bowler

IT WAS ALMOST 6:00 Saturday afternoon when Fred Moler and Charlie Horine drove up to the loading dock of the warehouse on South Wabash. Horine stayed behind the wheel of the squad car, and Moler got out and trotted up the steps. The boss spotted his uniform immediately and waddled up with a welcoming grin. "Why, hello, officer, I'd about given you fellas up," he said. "The set's over there by the door. I'll get you some help loading it." He patted Moler's left biceps and called over two black workmen with a loading truck. They loaded the color TV set onto the truck, jockeyed it out on the platform and down the ramp beside the squad car, and manhandled it onto the back seat. In its carton, the set was so bulky its reflection showed in the rear vision mirror.

"Big son-of-a-bitch, ain't it?" said Charlie Horine.

"Best color set money can buy," the boss said proudly, thrusting out his chin to reveal a boil previously concealed by a roll of fat. "Fully transistorized, never no tubes to burn out on you, and true-to-life color like you wouldn't believe. Tell the captain for me if he don't think it's the best picture he ever saw, I'll send him to the eye doctor and pay the bill myself."

"It's one of those made-in-Japan TVs," Moler said doubtfully. "They don't hold up like American TVs. Jap stuff always falls apart."

The boss demurred and quoted advertising claims establishing the superiority of his product. Horine interrupted impatiently: "All right, for Christ's sake. Magnavox ain't a patch on its Japanese ass. I believe it. Now can we get out of here?" His high, rasping voice had an added edge of nervousness.

The boss told one of the workmen to bring out two Model MA transistor radios. He gave them to Moler and Horine, saying expansively, "On the house, officers—in appreciation of your cooperation in this matter."

"Why, thanks," said Moler, clicking the off-on button and raising his unit to his ear. Country music burst tinnily from the speaker. "That's got a real nice sound for a transistor," he said appreciatively. The boss waved his hand as if dispersing a smell. "Much obliged," Moler said. The boss grimaced as if Moler's thanks caused him physical pain. "You didn't have to give us anything," Moler insisted.

"Will you get in so we can get started, for sweet Jesus' sake?" Horine snarled. "We ain't going to be in Sauganash till seven o'clock!" Moler settled into the seat beside his partner, closed the door, and waved to the warehouse boss. Horine burned rubber on the parking-lot pavement.

"That was darn nice of him, giving us these transistors, wasn't it, Charlie?" Moler said. "I mean, he didn't have to give us anything, you know?"

"That's because he's running a goddamned charitable institution. It's called Aid to Dependent Cops. Now will you shut up and let me drive?"

Fred Moler and Charlie Horine had been partners for more than a year. They were genuinely fond of each other, and also worked well together—two things that don't always, or even often, go together with policemen. Horine thought Moler was a little simple, and Moler thought Horine was a bit too hard on people, and both were right. Horine knew that Moler was genuinely delighted with his transistor radio, and Moler knew that Horine had shot a hillbilly kid in Uptown two months before when he hadn't really needed to.

They took the Outer Drive north. Moler looked at the sailboats moored in the harbor and thought that parts of Chicago were like a painting—white boats bobbing on blue water, and across the busy highway, the green richness of Grant Park, the glittering spray of Buckingham Fountain, the trees, the flowers; and beyond the park, the awesome backdrop of the Michigan Avenue skyline, sweeping north from the massive Conrad Hilton Hotel, past the serrations of the Loop, to the incongruously tall Hancock tower, and sedate Lincoln Park. A beautiful, beautiful city, Moler thought, with parks and statues and museums, and the zoo, and stylish shops and foreign restaurants, and Marshall Field's and the Merchandise Mart. How could anyone come to beautiful Chicago to cause trouble? It was a question Moler had returned to often during the past two weeks.

"I just don't understand it, Charlie," he said as they stopped for a red light. "Them hippies and Yippies in Lincoln Park— what in the world do they think they're doing? Practicing snake dancing, and taking off their clothes, and doing it right out where people can see them? And all that dirty talk, and smoking dope, and acting like juvenile delinquents? Why do they want to ruin the city for the people who live here? I mean, what's that got to do with politics?"

"It's the New Politics," Horine answered sardonically. "That's what they call it—the New Politics. And they're the New Left. Like in the New Deal, and the New Frontier. Everything with the word 'New' in it means you don't have to work, the government will support you, and if you're too proud to take charity, you're an asshole." The light changed, and Horine jerked the car forward.

Four miles west was the burnt-out ghetto where Mayor Daley had instructed his police to shoot to kill during the April riots; less than a mile west, in front of the enigmatic Picasso statue in the Civic Center, police had clubbed peace marchers a few days later.

Horine drove the car with great competence and supreme

contempt for physical comfort. His acceleration and decelera-
tion were jarringly abrupt, and he weaved across crowded lanes
only inches from collision. His small, wiry body was tense, and
his pale eyes never left the road. Watching him, Moler wished
he could drive as well as his partner; it was one of a number
of things in which he knew he would never be Charlie Horine's
equal. But that was all right, because there were things in
which Charlie would never be *his* equal either. Like bowling.
Charlie would never see the day he could bowl a 300 game.

Fred Moler had been born thirty-eight years before in a
neighborhood of run-down rooming houses that was later re-
juvenated as Old Town, an upper-middle-class Bohemia so ex-
pensively quaint the Molers could no longer afford to live there.
Fred joined a street gang, finished high school, and got a job
working for the city in the Streets and Sanitation Department.
The Korean war snatched him off the seat of a street sweeper
and equipped him with a gun and a uniform, each of which
he discovered to be a source of pride. After two years in the
army, he came back to Chicago and joined the Police Department. His acceptance on the force was largely due to an uncle
with clout in the 44th Ward.

Moler was a dutiful cop who did what he was told. He was
honest; even though he had been assigned to the Summerdale
Police District during the scandal that had almost destroyed
the force, no one had ever accused him of stealing anything.
He didn't shake down motorists or solicit bribes from tavern
owners. Even when he picked up payments for superior officers,
he didn't ask for an extra fin for himself. Consequently he
rarely received gifts such as Model MA transistor radios, and
the pleasure they gave him was innocent and unspoiled.

He may have been a little simple, but he wasn't dumb. He
knew that other officers didn't hold to the same standards he
did—even Charlie Horine augmented his income by a thousand
dollars or so a year—but he didn't hold that against them. For
the important thing about cops was their copness, and it did

more to bind them together than any ethical attitudes. And that was the way it should be, Fred thought. We know what it's like to do the job, and nobody else understands.

He shifted his big, well-muscled body on the seat, leaning forward to look past his partner out of the left-side window. They were passing North Avenue; Lincoln Park was on the left, North Avenue beach on the right. Normally Fred would have looked at girls in bathing suits; this day he looked at the hippies in the park instead. "Will you look at them all!" he said, marveling. "They're like ants! There must be five thousand of them!" Horine grunted, his eyes riveted on the road ahead. After a moment's silence, Moler went on: "They want to run a pig for President of the United States! You ever hear anything so crazy in your life?"

"Bunch of goddamned degenerates," Horine said flatly. "What they need is a good boot in the ass. Keep acting like that, they're going to get it, too."

The squad car skipped from lane to lane, continuing north. They passed the zoo, and the private gun club on the lake, and the crowded power boats in Montrose Harbor. A mile to the west, beyond the Rio-de-Janeiro-like façade of luxury hotels and condominiums that faced the lake and blotted up its summer breezes, lay the sweltering hillbilly slum where Horine had killed a boy, and Fred Moler had watched him die on the sidewalk, as the blood poured out of his stomach like tomato juice from a broken bottle.

When the Outer Drive ended, they headed north and west, past the broken windows of sprawling gray Senn High School, past the edge of the old Jewish neighborhood of West Rogers Park, and on until they crossed beneath Edens Expressway. From there it was only a mile or two to Sauganash, one of Chicago's few suburbs-in-the-city, where the roads curved with studied informality and there were small trees in the yards and basketball hoops above the doors of the garages. Horine slowed and turned into the captain's driveway. He stopped by the back door of the new redwood and fieldstone ranch house. A moment later the captain stepped out on the back porch dressed in a short-sleeved sport shirt with an alligator on the left breast and holding a bottle of beer. He stood drinking while Horine and Moler unloaded the color TV set and carried it into the house. They placed it where he directed, in a large living room furnished with limed oak furniture and a wall-to-wall gray rug and pictures of small children with huge eyes.

The captain offered them a beer in the kitchen, which they politely refused. "I want to thank you boys," he called after them as they were leaving. "When I'm watching the World Series this year in full, glorious, lifelike color, I'll think about you!"

When the car door was safely closed, Horine cursed the captain bitterly. Moler looked at his partner in surprise, opened his mouth to remonstrate, then thought better of it. He had learned that Horine had a capacity for rage disproportionate to the event that triggered it. He changed the subject to baseball.

They drove back to the station to check in the squad car and go off duty. Afterward, Moler suggested they stop for a drink at Maggi's, a neighborhood bar on Sedgwick Street where the alumni of his street gang met and reminisced about the days before the fags and hippies moved into Old Town. "We can have a couple of games on the bowling machine, too," Moler pointed out as the clinching argument.

The bar was nearly empty. The two policemen ordered steins of draft beer and carried them to a table near the long wooden bowling machine. On the wall beside the machine the name of the street gang was scrawled in lipstick: although pronounced "The Corps," it was invariably written "The Corp." Names of individual gang members were lettered around it—"Rubber Man," "Big Banana," "Little Turk," and "Charlie the Chink" were some of them. Seeing them there made Moler feel at home, and he smiled comfortably as he put two dimes in the coin slot and rested his fingers on the cool steel bowling puck.

On the first game he scored 279 to Horine's 240. He was in the sixth frame of the second game, with five strikes showing on the electric scoreboard, when a group of ex-Corp members entered the tavern. They picked up beers and came back to the bowling machine, where they kibbitzed throughout the remainder of the game, which Moler won with a 268.

One of the new arrivals asked if they were going over to the park tonight and move the freaks out. Moler shrugged his broad shoulders. "I'm off duty. The only thing me and Charlie are going to do is drink some beer and bowl a few lines on the machine."

"No, but what about the cops on duty?" the other persisted. "The paper said Daley ain't letting nobody stay in the park after eleven o'clock. What happens if they won't leave when they're supposed to? You guys gonna arrest them, or just bust their ass?"

"Ask Conlisk," Horine said dryly. Conlisk was the superintendent of police.

"No, but you got to have some idea," the other argued. "I mean, some of them people are real revolutionaries! You gonna treat them with kid gloves while they put LSD into Lake Michigan and turn everybody in Chicago into a drug addict? You gonna let them fire-bomb the Grant Park garage and close down the Loop, for Christ's sake? I mean, where do you draw the line?" He was so excited he spilled beer on the smooth wooden alley of the bowling machine. Moler quickly wiped it up with a paper napkin.

Horine looked at the man dispassionately. "You're so worried about revolutionaries, why don't you send over some of the Hippie Head-Hunters from the Corps to take care of them? They're great at working over hippies one at a time—how come they don't go in for mass production?"

"Law and order is your job, not ours," said the man accusingly.

"Then why don't you just shut up and let us handle it?" Horine concluded. He slipped two more dimes into the slot. "Okay, Fred, third time's a charm," he said to his partner. "Get us two more steins, and I'll beat your ass."

2

MUSICAL MOMENT
IN A CONFERENCE ROOM

MALCOLM TOLLIVER had come of age during the Eisenhower years and thought of them as a trough between two swells. If he had been born a generation earlier, he might have fought in the Spanish Civil War, or at least in World War II; he might have stood beside Walter Reuther at the Battle of the Overpass, building the UAW; he would have heard Woody Guthrie and read *The Grapes of Wrath* the first time around. Or if he had been born a few years later, he could have reached his manhood beside Martin Luther King in the Selma march, or called for insurrection through a bullhorn at Berkeley.

As it was, he sometimes thought to himself, his nostalgia was for "Rock Around the Clock" and "The Purple People Eater," his revolt had consisted of reading Jack Kerouac, and the struggle of his youth had been to land a copy job at an advertising agency.

It was time for the 10:00 news, and he turned on the TV and watched it half-comprehendingly. His brain was still sluggish from a pitcher of before-dinner martinis, and the announcer's voice was like a phonograph needle on a warped record, skipping whole bars of meaning. Pictures flashed on and off the screen with bewildering rapidity, too fast to allow his eyes to change focus from one to the next. The announcer was talking about protesters in Lincoln Park, and the police, and Senators Humphrey and McCarthy. Before Mal could untangle it all, the subject shifted to Vietnam.

"Oh, screw it," he said, switching the set off. "I'm going to make a drink."

"Great," said his wife Marilyn coldly. She was sitting across the room from him in the Mama Bear chair (as she had christened it in a more whimsical time), reading a woman's magazine, her long, slender legs tucked under her flat hips. Her chisled Nordic face didn't look ten years older than the wedding picture on the mantel—it looked ten years tireder, ten years more estranged.

Mal asked if she wanted anything. When she didn't answer, he went to the kitchen and made himself a strong bourbon and water. He returned to the living room and sat down. For a few moments the only sounds were the rustling of magazine pages and the clinking of ice. Then Mal spoke:

"Those kids—those Yippies. It's pitiful, you know? Them thinking they can buck the system. All they got to do is tell Hubert and ol' LBJ what they want, and that's the way it's going to be. Don't want to get killed in the war? Okay, just tell Hubert, Hubert ol' buddy, you better stop the war, 'cause we won't go. So Hubert, he stops the war, right? Shit." He drank from his glass. His wife looked at him expressionlessly. "Nobody's going to stop the war," he went on. "Nobody important *wants* to stop it. You know why? 'cause nobody important has to go! Only people have to go are immoral pot-smoking punks who aren't old enough to vote, right? Screw them! Who cares?"

"Why don't you go to bed, Mal?" Marilyn said impersonally. "You'll pass out if you keep on drinking."

"*In vino veritas*, my dear. You've never understood that. The only time I ever penetrate to the inner realities is when I'm sinking like a stone into an alcoholic stupor. My vision is crystal clear, but the hell of it is, it only lasts a few minutes. Then nighty-night. It's a stone drag."

"I've noticed."

"I've noticed you noticing," he said nastily. He took a drink.

Silence descended again, while he recalled an incident that had taken place at the agency the day before. He debated telling Marilyn about it. Experience had taught him that her reaction would probably be the opposite of what he hoped for; on the other hand, he felt a need to share the memory with someone.

"You won't believe what happened at the office yesterday," he said. "Talk about the *naiveté* of punk kids thinking they could buck the system! We were in the conference room, waiting to start the market research meeting. I mean it was wall-to-wall reactionaries, you know, everybody talking about the awful radicals in Lincoln Park, and how the city was going to have to do something about them before they bitched up the Convention, and like that. Everybody was giving his opinion, and finally somebody asked me what I would do if I were mayor, and I told them I'd bring over some spades from the S.C.L.C. 'What for?' they wanted to know. 'To teach the kids how to sing "We Shall Overcome," ' I replied with a dazzling smile."

"I'm sure they appreciated that," Marilyn said.

"No, listen—I'm getting to the important part of the story now," Mal said, excitement coloring his voice. "There they are, see, all looking at me as seriously as if I were reciting the Lord's Prayer, considering my suggestion, you know? Not wanting to leap to any irresponsible conclusions on insufficient evidence. And then Tobin, that little prick of an assistant account man, he says, 'You know'—Mal raised his voice an octave and pronounced his words prissily—'You know, I don't believe I've ever heard the words to "We Shall Overcome." How does it go, Mal?' And a couple of the others say, 'Yeah, Mal, how does it go?' And would you believe it, there's not a single damn person but me in that conference room who even knows the tune, let alone the words?"

He shook his head wonderingly and took a swallow of watered bourbon. Marilyn didn't say anything. "Dig this," he went on. "The year of Our Lord nineteen sixty-eight—Montgomery and Medgar Evers are past history. The Civil Rights

Bill and school integration are the law of the land. And there
I was in that goddamn mahogany boardroom, with fourteen
Brooks Brothers types staring at me like I was singing an
obscure Bulgarian folk song, belting the first verse of—" He
began to sing, in a bravura style:

> "We are not afraid—
> We are not afraid—
> We are not afraid, today.
> Deep in my heart
> I do believe,
> We shall overcome some day.

"How's that for a mind-blower? THEY HAD NEVER EVEN HEARD
THE SONG! NONE OF THEM HAD EVER EVEN HEARD THE GOD-
DAMNED SONG! But those kids in Lincoln Park expect their tinny
little voices to carry all the way to the Democratic Platform
Committee at the Amphitheatre! That's what I mean by pitiful!"

"Mal, how long do you think you'll hold down your job if you
do things like singing radical songs during meetings?" Marilyn
asked. Two small worry lines appeared between her eyebrows.
It was the nearest thing to emotion her face had shown all
evening.

He stared at her incredulously. "That's not the point of the
story! That's not what I'm talking about!" he cried. "I'm not
talking about me! I'm talking about this goddamn town, and
this goddamn country, and this goddamn world, can't you see?
Ten million people are willing to die for a song, and five miles
away nobody even knows the tune! Doesn't that mean anything
to you?"

They stared at each other. Mal's face was twisted with a
pain he couldn't articulate; Marilyn's face was cool and only
mildly concerned. Mal emptied his glass, spilling a trickle of
liquid down his chin. Marilyn stood up and placed her magazine on the end table beside her. "Well, I'm going to bed," she
said. "Don't stay up drinking much longer, dear. Remember,

tomorrow's the Beer-beque in Glencoe—you don't want to be hungover for the festivities." She turned off the light by her chair and left the room.

Mal stayed up another half-hour. He made himself a fresh drink and drank it walking back and forth through the first floor of the house, looking at the furniture and the books and the records and the pictures on the walls, at the framed copy-writing awards in his study, at the snapshots of himself and Marilyn, and then of himself and Marilyn and Lisa, at national parks and beaches and ski lodges. After a while it occurred to him that it would be fun to walk to the Friendly Neighborhood Saloon and see who was there. He was almost out the door when he remembered that the Friendly Neighborhood Saloon was fifteen miles away, down on the Near North Side. They had lived in their own house in Evanston for almost four years, and the nearest saloon was on Howard Street, and it wasn't very friendly, and it wasn't very neighborhood.

There was no point in trying to read anything, because he knew from experience he never remembered what he read when he was drunk. The only thing left was to go to bed. So he did. Marilyn was apparently asleep when he climbed in beside her.

Sunday was the kind of day that prompts wives in the sub-urbs to call one another and plan family outings. Mal reflected that Marilyn would have been on the phone before nine, if they hadn't already made plans to attend the Beer-beque—he winced at the word—at a colleague's Glencoe split-level. But since the day's social life was nailed down, she was free to sleep the sleep of the righteous. Wives are something else, he thought, shaking his head and wincing at the resulting stab of pain behind his eyes.

He had risen early to take advantage of the morning quiet and get some work done. He filled the coffee pot and plugged it in and then stood on the front porch waiting for it to perk. There was still a touch of dewy freshness to the air, but it was

fading fast, and the heavy August sense of overgrowth was
taking its place. *It's going to be a bitch,* Mal thought. It was
very quiet; except for the occasional unmelodic *creek* of star-
lings, the only sound he could hear was the murmur of traffic
on Sheridan Road two blocks away. *It's like a comedian's joke
about Philadelphia,* he thought. His eyes moved slowly across
the front yard, the dogwood bush, the maple tree, the gravel
driveway. *Goddamned grass needs cutting. It must be the
fastest growing grass in the world.*

He went back into the house, found that the coffee was done,
and poured himself a cup. He carried it to his desk, set it beside his typewriter, and forgot about it as he began to write
the 1969 Marketing Plan for HydroDent, the Hygenic Dental
Appliance *Your* Dentist Recommends. At most advertising
agencies, Marketing Plans (the words are invariably capitalized) are written, or at least assembled, by account executives;
however, at Mal's agency, the Pauncefoot company, some of
the accounts were handled on the Copy-Contact principle,
which meant that copywriters served as their own account
executives. Mal disliked the system, believing it undermined
a writer's professionalism by subordinating his creative ability
to his salesmanship. If he could have found another employer
willing to match the $20,000 annual salary he was making at
Pauncefoot, he would have gone like a shot. But the brutal
truth was that the ads he had in his sample book, created under
the Copy-Contact system, simply didn't look like the work of
a top creative man. So he stayed on at an unappealing job,
cranking out lusterless advertising he knew his clients would
buy, caught in a vicious circle of mediocrity, and slowly growing older in a young man's business.

He worked for half an hour, describing the marketing history
of the HydroDent appliance. He was beginning the section on
Sales Opportunities for 1969, when his six-year-old daughter
Lisa came downstairs.

She was a pretty child, but her appearance was so dominated
by her thick-lensed glasses it was difficult to remember any-

thing else about her. Also, the dentist said her molars would come in crooked, and in two or three years she would have to start wearing braces, and every time Mal thought about what she would look like then, it depressed him and he compensated for it by indulging her whims.

"Good morning, Daddy. Is Mommy up yet? What are we going to have for breakfast? What are you working on Sunday for?" Before she could think up any more questions, Mal stood up and opened his arms wide, and she jumped into them and hugged him until he groaned in protest.

"Hey, you're getting too darn strong! You ought to have those muscles licensed as deadly weapons, like a boxer's fists!" He set her down and took one of her hands, and they walked into the kitchen. "Mommy's still asleep, honey. What do you say you and I fix breakfast this morning, and surprise her?"

"Can we have waffles?" she asked eagerly. He made a face expressing comical helplessness, but she overrode it: "The recipe's in the book, Daddy! All you have to do is read it out, and I can make them!"

"Well, if you say so." As he found the page in the cookbook and took eggs, milk, and butter from the refrigerator, he thought once again that his daughter was his hostage to Fortune. He glanced at her, a bespectacled miniature Marilyn, wearing a flannel nightgown of robin's-egg blue, her honey blond hair tousled from the pillow, her face composed in an expression of firm concentration as she sifted flour into a mixing bowl. *Thus children doth make cowards of us all.*

He fried bacon to go with the waffles and sent Lisa upstairs to wake Marilyn. As he waited for them to come to the table, he switched on the kitchen radio and heard the report of a small disturbance in Lincoln Park the night before. In the course of clearing the park persuant to the mayor's orders, a policeman had hit a reporter, and eleven demonstrators had been arrested. Mal listened carefully, frowning. Marilyn came into the room before the report ended.

"Good morning, Mal. Well, aren't you glad we moved out

of Old Town? It sounds like it's not even safe to walk the
streets down there anymore." She looked, he thought, as if
the idea pleased her.

"Yeah? Just wait till the Gay Panthers take over Evanston.
Then you'll find out what real horror is. There's honey or
syrup for the waffles—how's that for class?"

She looked at him curiously. "My, we're feeling chipper this
morning, aren't we? The Marketing Plan must be going well."

"I guess I just love my work," he said, drawing a chair out
for his wife. A sudden feeling of hopelessness blew through
him like a winter wind, and he shivered. "Besides," he said
brightly, smiling at his two womenfolk, "there's the Beer-beque
in Glencoe to look forward to."

Mal hadn't finished the HydroDent Marketing Plan when he
left for the party that afternoon, but he persuaded himself he
would wrap it up when he got back home afterward. The Beer-
beque was about what he had expected; he drank beer until he
was tired of it and then switched to whiskey. To avoid talking
to Marilyn, he talked too much to the wife of an art director
from Leo Burnett; to avoid arguing about the hippies and the
Convention, he clownishly performed a Cossack dance on the
grass. He paid for both avoidances: Marilyn scolded him for
what she considered his ludicrous lewdness all the way home;
he acquired what were probably indelible grass stains on his
new white flannel pants when he fell over backward in the
middle of "Meadowland." When they got home, he announced
he was going to sit out in the back yard and have a resuscita-
tive drink before resuming his work on the Marketing Plan. He
was still there when Marilyn put Lisa to bed at 9:00, as well
as when Marilyn put herself to bed at 10:00.

The Marketing Plan remained unfinished when Mal stumbled
upstairs at midnight.

3

I SHOULD HAVE BEEN
A PAIR OF RAGGED CLAWS

OVER THE LAST TWENTY YEARS, Mike Rogoff had discovered that
if there was anything less lucrative than the radical book business, it was the porno business, and if there was anything less
lucrative than the porno business, it was the art film business.
At least that was true for him; other people may have made
fortunes selling *Masses & Mainstream* in the forties, smuggling
in copies of *Tropic of Capricorn* in the fifties, and exhibiting
Andy Warhol movies in the sixties—but for Rogoff, they had
only been parallel roads to the poorhouse. As he sometimes said
to himself with gallows humor: "Fourteen years in the Communist Party, and I had to quit before I found out what a disaster the Capitalist System really is!"

But the irony of his present predicament taxed even his saving ability to laugh at himself. He found himself facing bank-
ruptcy because his employees, in a motion picture theater spe-
cializing in revolutionary art films, had gone on strike against
him. And the cream of the jest was this—the union represent-
ing the employees was the IWW—the Wobblies! *The Wobblies!* he told himself incredulously. *A relic! Big with Sacco
and Vanzetti! My God, they were a joke by the time I went
to Harlan County in 1931! How did they get so unfunny again?*

He turned on the house lights in the empty theater and
limped into the auditorium, his eyes automatically noting the
slashed seats, the unidentifiable or unmentionable stains on the

carpeting, the carved graffiti on the armrests. It was an old theater, built in the late twenties as a neighborhood house, then, as the neighborhood declined, switching to ethnic films— first German, then Greek, then Mexican. When Rogoff had taken it over in 1965, the smell of poverty in the walls was beyond fumigation. But he had mitigated it with Lysol, decorated the peeling walls with agit-prop posters and portraits of Che and Mao, and renamed it the "cinéma vérité"—lower-case initials definitely intentional. For the first year, he thought he had something good going. In spite of an inconvenient location on Grand Avenue west of Halsted, he generally had good houses during the week, and lines formed on the sidewalk on Saturday nights. But business slacked off during 1966 and 1967, and this year he sometimes found himself exhibiting a film for an audience of ten or fifteen people.

And now there was this union trouble. When he had first found out that his young employees had all joined the IWW, Rogoff was amused, much as if they had taken to wearing raccoon coats and dancing the black bottom. But that was before he had discovered a continuing shortage in the receipts from the popcorn and soft drink machines. Investigation satisfied him that the source of the shortage was a provocative blonde with the unlikely name of Dagmar Correlli, and Rogoff fired her. She didn't choose to be fired, however, and the other four employees rallied around her in militant solidarity. At this minute they were on the sidewalk outside, picketing the box office of the cinéma vérité, and the theater had been closed for two days.

The hell of it, Rogoff thought, was that in similar circumstances any other movie house in Chicago would be doing business as usual. But he knew his customers. Although he could replace the striking employees and open his doors within hours, nobody would come to see his movie, because nobody who liked the kind of movie he scheduled would cross a picket line to see it.

The empty auditorium depressed him. He turned off the house lights and went to his cramped little office, intending to do some work. But he found it impossible to concentrate, and after five minutes gave it up and left the theater. On the sidewalk he turned to lock the front door behind him. The five pickets stopped walking back and forth. Four of them stood glaring, while Dagmar Corelli, wearing an army NCO's khaki shirt that almost concealed her brief tennis shorts, tossed her platinum hair and stepped up to him. "What's the matter, Mike? You get lonely in there, talking to yourself?" she asked in a husky, taunting voice.

He looked bleakly at the placard she was carrying, which read, "ON STRIKE AGAINST ANTILABOR PIGGERY." *Me, the antilabor pig*, he thought. *After Harlan County, and Teruel, and North American.* "Hello, Dagmar," he said. "It's a nice day for picketing. But I'm sorry if I'm keeping you from the park."

"Look, when are you going to get some smarts and stop acting like Orson Welles in *Citizen Kane*? We can keep you closed down for the rest of the summer, you know? When are you going to sit down and negotiate?"

"And take a thief back on my payroll? Not today, anyway. But keep in touch." He bobbed his head in the sketchiest suggestion of a bow and took a step around her. She moved to block his way.

"Don't give me that thief bullshit," she said in a louder voice. "You know the only thief in this society is private property! Why don't you admit you're a sellout, and the only thing you care about is squirreling it away and keeping your hook nose out of trouble? You old-time Communists—Jesus, what a put-on you are!"

Her usually sallow complexion had become swarthy with anger, and Rogoff reflected that it made her silver blond hair more unbelievable than usual. "Goodbye, Dagmar. Make sure nobody goes into the theater, will you?" He stepped quickly past her and walked along Grand Avenue toward the trolleybus stop on the corner, ignoring the cries of "Fascist" and "Pig" that followed him.

He rode east a half mile and walked two blocks north to Mary Cvetla's apartment. He let himself in with a key and called, "Mary? Are you home?" He was answered by a small boy in the living room, watching TV.

"Mamma's gone to the park," the boy said. He had large dark eyes in a wizened face, making him look like a marmoset. He was Mary's son, Stanley, and Rogoff was fond of him.

"Hi, Stash," Rogoff said cheerily. "What's purple and weighs twenty tons?"

"I give up."

"Moby Grape! Did your mother go by herself?"

"No, Johnny went with her. They only left a half-hour ago. You want to watch TV with me?"

"Okay. Let me get a beer first." He went into the cramped little kitchen and found himself a can of Meister Brau. *That goddamned Johnny*, he thought glumly, *he's circling like a vulture. If I don't watch out, he'll be in before I can say Boo. Maybe he already is.*

He carried his beer back into the living room and sat down on the couch beside the sickly ten-year-old. They watched an old western, Stanley with riveted concentration, Rogoff inattentively. *What do you expect?* his thoughts ran on. *You're a sixty-five-year-old man, and Mary's not forty yet—not even thirty-nine. She's an attractive woman—desirable—very smart for a Polack. It was only a matter of time until some guitar-playing schmuck took her away from you. Or did you think you were such a lover she'd never want another?*

He squirmed in embarrassment and drank most of his beer. A commercial came on, and Stanley asked him if he knew any more riddles. "Sure. How do you put six elephants in a Volkswagen?"

"I don't know. How do you?"

"Three in the front, three in the back." Stanley wrinkled his nose, indicating disapproval. "I guess Johnny's been coming around a lot lately, right, Stash? I mean, every day or so, right?" Stanley shrugged. "Does he ever spend the night here?" Rogoff went on, despising himself. "You know, like it was so late he just decided to sleep on the couch or someplace?"

Stanley frowned at him. "The movie's back on, Mike," he said sternly, and then glued himself to the screen again.

An hour later Mary let herself in the front door. She was alone. "Why, Mike, I didn't know you were coming over. You should have told me—I would have been back sooner." She was a good-looking woman, full-bodied but not fat, who wore her gray-streaked black hair around her shoulders in a too youthful style. Her myopia caused her to look worried even when she wasn't.

"It's all right—Stash and I have been watching Randolph Scott cut 'em off at the pass. You been over to the park?"

"Yeah, wow. You should see it over there. It's wild. There's got to be two thousand kids there doing their thing, and police riding around on their three-wheelers, right on the grass, but all good-humored, you know, nobody mad or anything." Mike asked if she thought there was going to be any trouble, and she said it didn't look like it to her. A lot of the kids were stoned, but there were neighborhood people there too, having picnics, playing ball, and pushing around baby buggies. "It's just a beautiful Saturday afternoon in the park. I wish you'd been there, Mike."

He took a deep breath. "Oh, I don't think that would have worked out," he said in a flat voice. "If Johnny was with you, I think three would have been a crowd, don't you?"

She glanced at him sharply, then looked away. "I don't know why. We were only taking a walk. It's not as if we were making out in the bushes."

"Like other times, you mean." *Why are you doing this now?* he asked himself. *Haven't you got enough troubles without bringing this to a head too? Because,* he answered himself,

*there are times when you've got to dump it all on the table and
look at it.*

"Mike, I think we better have a talk," she said calmly. She
opened her purse and took out some change. "Stanley, run
over by the 31 Flavors and get yourself an ice cream cone."
After the boy had left the apartment, she sat down beside
Rogoff on the couch. "I don't think it's working out," she said.
"I don't think we're good for each other anymore, Mike."

The dull certainty of loss flowed through him like nausea.
"Good for each other? You sound like McCall's magazine."
He stared unseeingly at the TV screen. "Look, don't give me
'Good for each other,' all right? If you like it better with
Johnny, just say so. I can understand that. You think I'm not
perfectly aware I'm sixty-five years old? It's been a while since
anybody called me the Wild Bull of the Pampas. A woman
with healthy desires, I can understand how she might want
it more often than a man of my age can oblige her—"

"Mike, listen and shut up. Don't start off feeling sorry for
yourself because you're sixty-five. That's not what we're talking about. It's not how potent you are, it's your attitude. You
think like an old man, and it's no fun making love to an old
man."

They talked about it for ten minutes, Rogoff bitterly making
a case for her need to have a youthful lover and Mary denying
the need. Then Stanley came home with the last half of his
ice cream cone, and the three of them sat in front of the TV
set together. After a few more minutes, Rogoff got up and
made ready to leave. Mary said, "Let me have the key to the
apartment, Mike."

Rogoff separated it from his key chain. "Somebody waiting
for it?" he asked innocently. She looked at him levelly, frowning her habitual slight frown, and shrugged. He handed her
the key and smiled at the boy. "So long, Stash—I'll see you in
the funny papers," he said.

"So long, Mike," the boy answered. Rogoff left the apartment, closing the door behind him, and walked down the stairs into the warm early evening air.

The next day Mike stayed in his apartment all morning and afternoon, leaving only to buy lox, bagels, and cream cheese for his ritual Sunday brunch. While he ate, he listened to records on his monaural, lo-fi phonograph. He played old 78s with Asch, Okeh, and Vocalion labels—Big Bill Broonzy, the Honeydripper, Leadbelly, the Almanac Singers, Woody and Pete, Songs of the Lincoln Battalion. He sat in a worn maroon easy chair, head back, eyes closed, and sang along, his fingers tapping the rhythm on the upholstered arm: "Die Heimat ist weit,/ Doch wir sind bereit./ Wir kämpfen und siegen für dich:/ FREIHEIT!" *We're fighting and winning for you— FREEDOM!*

So long ago, so long long ago! The kids talked about The Movement as if it had just burst squalling into the world last Wednesday. But he remembered it when it was called The Party. He had been an organizer in the early thirties, before he had gone to Spain, and his body still bore scars both of eastern Kentucky and Aragon. But no scars of World War II, he thought ironically—even though he had left The Party in 1940, he was considered a "premature anti-Fascist" by the War Department and sidelined throughout the war.

In *Darkness at Noon*, Koestler writes about revolutionaries who fall out of the swing. The swing is society, pushed off from tyranny by the French Revolution, ascending with apparently uncheckable impetus toward the blue sky of freedom. But gradually the rate of ascent slows down; the swing hesitates, becomes immobile for a second, then begins to fall backward with ever-increasing speed, carrying its passengers from freedom back toward tyranny.

He who has gazed upward instead of clinging on, Koestler says, becomes dizzy and falls off. Rogoff fell off when Hitler and Stalin agreed to divide Poland between them.

He finished his brunch and opened a can of beer. *I am an old man,* he thought. *What did Eliot write?* "*Here I am, an old man in a dry month.*" The beer tasted good. *Or maybe just* "*A dry old man,*" he added, taking another swallow and sighing. "*I should have been a pair of ragged claws—*" *That's another good one. And how about* "*stale, flat and unprofitable*"? *It's not Eliot, but it's got that same joyous lilt.*

The last record on the changer ended, and he replaced the stack with another stack, this time consisting of cherished old jazz records with Commodore and Blue Note labels—Bechet, Tommy Ladnier, Pee Wee Russell. *Pounding Hearts Blues* dropped first, with Sid Catlett's thudding drums, Teddy Bunn's insinuating guitar, the clear trumpet of Frankie Newton and the burred trombone of J. C. Higginbotham, all tied together with the magic of Sidney Bechet. When it was finished, he thought, *My God, but that was music!* And before he could stop himself, he added meanly, *What have they got today— Engelbert Humperdinck and The Fugs!*

His attention began to wander. He stood up and looked at titles in his bookcase but couldn't find anything that interested him. He considered going to the cinéma vérité to do some work, but the prospect of meeting Dagmar Correlli and crossing the picket line was more than he could face, and he opened another beer instead.

Remembering, worrying, fidgeting, pacing, changing records, and looking out of the window, Mike Rogoff wasted half the afternoon, until he had consumed enough beer to feel sleepy. Then he took a nap.

It was almost dark when he woke up. He sat up on the couch, pulled on his long nose and sucked his teeth, and gazed with distaste at the unwashed brunch dishes and leftover food. He didn't want to clean up the mess, he wanted to escape from it, so he left his apartment and went to Mister Dooley's.

Like many Old Town saloons, Mister Dooley's was built around a gimmick. Six-foot photographic blowups of old-time

Irish politicians decorated the walls: "Bathhouse John" Cough-
lin and "Hinky-Dink" Kenna, the lords of Chicago's First Ward;
"Honey Fitz," the Kennedys' progenitor in Boston; Mayor Curley giving a last hurrah from behind bars. Between the blowups hung framed broadsides, sheet music of forgotten campaign
songs, and menus from political victory banquets. Apparently
there were plenty of people in the neighborhood who found it
comforting to do their drinking under the benign gaze of Hi-
bernian Democratic machine politicians. Rogoff had never
understood why, but he liked the place anyway.

It was a little after 8:00 and Mister Dooley's was filling up.
The air was smoky, and the juke box was playing an Irish bal-
lad. Rogoff made his way to an empty stool beside a woman
with tousled hair and a pug nose, who sat with her heels
hooked over the top crossbar of her stool, her chubby knees
wide apart and her skirt hiked up over her thighs. As he sat
down, she glanced at him, grinned widely, and shouted,
"Rogoff! How the fuck are you?"

Rogoff smiled in spite of himself. "Mamma told me there'd
be days like this, but I thought she was just anti-Semitic," he
answered. He signaled to the bartender to draw him a stein of
draft beer. "Hi, Goody—where's Frank?"

"Probably out balling a chick somewhere. Haven't seen the
son-of-a-bitch in a week."

Goody's smile vanished and she stared glumly at the glass in
front of her, her mercurial spirits plunging at the thought of
her ex-husband's probable activities. Robin Goodpasture and
Frank Finley had been married for five years, an almost inter-
minable period for both of them, marked by spectacular drunks,
fights, adulteries, separations, and reconciliations. Finally
Frank had reached a point where he had had to choose between
getting a divorce and becoming a West Madison Street wino.
He chose the divorce, and he and Goody set up separate apartments. Neither was strong enough to sever the relationship
completely, however, and they remained awkwardly bound to-

gether, in an estate that sometimes provided sex without love, and sometimes love without sex. Frank wrote a column for a Chicago daily newspaper; Goody divided her working hours between a loan company office on the Near West Side and a woman's group opposed to the Vietnam war.

Rogoff frowned at a gigantic blowup of Jim Farley at the 1932 Democratic Convention. "What the hell are we doing in here with those goddamn mick crooks on the walls, while the Great Dumpling is outside shafting the whole democratic process?" The Great Dumpling was a current epithet for Mayor Daley. "You'd think we would have had it up to here with Irish machine politics."

"It's not just Irish machine politics," Goody replied, glad to shift her thoughts from her ex-husband. "The Irish only add the ineffable charm—they're the spoonful of sugar that makes the medicine go down. It's also the Polack machine, and the Wop machine, and the Nigger machine, and the Wasp machine, and the whole motherless capitalistic machine. Shit, Mike, they've all sold out! Napalm the gooks! Napalm the goddamn gooks!" She made a sweeping gesture with her arm, almost upsetting Rogoff's beer. "Why the hell not? It's not as if they're human!"

In most bars people would have been staring at Goody by this time, but to the clientele of Mister Dooley's, she was unremarkable. "Watch your right hook," Rogoff said, as he prudently moved his stein a foot down the damp bar. "Look, don't New-Left me to death tonight, all right? Your friend Dagmar Correlli and her buddies are taking care of that department very nicely, thank you. Just let me sit here and drink my beer with a pretty girl."

Goody's sympathy was as spontaneous as her indignation. Her face showed instant concern: the bold eyes softened, the pretty mouth pursed. She put one small hand over his. It was cold from cupping beer steins. "Look, Mike, that strike is a bummer," she said earnestly. "I know how you feel about it—

but think how Dagmar feels. You're attacking her identity as a responsible human being. Nobody should ever do that to another person."

"I beg to differ. I'm attacking her competence as a thief, and any inept lawbreaker should have the right to do that to any more inept lawbreaker, particularly if it's his money that's involved." She opened her mouth to argue, but before she could say anything he went on: "Enough about Dagmar, please. I'll put some money in the juke box. What do you want to hear? 'The Rising of the Moon'?"

"How about *Johnnie, I Hardly Knew You*"?

"Okay, that will keep us in stitches." He went to the juke box, put in a quarter, and pushed the buttons for *Johnnie, Hey Jude*, and *Gentle on My Mind*. Threading his way back to the bar, he exchanged greetings with a number of newspaper people. He commented on this to Goody: "We're up to our ass in the press here tonight, have you noticed? I wonder who's back in the city room minding the store."

"Well, there's nothing happening at the hotels or at the Amphitheatre tonight. I guess some of the guys think the action may be up here, in the park."

"What do you think, Goody?"

"Well, here comes Richard Harding Davis—why don't you ask him?" She nodded toward a tall, red-haired man who had just stepped through the street door. Her eyes sparkled, and her chunky body straightened from its boneless slouch. She raised herself six inches from her bar stool. "Hey, stud—over here!" she called.

Frank Finley saw them and spread both arms in a gesture of welcome appropriate to greeting prodigal sons. He was a notably ugly man, whose oversized features gave him the look of a wrestler with acromegaly. His large hands and feet appeared to be too heavy for the thin bones attached to them. He was wearing a dirty seersucker suit and a very narrow tie almost a yard long. He pushed against the bar between Rogoff

and Goody. "My cup runneth over," he said happily. "The
quondam wife of my bosom and Tiresias the sage together in
the same oasis! Ah, there's balm in Gilead tonight!"

"If you won't butcher any more classical phrases, I'll buy you
a beer," Rogoff said. Finley agreed, and Rogoff signaled the
bartender with three fingers and put money on the bar.

"What's going to happen in the park tonight, Frank?" Goody
asked. The noise level had risen, and she had to shout to make
herself heard.

"The fuzz plan to kick some ass, and I wouldn't be surprised
if they do." He took a long swallow of beer from Goody's glass,
and when he lowered it, there was a white foam mustache
under his nose. "I talked to Rennie and Jerry Rubin, and they
say they're not going to try to move the kids out tonight. They
figure if it's going to happen, let it happen now."

"They see themselves as martyrs, right?" Rogoff asked sardonically. "Some martyrs."

"I don't know from martyrs, but they think it's time to find a
place to stand. And, man, all you got to do is look at the week's
casualty report from Nam, and you got to admit they have a
point."

"You think finding a place to stand means nominating a pig
named Pigasus for President of the United States?"

"That was last week. This is this week. You watch—it's going to be a whole new ball game."

"And the name of the game is Revolution!" cried a deep,
histrionic voice beside them. They recognized Aaronstein, a
well-known semiprofessional actor and neighborhood character.
He was obviously three-quarters in the bag. "Tremble, ye
Philistines, ye scriveners and publicans and toss-pots and hus-
sies—the Lion is in the Streets! The Little Foxes are spoiling
the Tender Grapes! The Wolf is in the Fold, and the goddamned Goose Hangs High!" He turned his profile to them and
thrust out his chin.

"Jesus, dig Mount Rushmore!" said Goody. "Hey, Aaronstein, stay loose, man! There's a long night ahead."

"A Long Day's Journey into Night, you mean—the Night of the Long Knives!" the actor said scornfully. "What do you say to that?"

"I say you've got more shit than a Christmas turkey," Goody said firmly.

Rogoff told the bartender to give Aaronstein a beer before he started doing the porter's scene from Macbeth. Then he turned away from the performance and resumed his conversation with Goody and Frank.

Time passed beerily. The folk music from the juke box gave way to acid rock. More people pushed into the already crowded tavern. The toilet in the men's room became clogged. The smoke was so thick it was difficult to see Mayor Curley's picture from the end of the room. Aaronstein made a florid farewell and wheeled his bicycle out from behind the door, where he always kept it, and rode unsteadily away.

At about 10:00, Dagmar Correlli and Mark Phillips came in. Phillips was a big, curly-headed young man who looked like a football lineman from an Ivy League college. He came from an Eastern family with money, had received an excellent education, and used his considerable abilities to radicalize the street gangs of Chicago, by means of an underground newspaper he edited and called *Grease*. Rogoff had met him once or twice before and considered him both unprincipled and dangerous.

Rogoff and Dagmar recognized each other simultaneously. Rogoff half rose from his stool and reached for his change on the bar. Dagmar tugged Phillips by the arm and butted her way toward them through the crowd. Before she spoke, Rogoff recognized the slack-lipped belligerency in her sallow face. She was, he reflected with resignation, a mean drunk. He sank back on the stool.

"Well, if it isn't the famous American radical and well-known humanitarian, Old Fart-Face What's-his-name." Dagmar sneered. "Look, Mark—you ever wonder what happens to old Communists? They don't fade away, they just turn to crud."

Rogoff turned his hands toward her, palms up, as if to show

he wasn't armed. "Dagmar, this is neutral ground. I don't want
to fight with you. I'll even buy you a beer. So be nice."

"Up yours, you cop-out bourgeois son-of-a-bitch!"

Mark Phillips put his hand on Dagmar's buttocks and patted.
"Baby, don't be a hard-nose—if the man wants to buy us a
beer, let him buy us a beer. A beer doesn't know who's buying
it." He spoke with an edge of mockery to his voice, and Rogoff
wondered whether he or the girl was being mocked. Dagmar
glowered, but accepted the offered stein. Phillips ordered a
half-and-half, which cost twenty cents more than a beer. Rogoff
paid.

A booth opened up, and they all moved into it. Goody, Dagmar, and Phillips began an argument on civil disobedience.
Goody argued that the act of protest should have some relationship to the injustice being protested—as for instance, the
burning of draft records was related to the injustice of drafting
men for an imperialist war. Dagmar and Phillips disagreed;
they refused to grant that draft-record burning was inherently
any more suitable a protest against the draft than fire-bombing
an underground parking lot or stink-bombing the board of trade
at high noon. Rogoff kept out of the discussion because he had
had enough of theoretical arguments in his life. Frank Finley
left the table and returned with five shot glasses of tequila, and
they all had Mexican boilermakers. The noise increased, and
the pounding juke box became almost inaudible.

Then Frank looked at his wristwatch and announced that it
was after 11:00. "I've got to go see Abbie Hoffman turn into a
pumpkin. Who's coming with me?"

Rogoff's immediate feeling was that it was time to go home.
He began to excuse himself, but Goody and Frank both urged
him to come along. Dagmar pointedly looked away and didn't
say anything, so partly to spite her, Rogoff allowed himself to
be persuaded.

Other customers followed them out, and the group that

headed down North Avenue toward Lincoln Park numbered nearly twenty, of whom three besides Finley were newspapermen. Everybody was at least half drunk, and it was a fine summer night.

4

CITYSCAPE
A Summer Sunday

SUNDAY IN THE CITY had begun sunny and cool, with a brisk breeze off the lake. The few early-morning swimmers and sunbathers on the beaches lay in the sand or on the rocks watching the tiny white triangles on the horizon execute their maneuvers. Tardy gulls sat on the pilings, scanning choppy waves for a late breakfast. The sky looked freshly scrubbed, and visibility was so good that from the point at North Avenue Beach, near Lincoln Park, you could see clearly as far north as Uptown, and as far south as Grant Park and the Conrad Hilton Hotel.

At the Hilton, most of the Democratic Convention delegates had arrived and were asleep in their rooms. The McCarthy people were exceptions. Bright-eyed and wearing fresh aftershave lotion or cologne—"Clean for Gene"—they clustered in the corridor outside the fifteenth floor McCarthy suite, in the coffee shops, and in the lobby, talking about the issues that concerned them: the Vietnam plank in the platform, the seating of the rival delegations, Teddy Kennedy's plans. Occasionally someone would mention the news about the police clearing the demonstrators out of Lincoln Park the night before, but it was not a major subject of conversation.

Some of the wives of Humphrey delegates went sightseeing. The Museum of Science and Industry and Maxwell Street were two popular attractions. Visitors to the museum were not aware of the great non-Wasp subcity curving around them, because the trees of Jackson Park screened the black slums of the Bronze-ville ghetto from sight. But on Maxwell Street there was a delicious sense of foreignness. Not as many Jews as they had expected, but more of everything else—Gypsies, blacks, In-dians, Latins, Arabs, hillbillies.

And, sandwiched between a bridge table piled with defective rabbit-ears TV antennas and a ten-foot monolith of worn auto-mobile tires, a woman of indeterminate race, dressed in the robes of an Aztec princess, wrapped a defanged rattlesnake around her neck.

A Negro man in an apartment on Drexel Avenue got out of bed and went to the bathroom down the hall. On his way back to bed he turned on the radio and picked up a half-filled bottle of Richard's Wild Irish Rose wine from the table. He lay down beside the naked woman on the bed and tilted the bottle to his lips. Then she drank, and then he drank again, as the radio announced that the police had been forced to clear Lincoln Park of demonstrators the night before.

The man laughed. "Ain't that just tough shit, though? Now the pigs are messing over their own people!" He set the bottle on the bedside table and slid one arm around the girl's shoul-ders. Her eyes crinkled at the corners with amusement as she waited for his kiss.

In the early morning, the only people in Lincoln Park were neighborhood dog walkers, but about 9:00 the hippies, Yippies, and Mobe people—short for National Mobilization Committee to End the War in Vietnam—began to reassemble. By noon, as the temperature rose into the eighties, the crowd was larger than it had been the day before, and still growing. Uniformed police, helmeted and dressed in short-sleeved blue sport shirts, were present in large numbers on the streets that bordered and intersected the park—Clark, Stockton Drive, Cannon Drive,

Ridge Drive. Police motorcycles threaded through the crowd, motors roaring.

Overnight, the mood of the demonstrators had changed. During the preceding days, in spite of the apocalyptic New Left rhetoric, a holiday mood had hung over the park. A Yippie leaflet announcing projected activities offered "Pin the Tail on the Donkey, Pin the Rubber on the Pope, and other normal, healthy games." There was an overabundance of scatological talk, which made the serious Peace people suspect the Yippies were frivolous, which, in turn, made the Yippies suspect the Peace people were square. Until Saturday night, this polarization was an important fact among the assembled dissidents.

But on Sunday the people in the park were annoyed. Not angry, not frightened, but annoyed. Annoyed with the mayor and the police for running them out the night before, annoyed with Abbie Hoffman and Allen Ginsberg for advising them to leave, and annoyed with themselves for the docility with which they had trooped out.

This common annoyance worked against the tendency toward polarization. As the heat rose to the low nineties, and the afternoon sun lowered in the sky, freaks and straights looked at each other speculatively, each group wondering what kind of ally the other would make in the days and nights ahead.

Mayor Richard J. Daley caucused with the Illinois delegation. He enjoyed himself enormously, because he didn't often get the chance to play the role of national, as well as local, leader. He listened to two hours of panegyrics and saw himself elected chairman of the delegation. When he left, his face was as pink and round and smiling as a Toby mug.

5

RED ROVER, RED ROVER

SARI SCHRAM AND TED BAKERFIELD arrived in Lincoln Park about 1:00 Sunday afternoon. They had been hitchhiking west since Friday morning, and they were tired and grubby. They were both dressed in blue jeans and carried knapsacks, so the things that distinguished them most from one another were Ted's beard and Sari's guitar.

Sari was twenty-one, with a long-legged dancer's body and a face like an Old Testament queen. Her father was a successful Broadway director and play-doctor, and she had grown up in a luxurious and intellectual home. She had attended private primary and secondary schools and had completed her sophomore year at Barnard when she became active in SDS and dropped out to help establish a Free School in the Bronx. The Free School had been a success, but Sari found it gave her no satisfaction—her sense of guilt over the privileged life she had led required a more violent commitment to counterbalance it. She had been searching for such a commitment in the East Village when she met Ted Bakerfield.

Ted was a doctor's son, born and raised in a small town in southern Michigan, and also an only child. He was twenty-four, a diabetic, and had graduated from Oberlin two years before. Since then he had sampled a number of dishes on the New Left smorgasbord—drug and draft counseling, underground newspapers, two months in an Arizona commune, and two weeks of Chavez-watching in Delano, California—but had failed to find what he was looking for. When he met Sari, they had both heard plans for the Yippie "Festival of Life" to be celebrated in Chicago in August as the counterculture's answer to the Democratic National Convention. They decided to attend it together.

Hand in hand, they stepped off a Clark Street bus and walked into the park. After a few steps, as though by unspoken agreement, they stopped and stared about them. "Oh, wow!" said Sari. "How about this?"

As far as they could see, the green grass was hidden from sight by the packed humanity that walked, stood, sat and lay on it, mostly teen-agers and young men and women in their early twenties, but with a leaven of children, the middle-aged, and the elderly. Rock music throbbed in the air like a single, collective pulse. A tightly packed crowd of three or four hundred surrounded an improvised speaker's platform, but within a few yards the amplified oratory lost its content and became merely another line of musical counterpoint. Policemen, some grinning and some grim, gunned their three-wheelers, skirting picnic blankets and hootenannies. Frisbees sailed lazily through the air, thrown and caught by men who looked like unfrocked fraternity members. Balloons popped. The breeze was spiced with marijuana and charcoal cooking.

Sari and Ted began walking toward the Garibaldi statue looking for someone they knew. They had come to Chicago without coordinating their plans with either the Yippies or the Mobe and had no idea where they would crash for the night. This didn't worry them, because they assumed they could always sleep in the park.

"Hey, Sari, baby, what's happening?" called a boy with a thin, large-pored face and a Ho Chi Minh beard. He was sitting on the grass with five or six companions, drinking beer. As Sari approached, he tilted his head to one side and touched his cheek with one finger. "Just lay one on me right there," he said.

Sari bent and kissed him. Ted smiled tolerantly. "Oh, wow, Lucky Lindy!" Sari said. "I should have known you'd be here. You're a bird of ill omen if I ever knew one."

"Wherever the shit is preparing to hit the fan, I'll be there, Ma," Lucky Lindy said, imitating Henry Fonda in *The Grapes of Wrath*. "Wherever little potheads are sucking their joints, I'll be there—"

"You're too much, Lindy. Listen, this is Ted. Ted, this is Lindy. Ted was in Delano with Cesar. We're together." She smiled proudly and smoothed her heavy dark hair as Ted and Lindy shook hands, using the Black Panther grip.

"Glad to meet you, man," said Ted politely.

"Like park it and have a beer, babe," Lucky Lindy answered. He pointed to each of the others in the circle around him and introduced them, using first names and nicknames only. Ted and Sari nodded to each in turn and accepted two cans of beer.

"Where you figure to crash?" Lindy asked Sari, his small, red-rimmed eyes moving down her body in frank appraisal. She shrugged. The park, if they couldn't find any place else, she guessed. "Yeah, well, there may be a little flak about that," Lindy said, grinning. "The Great Dumpling says nobody sleeps in the park on account of a historic old ordinance which he passed yesterday. The word is, the fuzz is going to bust anybody who tries to sack in here tonight."

"What are they going to do, bust two thousand kids?" asked Sari unbelievingly. "No way, man—they don't have that much room in the jails!"

"Maybe they don't plan on putting them in jails. They didn't last night. Look, all I'm saying is there's a bunch of us staying in a church over on Sedgwick, about three blocks due west of here. You're welcome to fall in there tonight, if you want to."

Aware of Lindy's eyes upon her, Sari reached for her guitar and tuned it. Ted stretched out beside her and closed his eyes, wrapping one arm around her hips with casual possessiveness. His silky beard lay on his thin chest like a friendly animal. Lucky Lindy opened another beer and sat on the grass beside

Sari. She began to sing, in a strong, true, but not especially melodic voice:

> "When the moon is in the seventh house,
> And Jupiter aligns with Mars,
> Then Peace will guide the planets,
> And Love will steer the stars—"

The voices of Lindy and his friends joined her in the familiar chorus:

> "This is the dawning of the Age of Aquarius,
> The Age of Aquarius . . .
> Aquarius . . . Aquarius . . ."

Only Ted was silent. Behind his closed eyes and peaceful expression, his mind worked restlessly. What was going to happen tonight, he wondered. Would the police try to drive them from the park, and would they resist? Would there be violence, and if so, how much? Shooting? Killing? Was this what happened in the Age of Aquarius? And if so, then how did the Age of Aquarius differ from the Johnsonian Age, the Age of MacBird, Defoliation, and the Free Fire Zone?

Ted wasn't any more of a coward than most of the other people in the park, which meant that he had a bit more courage than the national average. But violence upset him, both intellectually and emotionally. When he thought about it, he felt much the same as when he went off his diet and his sugar level dropped—his muscles became rubbery, his head light, his skin both cold and sweaty. It seemed to him that violence was outside the area of permissible human interaction, any time, anywhere, regardless of justification or rationalization.

He had felt that way as long as he could remember, and in his mind his abhorrence of violence was somehow connected with his diabetes, because he became aware of the physical effects of both at the same early age. His belief in The Movement was based in his vision of it as nonviolent, and his uneasiness came from his knowledge that not all of his fellow New Left radicals agreed with him.

Most especially, and most importantly, Sari didn't.

Passive resistance, he knew, would fit her character the same way it would have fitted Irgun or the Stern Gang in Palestine in 1948. There was an ancient pacifist tradition running through the history of the Jews, but it was not the tradition that nourished her; she drew her sustenance from Esther and the Maccabees and Masada.

Sari put her guitar aside, and the conversation was resumed. Ted kept his eyes closed. One of Lindy's friends launched into a surrealistic flight of fancy that involved dosing all the Democratic delegates with Spanish fly during TV prime time. This prompted the other members of the group to try to top the original suggestion, and Ted gradually slipped off to sleep on a wave of Rabelaisian excess.

When he awoke, dusk was falling, and people were starting to light trash fires on the grass. Ted got to his feet, and he and Sari found a wastebasket full of newspapers, leaflets, mustard-damp paper napkins, and empty beer and soft-drink cans. They brought it back and fed whatever was inflammable to the little flame Lindy had kindled.

Looking at the young faces around the fire, washed by flickering light and shadow, Ted was reminded of chilly summer evenings at Boy Scout camp in Michigan, when he was a boy. It had been exciting to be away from home, huddled close to a campfire, surrounded by vast darkness and unknown dangers. Beside him, Sari's face was exalted. He took her hand and squeezed it.

The police motorcycles no longer roared through the crowd, but on the roads that bordered Lincoln Park the police Task Force assembled in strength, quietly. When the curfew announcement was read over a loudspeaker at 10:30, there were

more than 450 policemen prepared to sweep approximately
1000 protesters out of Lincoln Park. Half the police were armed
with shotguns and tear-gas canisters; all, of course, carried
service revolvers, Chemical Mace, and "batons," which once,
in less image-conscious times, were called "billy clubs."

By that time there had already been two miniconfrontations
between police and protestors, neither one of which Ted and
Sari had seen. The first had taken place when some Yippies
tried to move a flat-bed truck into the southeast end of the
park to use as a rock-band platform. A squad of ten officers
halted it. A crowd immediately surrounded the truck, pressing
close to block its withdrawal with their bodies. Blows were
struck, and two men and a girl were roughly flung into squad
cars and driven away. The episode dwindled to cursing and
shoving.

An hour or so later another group of young demonstrators
pushed twenty-odd policemen up against a fieldhouse wall and
immobilized them there for half an hour, until reinforcements
charged the crowd, clubbing as they came. They broke through,
leaving a trail of bloody heads behind them. The white-jacketed medics from the Medical Committee for Human Rights
began bandaging wounds.

Sari and Ted were crouching in front of their dying trash fire
when the curfew announcement sounded through the park.
Around them in the darkness was the sound of constant movement, as medics and clergymen circulated giving advice, much
of which was contradictory. Some people were talking about
a march to the Loop; others insisted that everyone stay in the
park and defy the curfew; the preachers offered their churches
as dormitories. Amplified voices called out appeals to reason
and incitements to riot in bewildering succession.

Although they were both eager and both frightened, in Sari
the eagerness outweighed the fear, because nothing in her life
had prepared her to believe she could be hurt. Ted, who knew
better because he was a doctor's son, shivered from the adrena-

lin chill that comes with helplessness in the face of danger.

They were debating what to do when a startling apparition appeared in the firelight. It was Aaronstein the actor, straddling his bicycle, his hair disheveled, his body atwitch, his eyes wild.

"Here's where it begins, you yellow Yippie bastards! Revolution! Revolution now! Stay in the park and fight the pigs! Parks belong to the people! Are you going to let them piss all over you, or are you going to stand up and fight?"

"Jesus Christ, man," said Lucky Lindy reasonably, "you're really wigged, you know? Stay loose, or you'll take off like a goddamned Roman candle."

Aaronstein raised his clenched fist over his head. In his mind he saw the Bastille before him, or possibly the Winter Palace. "Pigs eat shit! Dump the Hump and Hump the Dump! There's a new world being born tonight, you assholes—are you going to turn your back on it? It's the Revolution! Make way for the Revolution!" He put one foot on a pedal and began to move forward into the darkness, fist still thrust into the air. "Make way for the Revolution!" he called repeatedly as his voice dwindled in the darkness.

Sari looked at Ted, her large dark eyes gleaming in the dying firelight. "What do you think—do we stay here and bear witness? Or do we go trashing in the streets?"

Ted licked his dry lips. He took a deep breath and said, "I'm scared shitless, but I'm not just going to walk out of here because they say so. Let's stay and see what happens."

There were murmurs of agreement from Lindy and his friends. The circle of seated bodies contracted around the embers, as each of the waiting young people sought to lessen the distance between himself and his neighbors.

Shortly after 11:00 the police skirmish line moved westward across the park. Motorcycle police weaved back and forth fifty yards in front of the line. At first, everyone retreated before them, but, as they approached Stockton Drive, near the western edge of the park, they found the young people had stopped running. The motorcycles drew off, and the police line approached the protesters who awaited them on a gentle incline sloping upward toward the road.

Fred Moler and Charlie Horine were near the center of the police line. Moler was tired and confused. He had been on duty since 10:00 that morning, and he couldn't understand why these people wouldn't leave Lincoln Park when they were told to. He saw no connection between a war that two of his nephews were involved in 10,000 miles away and the four-letter insults thrown at him by disrespectful upper-middle-class hoodlums. Most of all, he couldn't understand why all the people of Chicago, including the newspapermen and TV reporters, and especially the priests and preachers of the city, weren't standing behind their police force, giving them support and encouragement in this battle against anarchy.

His pride was hurt, and this made him feel betrayed. He wasn't a bloodthirsty man, but it was easy to tell himself these kids needed to be taught a lesson. And as long as nobody was killed, it was permissible to enjoy the instruction.

Horine, he knew, felt much more bitterly about it. Ever since the Summerdale police scandal, Horine had nursed a special hatred for newspapermen, whom he put on the same moral level as pimps, pushers, and the American Civil Liberties Union. Hippies and peaceniks he simply considered vermin, to be brushed out of sight any time they had the temerity to appear around decent people.

The difference between him and his friend, Moler realized, was that while he was shamefacedly anticipating a little ass-kicking, Charlie wanted to hurt people—a lot of people—and hurt them bad.

Ahead of him, Moler saw the protesters formed in a long line, facing the police, waving their hands and shouting: "The parks belong to the people!" and "Hell, no, we won't go!" A pretty girl with long blond hair called out an obscenity that shocked Moler, another oinked like a pig, a third yelled an invitation to "Join us!"

A lieutenant with a bullhorn ordered them to move within thirty seconds. The reply was increased defiance. The lieutenant waited until the time was up, then looked over his shoulder at his men. "Let's go get them!" he ordered.

The skirmish line charged up the slope into the crowd. Moler was suddenly wildly excited, his breath short, his blood racing. A boy with an Indian headband, seventeen or eighteen years old, was in front of him. The boy looked at him with flinching defiance until Moler raised his club to strike. Then, too late, he ducked and tried to run. Moler caught him on the back of the head, and the boy fell to his knees and crossed his arms over his head to protect it. Moler hit him on the side, just over the kidney, and the boy rolled over on the ground, assuming a fetal position to escape further injury.

That'll give him something to remember! Moler thought jubilantly. A girl thrust her face close to his and screamed "Fascist!" Disfigured by rage, her face looked more animal than human. She spat at him, and saliva speckled his face. Startled, he pulled back, swinging up his club between them. The wood struck her under the nose, throwing her head back and tumbling her down on the grass. Blood erupted from her nose and mouth. "Pig! Murdering, filthy pig!" she shrieked, her eyes wide and unbelieving.

Moler stood stock still, staring back at her. *I shouldn't have done that!* he thought. Then a second later he amended, *No, I didn't do anything—she did!* He raised his club, and the girl scurried away like an injured crab.

Beside him Charlie Horine called, "Fred, here!" He turned to see his partner kneeling on a prostrate young man in bib overalls, one uniformed knee in his crotch, the other in his stomach, one hand clutching a thick black beard, the other bringing down a baton across the side of a face. The man writhed desperately, trying to shield his head with his arms. "Help me, Fred—hold this cocksucker's arms for me!" Horine yelled. Obediently Moler pinned one arm with his foot, and Horine, by releasing the beard, was able to immobilize the other arm with his left hand. Then he began to work on the man's face, laying the wood across the nose, the upper teeth, and the side of the jaw. He would have ground the end of the stick into the man's eye sockets, but Fred stopped him. "That's enough, Charlie! Don't kill him!" Panting and cursing, Horine rose to his feet, the wooden club dangling loosely from his hand. Fred took his arm and pushed him forward. "Come on, buddy! Let's go get us some more!"

The police line swept the park clean. Driving the crowd before them, the club-swinging officers crossed Stockton Drive and the parking lot west of it, only stopping when they reached Clark Street. There, on the sidewalk with the park behind them, they re-formed. The street was jammed with cars, most with their horns blowing. On the far side of the street, overflowing the sidewalk, were between one and two thousand people—Yippies, hippies, peaceniks, neighborhood residents, reporters, street-gang members, Mobe marshals and medics, TV cameramen—all packed together in a yeasty mass of fear, anger, and exhilaration. Photographic strobe lights blazed from the crowd, illuminating police and protesters alike.

"Red rover, red rover, let Daley come over!" the young people shouted. "Streets belong to the people! Pigs eat shit!"

For ten minutes the police maintained their position on the east side of Clark Street, while the crowd continued to shout taunts at them. Then, without warning, they charged into the street, zigzagging their way through the jammed cars, and tore into the packed humanity on the far sidewalk.

Mike Rogoff was standing with Goody and Frank Finley near the Eugenie Triangle when the police attacked. One officer charged straight at Goody. In the press of the crowd she was unable to back away, and Frank pushed himself in front of her. "I'm a reporter!" he yelled. "Here are my press credentials!"

"Fuck your credentials!" The cop struck Finley on the side of the head, sending him to his knees. "Goddamned reporters, we're going to fix your ass!" He raised the club again, and instantly Goody leaped at him, her fingers clutching at his face. He warded her off with one arm and swung his club viciously. The blow caught her on the upper arm, sending her lurching against Rogoff. "Whore! Whore!" the policeman yelled, striking at her again. "How do you like that, you Commie whore?"

In avoiding his second blow, Goody lost her balance and sprawled backward on the concrete, momentarily as helpless as a turtle turned upside-down. The policeman leaped toward her. Rogoff, mastering the fear that thinned his blood and tasted like bile in his mouth, interposed his body between the woman and the cop. On hands and knees he straddled Goody, accepting the blow that exploded against his back, the kick that jarred his hip, the second blow across the ribs. *Nothing ever changes. It's Harlan County again—it's the Ebro again. Maybe this time I'll die.*

He lay on the sidewalk with Goody's body stirring feebly under him, and Frank Finley kneeling beside him and staring at the blood he had wiped from his head. The policeman charged off after a new target, and Rogoff struggled to his feet. The pain in his lower back was incredible. "Frank, we've got to get out of here!" he said to the reporter. "That crazy bastard could come back and kill us!"

Frank slowly rose. "I told him I was a reporter. You heard me, Mike. I told him I was a reporter!"

"So next time don't tell him. Here, let's get Goody up." The two men raised the woman to her feet, and Mike supported her until she found her equilibrium. She was crying, and the sobs shook her body like a chill. "You're all right, honey. Come on, let's get away from here," he said soothingly. He put an arm around her and drew her down the sidewalk toward Wells Street. Frank followed them, his tall, thin body lurching awkwardly, his wrinkled seersucker suit splashed with blood. They stepped over unconscious bodies and hurried past a group of four policemen beating a white-jacketed medic. A few feet further on, two officers had a fifteen- or sixteen-year-old boy pinned against the side of a parked car and were taking turns hammering his head. They saw another policeman corner a newspaper photographer and smash his camera to pieces.

"Mike, the cops—they've taken off their name tags!" Finley said suddenly. "There had to be an order for them to do that!"

"You can write about it tomorrow. For tonight, can we please get away from here?" They pushed their way through the congested traffic on Wells Street and continued west on Eugenie until they were out of the immediate neighborhood of the police attack. As the sounds of violence receded in the summer night, it was as if they were awakening from a collective nightmare. Goody stopped crying and started cursing.

After a few moments Frank said, "What you're saying is absolutely true, and very well put, but I would rather hear it over a drink." Rogoff agreed, and they headed for Mister Dooley's.

Violence swirled along Clark Street like white water over rapids, and the crowd melted away under the force of the police charge. Not only were young people assaulted—area residents, sitting on their front porches, or retreating into their own apartment house vestibules, were clubbed and sprayed with Chemical Mace. Dazed newsmen discovered the hatred the Chicago police had concealed from them for years, and clergymen found that their dog collars, like the white jackets of the medics, served only to invite attack.

Half the people on the street had disappeared when a bizarre incident occurred, which promised to move the action back into Lincoln Park again. Aaronstein the actor, now half out of his head with role-playing, liquor, and a sense of personal invulnerability, suddenly appeared behind the police line, on the sidewalk beside the park. He was accompanied by a twelve-year-old boy waving a Vietcong flag, and the two were illuminated by a hand-held floodlight carried by a TV technician beside

them. "Revolution . . . NOW! Revolution . . . NOW!" bawled
the actor. He was dripping wet from having been thrown,
along with his bicycle, into Lincoln Park lagoon. His long hair
was plastered down over his bony forehead, and his heavy-
lidded eyes were shut in a transport of dramatic intensity.
"What do we want? REVOLUTION! When do we want it?
NOW! Back to the park, you yellow-bellies! REVOLUTION
. . . NOW!" He strode down the sidewalk with long, loose-
jointed steps, with the boy beside him grimly waving his flag,
and the media technician trotting to keep up.

A handful of Yippies dashed across Clark Street to join him,
but before a group could accumulate, policemen attacked the
actor from both sides, driving him off the sidewalk and into the
street, with his long arms wrapped around his head, elbows
as angular as the knees of a grasshopper. He ran stumblingly
through the stalled traffic, disappearing down a side street. The
boy with the Vietcong flag dropped it and scampered after
Aaronstein. A policeman broke the TV technician's floodlight.

The demonstrators remaining on the street had either pulled
back north of Lincoln Avenue, or were herded into LaSalle
Street, in the short block between Eugenie and North Avenue.
Policemen harried the outer edges of the crowd, striking at
legs and buttocks, pushing frightened people south, where another police detail waited to disperse them to the right and left.
In fifteen minutes LaSalle Street was clear.

Two blocks north, on Wells Street facing the park, there was
a narrow empty lot sandwiched between Oxford's Pub and the
Second City's theater. The summer before, Second City had
operated a beer garden there, but the experiment was a failure,
and this summer the lot had stayed empty until The Movement, with the consent of the owners, converted it into a command post and medical station. Behind its seven-foot wall and
iron-barred gate were crowded seventy or eighty young men
and women, the larger part of whom were injured. Volunteer
medics worked busily over them. Mobe leaders and Yippies

argued demonstration strategy, and correspondents for the radical and underground press interviewed them and one another
on the night's happenings. Aaronstein the actor, tilted back
against the wall in a broken kitchen chair, smiled with closed
eyes, and said repeatedly, in his resonant baritone, "Oh, hairy,
man—oh, shit!"

Ted Bakerfield and Sari Schram squatted close together in a
corner of the patio. Lucky Lindy was with them, lying quietly
on his back, with eyes inflamed and a bandage around his head.

Ted's voice was an exhausted monotone; he sounded as
though it was all he could do to form the words. "The thing
that wipes me out," he said, "is the sheer *viciousness* of it. I
mean, Christ, they wanted to *kill* us!"

"Oh, no, they didn't!" Sari answered harshly. "If they'd
wanted to kill us, they'd have done it. They didn't want to
kill us, only scare us and make us run away. And they did,
they did—oh, goddamn them, they did!" She shook her head
furiously. "We've got to go up against them again, Ted—we've
got to show them they can't push people around this way!"

Ted was silent a moment. He put one hand over his eyes
and squeezed gently on his eyeballs. "You think it'll come out
any different the next time?" he asked quietly.

"Hell, yes, it'll come out different! You better believe it!"
She glared at him furiously, as if daring him to disagree. He
continued to shield his eyes with his hand. Her expression
changed, softened, and she touched his forehead with her fingers. The skin seemed hot and dry to her. "Ted, have you had
your shot today?" she asked. He shook his head slowly. "You
idiot, do you want to go into shock?" she scolded. "For heav-
en's sake, Ted, you need a keeper!" She hurriedly unbuckled
the straps of his knapsack and dug inside it; in a few moments
her hands emerged with a disposable plastic hypodermic syringe and a vial containing 10 cc's of NPH insulin. She set them
on the bricks beside her and rummaged through the knapsack
again until she found a package of cotton balls and a bottle of

rubbing alcohol. She dampened a cotton ball with alcohol, pulled up Ted's sleeve, and rubbed a spot on his upper arm. "Here, hold your sleeve up now!" she ordered. She was filling the syringe with Ted's daily dose of eighty units of insulin when a voice beside her barked, "Jesus Christ, do you damn junkies want to get us all busted?"

She looked up angrily. A Mobe marshal, a straight with horn-rimmed glasses like Rennie Davis, glared down at her indignantly, his lips pursed in disapproval. "It's insulin, you schmuck. He's a diabetic. Do you mind if he doesn't die?"

The marshal's expression changed to one of discomfort. "Well, get rid of that needle when you're done, okay? There's no telling what the fuzz would do if they found it lying around in here." Sari snorted, and the marshal turned away.

Sari administered the injection, and Ted sighed deeply. Then she repacked the syringe, vial, cotton, and alcohol in the knapsack. They sat in silence for a moment, and then Sari said plaintively, "They got my guitar. I think I dropped it in the parking lot. It cost me two hundred dollars—it was a Gibson."

"Maybe it's still there," said Ted.

"Fat chance—those pigs would stomp it just for laughs." Lucky Lindy groaned and wiped at his eyes with his fingers. A passing medic stopped and bent over him, warning him to keep his hands down if he didn't want to do himself permanent damage. Lindy put his hands back at his sides, the fingers trembling against his blue denim pants. Sari touched his shoulder. "Take it easy, Lindy—try to go to sleep," she said.

For a few minutes Ted and Sari sat watching the activity around them. Then Sari asked, "Were you very scared tonight, Ted?"

Ted laughed shortly. "You're fucking-A I was scared."

"So was I. Oh, Jesus, was I ever! But you know what? I think they were, too. The pigs. I think they were as scared of us as we were of them. You know?"

"I didn't see any of them running away."

"That's because they had the guns and the clubs and the Mace, and we didn't have anything. But they were scared anyway. They wouldn't have acted the way they did if they weren't scared."

Just then, on the other side of the wall that separated the patio from Wells Street, Fred Moler and Charlie Horine walked along the sidewalk. The street was nearly deserted; the long Sunday night was nearly over.

"In there is where their medics hang out," Horine said. "Used to be a beer garden. Now they've made a fucking hippie hospital out of it."

"Yeah?" said Moler. "I bet it's full up tonight."

"You know it." Then, as an idea struck him, Horine stopped and detached his aerosol spray can of Mace from his belt. Grinning at Moler, he rose to his tiptoes and stretched his arm above his head. The spout of the Mace can was an inch or two above the top of the wall.

He pressed the release button and walked slowly along the full length of the wall.

6

CITYSCAPE
Workday

FOR MOST PEOPLE in Chicago, Monday, August 26, was like all other Mondays: they had to go to work. Many of the people who worked downtown came in cars and buses that sometimes sped and sometimes crawled past Lincoln Park. There wasn't much to see there: a few hippies, a few policemen, a few neighborhood citizens walking dogs. It was difficult to relate the quiet scene to the reported violence of the night before. Since the newspaper stories were more interesting, the passengers in the cars and buses reburied themselves in their *Tribunes* and *Sun-Timeses*.

The park was very pleasant. The police had used little tear gas the night before, and an off-shore breeze had dispelled most of that. Only by sitting or lying down in a sheltered area close to trees or bushes was it possible to smell the gas at all—although after fifteen or twenty minutes in the park one did become conscious of smarting eyes and a rasp in the throat not much worse than is experienced by a smog-breathing Los Angelino most days of the year.

After 9:00 the kids began to come back from the crash pads and church basements where they had spent the night. Those who could afford it stopped for breakfast on Lincoln Avenue or looked for relevant paperbacks at the drugstore in the Lincoln Hotel; those who couldn't came hungry and bookless. A few of the more militant wore crash helmets.

By noon the rock groups were playing and the speech-making began. The police on the three-wheelers and in the squad cars watched the increasing activity sardonically, thinking, *If they want more, we'll give them more.* Police and protesters were as tightly bound in symbiosis as the crocodile and the crocodile bird, the one lazily yawning as the other darts among its teeth to feed.

A mile away a caucus of neighborhood ministers met at St. Paul's church to discuss plans for preventing, or at least alleviating, the violence they feared would erupt that night. After some discussion, they agreed to meet on Clark Street, opposite the park, at 10:45, fifteen minutes before curfew.

As the day progressed, there were rumors among the police of Yippie plans to paralyze the city—opening fire hydrants, calling in false alarms, fornicating in the middle of the main streets during the afternoon rush hour.

People believe what they want to believe.

About 2:45 in the afternoon, Tom Hayden and Wolfe Lowenthal were arrested while trying to organize a march on the Conrad Hilton Hotel. The charges were obstructing the police, resisting arrest, and disorderly conduct—for allegedly letting the air out of a police car's tires.

They went off to jail, and shortly thereafter Rennie Davis led 500 young people to Central Police Headquarters in protest. The march was so orderly that office workers along the route didn't know it had occurred until they saw it on TV that night.

7

THE IMAGE-FACTORY

MAL TOLLIVER began his Monday with the *Today* show, sipping coffee and wishing he hadn't stayed so long, and drunk so much, at the Beer-beque. Most of the news was about Chicago, and he couldn't keep his mind on it.

"Well, today's the big day," Marilyn said brightly. Unlike Mal, she was a morning person. "I wonder which Georgia delegation they'll seat. That will certainly show which way the wind is blowing, won't it?"

"Hmmmh?"

"Whether the convention votes to seat the Julian Bond people or the regular party hacks," Marilyn explained pleasantly, "will show how much strength the liberal wing has. If they win on the Bond seating, it means they have a better chance of passing an antiwar plank for the platform."

"Oh." Mal looked at her morning-fresh, attractive face with mild incredulity, thinking, *How does she stay on top of everything all the time? She must represent the ultimate triumph of the Media: unconscious force-feeding.* "Yeah, well, I hope old Julian makes it—I've always been a fan of his brother, James."

Marilyn frowned. "James? I don't think I've ever heard of him."

"James Bond—you know, secret agents, sexy ladies, fiendish tortures. Bang, bang," he said spiritlessly. "Let it pass."

They watched the program until quarter of eight, when Mel

left for the el station. He bought a paper, waited on the platform for three minutes, and jockeyed for position in front of the sliding car doors when the train pulled in. He was successful enough to claim one of the few remaining empty seats. He arranged his paper in the commuter's fold and moved his eyes down the columns of type. The train screeched and swayed along the venerable tracks.

At Howard Street he put the paper aside and looked out the window. *From here to the Loop there's eight miles of back porches. If you only traveled by el, you'd never know Chicago apartment buildings had fronts to them. Hell, maybe they don't.* He remembered the punch line of the old psychiatrist joke: after the poor paranoid leaves, reassured that the cities of America really do exist, the shrink dials a telephone number and whispers conspiratorially, "Set up New York." *Set up Chicago—back porches only,* he thought. *Reverse Potemkim— the ass-end view.*

He left the train at Grand Avenue and walked east to Michigan. As he drew nearer the office, he began to worry about the unfinished Marketing Plan for HydroDent and the meeting that was scheduled in the afternoon to discuss it. He had a full two hours' work to put in before the plan could be typed up, and he wasn't sure he would be granted two uninterrupted hours. *Why didn't I finish it yesterday? For a while there, I was really rolling.*

He stopped at the coffee shop on the first floor of his building and picked up a large carton of black coffee and a sweet roll. It was ten minutes to nine when he sat down at his desk on the twenty-ninth floor, and the office of Pauncefoot Associates was so quiet he could hear the hum of the central air conditioning. The people who made all the noise never arrived before nine.

He opened the coffee carton, burning his fingers and spilling a few drops on the desk. "Damn." Sipping the coffee and munching the sweet roll, he leafed through the pink job-requisition forms awaiting his attention. It was worse than he had expected. In addition to the HydroDent Marketing Plan, four other requisitions also had Monday due dates: a mailing to dentists announcing a new model HydroDent appliance; a group of commercials using the talent on Captain Kangaroo to sell Brek-first, the breakfast you pour from a package—Mister Greenjeans and Mister Moose to be featured; suggestions for a name and associated image for a proposed shopping center in Scottsdale, Arizona—the Chairman of the Board of HydroDent had an interest in this; and a TV commercial promoting the annual chocolate festival of Clutter's Candies—this year's theme, The Little People Invade Candyland. Close behind the five front-burner jobs were six others requiring action by the end of the week.

The sweet roll tasted like saccharin-flavored newsprint. He washed it down with the last of the coffee and shuffled the requisitions into a neat stack. Loud voices came from the hallway, indicating it was 9:00. *Time to go to the john,* he thought gratefully. He took a copy of *Life* from his in-basket and walked quickly to the fire stairs—the men's room was on the floor below. He was glad to find the booth directly under the ceiling light unoccupied, because it was the only one of the three bright enough for comfortable reading. He locked the door, lowered his trousers, and opened the magazine. King's-X; he was safe.

But he wasn't. The hall door opened, and a pair of brown and white saddle shoes with red rubber soles entered the washroom. Mal recognized the shoes, and thought about raising his own feet above the bottom of the cubicle door to prevent similar recognition by the man outside. He realized the newcomer, confronted by a closed door with eighteen inches of feetless space below it, would immediately penetrate the deception. He sat motionless, hoping the saddle shoes would walk to the urinal and walk out again.

"Mal? Mal Tolliver? Is that you in there?" asked Loren Price

in a querulous voice. Loren was the assistant account executive
on Clutter's Candies. Normally easygoing, if a little lightweight,
he panicked under pressure.

Mal didn't answer. Loren said doubtfully, "Mal? Mal, answer me! I know that's you!" Mal held his breath. Loren said,
"Mal, don't be this way! Goddamnit, you're not fooling anybody!" Mal coughed in an artificial tenor voice.

Then, incredibly, Loren's face appeared between Mal's knees.
"You son-of-a-bitch, you can't fool me!" he said in bitter triumph, glaring up red-faced from below the cubicle door.

"Good morning, Loren, what can I do for you?" Mal asked
pleasantly, spreading his knees wider and moving his magazine
to one side.

"The proof of the Halloween ad just came in, and Mr. Clutter wants to see it right away. I'm taking it out to the plant for
a ten o'clock meeting."

"Go with God."

"It's got *widows*, Mal! Three separate widows on three different paragraphs! You know how Clutter feels about widows!"

"Tell the silly bastard they help the eye bridge the paragraph
spacing. Does he want all his ads to look like *Literary Digest*,
nineteen thirty-six?"

"Mal, you've got to cut the widows for me. You've got to
make all the copy flush right!"

"The only thing I'm going to make flush right is this biffy
I'm sitting on."

"Mal!" Loren's expression changed from accusing to implor-
ing. His hand materialized next to his face, holding the proof
of a full-page magazine ad. "Here, it'll just take a minute. I'll
wait for it." He thrust it into Mal's free hand. "Have you got
a pen?"

"I've got a pen." Mal sighed and took a felt-point pen from
his breast pocket and uncapped it. He saw that Loren's head,
sideways, was still looking up at him. "Christ on a crutch,
Loren! I'm not going to do anything until you stop staring at

me like that! You look like a damn *pre*-vert." Loren's head withdrew, and Mal began to edit the copy.

Five minutes later Loren left with his widowless ad, and Mal zipped up his pants and returned to the twenty-ninth floor. He started working on the HydroDent Marketing Plan. The writing went well for twenty minutes, then began to sputter out, as Mal's mind grasshoppered from subject to subject.

He decided he needed a change of pace. "A little pure logic to blow away the cobwebs," he said aloud. He took a blank sheet of paper, drew a triangle on it, and labeled the three corners A, B, and C. He began to solve one of his favorite puzzles, the Great Triangular Duel. He had solved it ten or fifteen times before, but he always forgot the solution as soon as he achieved it, so his zest in reattacking it was first-time fresh.

The situation upon which the puzzle is based is provocative, if not entirely believable. Three men are prepared to fight a duel with pistols. The first man, A, is a dead shot—he absolutely never misses. The second man, B, hits his target 80 percent of the time. The third man, C, can only hit what he shoots at one out of every two tries. The duelists are to fire in turn, a single shot each, and continue until only one remains alive. Problem: if C fires first, what is his best strategy, and what are the odds of each man's survival under all circumstances?

All right, if C shoots at A and hits him, then B will have the next shot, and he'll have to shoot at C, and the odds are four out of five he'll get him, Mal reasoned happily. *But if C misses A, then either B or A will have the next shot, and whichever it is will have to shoot at the other one . . .*

He was so engrossed making notes under the triangle he didn't notice when Toby Tobin, the assistant account executive on HydroDent, entered his office. He had wiry, wavy hair, like Nixon's. "We shall over-cuh-a-um, we shall over-cuh-a-um . . ." he sang softly. "You in good voice for the meeting this aft, leader?"

Mal made an instinctive gesture with his hand to cover the Great Triangular Duel. Tobin noticed and grinned, and Mal moved his hand away guiltily. "Meeting? Oh, you mean the HydroDent meeting?"

"Well, I don't mean a meeting of the Democratic National Committee. I hope the Marketing Plan is ready. Gordon Goodguy was asking about it already this morning. I told him I was sure you had it in the works."

"Gordon Goodguy" was this week's name for A. B. Pauncefoot, the Chairman of the Board. Other weeks it was "Desperate Desmond" or "Foxy Grandpaw." Thinking up names for the agency's senior executives was the nearest Tobin ever came to creative work.

"I'm not sure it will be run off by then, but the writing's all done," Mal lied. "I'll be able to talk it, at least."

"I hope so, friend. But I got the impression the man expected to hold the papers in his hot little hand. And when he's disappointed, *everybody's* disappointed, you know?" Tobin flipped through the pages of a magazine on Mal's desk. "Little lunchyboo today, or don't you plan on going out?" he asked casually.

Not with you, you sneaky little creep, Mal thought. "Like to, but I've got a date," he said. "Take a rain check, though."

"Good-O." Tobin sauntered out of the office with a wave. Mal stared out the door after him. *If he's going to keep breathing down the back of my neck, I'll have to buy him a bottle of Listerine.* He picked up the Great Triangular Duel again, but the edge of his enjoyment was blunted. The unfinished Marketing Plan lay too heavily on his mind to permit escape. He felt the first chilly edge of panic. *What happens if I don't get it done?*

He worked steadily until 11:30, when he received a phone call from a friend at another agency. The friend wanted to meet him for lunch, but Mal begged off. He was about to say goodbye, when the voice on the line asked if he had heard about Biff Maull. "Biff? No, I haven't heard anything. What's with Biff?" "He's dead." "Dead? Jesus Christ, what happened?" "Burned to death on a couch in his living room." "*What!*" "No lie—he got home loaded, and must have taken some pills and crapped out on the couch to smoke a cigarette and watch the tube for a minute. He went to sleep and the couch caught on fire. Phyllis woke up and smelled the smoke, and called the fire department. When they got there, Biff was dead."

"Jesus Christ," Mal said again. He pressed his forehead against the earpiece of the telephone. He felt as if all the blood in his body had drained down into his legs. "Listen, I've got to go," he said in a thick voice. "Thanks for calling. We'll do lunch another time, okay?" He put the phone back on the hook and sat looking at his typewriter unseeingly, his hands lying open in his lap.

Biff Maull and he had started out together as copy cubs, sharing an office in the old Mason-McDonald agency on Jackson Street. It was just after the Korean war, and both of them were eager for success in the un-self-conscious manner of the time. They were friends and competitors, striving to top each other in their work, and sharing their problems and hopes over lunch. Biff was writing a novel on the side, getting up at 5:30 every morning and working for two hours before breakfast. Mal had thought that was the most dedicated thing he had ever heard of, although he never would have admitted it to Biff.

The time came when they both left Mason-McDonald for better paying jobs, but they had kept their friendship alive with weekly lunches at Henrici's or the Berghoff. Biff married, bought a house in Lake Bluff, and changed jobs again, becoming a copy group head at the best creative shop in Chicago. He had a child, a lovely little girl whose mind would never grow beyond that of an average six-year-old. His wife went to a psychiatrist, who told her she had to start being her own person, which she did. Biff moved into positions of increased responsibility, until he was supervising copy and art on $20,000,000 worth of advertising a year. The novel was set aside, and the weekly lunches spread out until they became monthly, and then bimonthly.

Of all the young writers Mal had known, he believed Biff was the best. *He could shovel shit, and he could bay the moon, and he was going to write something great some day, something with his own name on it.*

Sure he was.

Mal sat quietly for ten minutes, then rubbed his face with both hands, as if he had just awakened from a nap. He left the building and went to a nearby saloon with a steam table in the back serving a lunchtime clientele of admen and construction workers. He ordered a double martini at the bar, and then another one. As he was finishing the second, and preparing to walk back and pick up his rare roast beef sandwich and coffee, two men he knew sat down beside him and offered to buy him a drink. It seemed rude to refuse.

It was 1:40 when he returned to the agency and resumed work on the HydroDent Marketing Plan. His typing was slower than it had been in the morning, and he made considerably more mistakes. He pounded doggedly along, unreeling sentence after sentence of the type of Business English built of plural nouns and passive verbs, which is favored for conference reports and marketing plans.

He finished at a quarter of three and was leaning back in his chair with his eyes closed when his secretary buzzed him with the information that he was wanted in Mr. Pauncefoot's office for the HydroDent meeting.

He collected the typed sheets of the Marketing Plan, and the research data and contact reports it was based upon, and placed them all in a manila folder. As he was going out the door, a young writer named Gomez stopped him to ask a question about a Brek-first commercial. "Later, man—it's front office time," Mal said. He walked quickly down the hallway toward the Art Department, where there was a sink and a mirror and a paper towel dispenser. He inspected himself in the mirror and grimaced.

Looking back at him was a thirty-six-year-old man with hollow, bloodshot eyes, a skinny nose, and prominent cheek- and jaw-bones. The tawny hair was long enough to cover the tops of his ears, and a full mustache curved around three sides of his thin-lipped mouth. He was dressed in what he hoped was an acceptable compromise between account-man conservatism and creative-man raffishness: a blue denim sport jacket over a red-checked shirt, open at the neck to show a loosely tied Montgomery Ward bandanna; a wide belt with an engraved brass buckle; hip-high corduroy pants and desert boots.

He inspected the image without enthusiasm. *It wouldn't have been too dumb to wear a suit today,* he thought. He splashed cold water on his face and around his neck and combed his hair back from his eyes with his fingers. At a nearby fountain he rinsed his mouth out and spat the icy water down the drain. *I dare do all that may become a man,* he thought incongruously. *Who dares do more is none. Well, hello dere!*

The walls of A. B. Pauncefoot's office were covered with sharkskin, according to the management of the building—but whether that meant the worsted suiting material with the hard, sleek finish, or the actual epidermis of the carnivorous *Elasmobranchii,* Mal had never discovered. It didn't really make any difference, because the point was the expense. It was enough if you were aware of that.

When Mal entered, Pauncefoot and two of his vice presidents were standing by the windows overlooking Michigan Avenue, watching a line of two or three hundred demonstrators marching south—the group led by Rennie Davis, heading for the Central Police Headquarters to protest the arrest of Hayden and Lowenthal. Police squad cars and three-wheelers followed them like cowboys herding cattle, and, even with the office windows open, the shouts of "Ho! Ho! Ho Chi Minh!" were barely audible.

"It's a matter of respect," A. B. Pauncefoot was saying. "If you have no respect for yourself, you can't be expected to respect your home or your parents or your church or your country." The vice presidents nodded, and Pauncefoot went on, "As ye sow, so shall ye reap. There you see the results of a whole generation of permissiveness. All their lives it's been gimme, gimme, gimme—whatever they wanted, they got, and nobody expected anything from them in return. Their ids rotted out their egos, and their egos rotted out their superegos —no wonder they have no respect!"

Mal sat down in an easy chair away from the windows and observed the chairman of the board pass judgment on the marching protesters twenty-nine floors below. He thought it was interesting to see a man who had spent forty years persuading children to demand certain candies and breakfast foods condemn them because they had been persuaded.

The large room filled up; counting Pauncefoot, there were ten people at the meeting. Media, Research, Art, Copy, TV Production, Traffic, and Contact were represented, and Pauncefoot's cold-eyed secretary was on hand to take notes.

Pauncefoot sat at the head of the gleaming walnut conference table. He was a heavy, narrow-shouldered six-footer with crewcut gray hair and a face that looked almost noble, until one noticed the eyes, which were greedy, and the nose, which seemed boneless. He had reached his present position of eminence in advertising by deferring to his clients' judgment on all creative matters. He was like a doctor who asks his patients what disease they think they have and prescribes accordingly; he is bound to lose a few patients that way, but the ones who stay alive have a high opinion of his no-nonsense professionalism.

The meeting began. The Media and Research people had some things to get out of the way, and there was an explanation of a TV cost overrun. Toby Tobin brought up the question of the agency's participation at the trade show in October, and after some discussion it was decided that Pauncefoot Associates would pick up the tab for a cocktail party promoting the Hydro-Dent Professional Model. Then it was time for Mal to present the Marketing Plan.

He cleared his throat nervously and opened his manila folder. Before he could begin, Pauncefoot asked if he wasn't going to distribute copies of the plan. Mal explained he hadn't been able to get it through typing, copying, and distribution in time for the meeting, and rather than hold things up unnecessarily, he would read his original copy to the group. Pauncefoot didn't like that. He asked who was responsible for failure to have copies available. Mal stoutly answered that the responsibility was his, hoping Pauncefoot would believe he was shielding some unfortunate but deserving menial down the line. Pauncefoot studied his face as if he wanted to be sure not to forget it. "All right, go on," he ordered curtly.

The reading went badly. Some of the pages were out of order, and once Mal had to stop for thirty seconds, riffling through the folder twice before finding the page he needed. When he reached the itemized figures on the recommended media budget, he had to wait while everybody around the table wrote them on their scratch pads and added them up; the Media vice president found a mistake in the totals. "Just a typo, Fred, but thanks for spotting it," Mal said, forcing a smile. Under his shirt he could feel drops of sweat skittering down his ribs.

After what seemed like hours, Mal got past the statistics and into the creative strategy. Pauncefoot leaned back in his massive leather chair, his small eyes almost disappearing between lids and pouches. He waited until Mal finished the section before asking, "Is that what they want? Is that the consumer copy story they want, and is that what they want to tell the trade?"

"Yes, sir—that's the way they spelled it out to me."

"You're sure now? I'd hate to go back to them with a copy platform put together by some young, beatnik, ivory-tower copywriter trying to be creative. Some of the far-out stuff that comes out of this copy department—" He shook his head to indicate that, with the best will in the world, he couldn't comprehend the irresponsibility of today's young writers. "Why, if I'd written stuff like that thirty years ago, the men in the white coats would have trundled me off to the funny farm. I mean it! But of course we were old-fashioned," he went on with heavy sarcasm. "The idea then was to move merchandise, not paper your walls with awards from the Copywriter's Club!"

Mal answered, dry-mouthed, "I put this together myself, Mr. Pauncefoot. It represents ideas the client and I have developed together in meetings over the past three months. There won't be any surprises in it, as far as HydroDent is concerned."

The chairman of the board leaned forward, elbows on the table, fingertips pressed together, and his eyes glittered maliciously. "I'm glad to know who's responsible, Mal," he said. "I always like to be able to give credit where credit is due—*if* it's due."

The meeting was over. Mal saw Toby Tobin coming around the table and quickly left the office before the assistant account executive could reach him. *The little son-of-a-bitch will start singing "We Shall Overcome," and I'll club him to the ground,* he thought.

It wasn't quite 5:00, but Mal headed for the Wrigley Restaurant bar, pausing only long enough to drop off his manila folder on his secretary's desk. She looked at him enquiringly. "You know where I'm going, Linda," he told her. "I will not pass Go, and I will not collect two hundred dollars."

He arrived ahead of the crowd and slipped into an empty booth. The waiter brought him a double martini without bothering to ask for his order. He sipped it slowly, enjoying his solitary inactivity amid the purposeful preparations of the barman and waiters. He felt remote and safe, at least for fifteen minutes; it was King's-X again, as it had been in the john cubicle that morning.

Well, you blew it, he thought. *When the old man gets his hands on that Marketing Plan now, he'll take it home and put*

it under a microscope, and find a hundred mistakes. Jesus,
why didn't I get it written over the weekend?

People began to arrive—a lady copy supervisor from Burnett,
a bearded art director from Foote, Cone, a TV producer and his
girl Friday from Meyerhoff. He called them to join him, and before long there were eight people crowded in the booth and
on chairs in the aisle. They talked about the convention, and
the people in the park, and the police, and whether the scene
in Chicago resembled the scene in Prague, where Russian tanks
rumbled up and down the city streets. Their voices grew louder
as they tried to make themselves heard above the escalating
noise in the room, and Mal's eyes began to smart from the
cigarette smoke. He ordered double martinis at brief intervals,
and by 6:00 he was drunk.

The lady copy supervisor said we can't just walk out on
Vietnam, we have obligations to our ally there. Mal answered
her rudely in an intense four-minute monologue. While she
was leaving, the TV producer said he had supported Bobby
Kennedy, but he couldn't take McCarthy seriously. Mal explained why he was wrong and ordered another drink. While
the TV producer and his girl Friday were leaving, an account
executive came over and told an ethnic joke. Mal informed
him that it was upper-middle-class prejudice like his that supported the Ku Klux Klan. They argued about it, and the account executive left. Mal and the bearded art director talked
about friends in the business, until Mal said, in a voice that
rang loudly through the now sparsely filled bar, "Fuck advertising!" The art director left to catch the 7:14 commuter train
to Glen Ellyn.

Mal ordered a double martini. "Last one," he explained to
the waiter, who accepted the information expressionlessly. "Got
to get myself something to eat. A man can only drink so much
on an empty stomach."

The waiter cleared the empty glasses off the table and
brought Mal a fresh drink. Mal sat alone in the booth, turning

the glass to make interlocking rings of moisture on the table-top. A little over two hours before, he had been sitting alone with a glass before him, just as he was sitting now.

But he didn't feel as if he had King's-X anymore.

CITYSCAPE
Chicagoland Briefs

THE MARCH that A. B. Pauncefoot had watched from his office window continued south until it reached Central Police Headquarters at 11th and State. There the demonstrators demanded that Hayden and Lowenthal be released immediately. The police received the demand with stolid indifference, their brawny bare arms folded across their baby-blue sport shirts. Baffled and angry, the demonstrators straggled across Michigan Avenue into Grant Park. When they saw the huge statue of Civil War General John A. Logan straddling his charger and waving his banner at the Conrad Hilton Hotel, they decided to capture the general.

Two or three hundred young men and women surged up the little hill and engulfed the base of the statue, and five of them shinnied up General Logan's massive jackboots and occupied the high ground on the horse's back, waving Vietcong flags and red revolutionary banners and shouting their now-familiar slogans—"What do we want? PEACE! When do we want it? NOW!" and "Dump the Hump and Hump the Dump!"

Either to protect General Logan or to remove the protesters from the view of the delegates' wives in the hotel across the street, the police formed a skirmish line and swept north to the statue, pushing the crowd before them. Their behavior was disciplined and restrained until they had isolated the young men on the statue from their sympathizers. Then they turned ugly. When one seventeen-year-old was slow to obey the command to climb down, a policeman grabbed one of his feet and began to pull him off the statue. The boy's arm caught behind General Logan's scabbard. As he hung helplessly, crying in fear and pain, the policeman continued to tug with all his strength. Other policemen joined him, and in a few moments the boy lay on the ground with a broken arm. He was then deliberately kicked in the groin and in the head, taken to jail, and booked for aggravated assault.

Meanwhile the crowd drifted north, heading back to Lincoln Park.

At the Amphitheatre, the fight over the seating of the Georgia delegation began in the afternoon. As it progressed, the velvet glove of Mayor Daley's hospitality began unraveling to expose the ferrous fingers inside. McCarthy delegates on the floor could only reach microphones with difficulty, and when they did, the microphones often went mysteriously dead. At signals from the mayor, sitting with the Illinois delegation in the front of the hall, the packed gallery burst into furious applause, or shouted down opposition speakers with First Ward finesse ("Shut up, you asshole!"). When one delegate entering the Amphitheatre, tired of the security rigmarole at the gates, tried to use his Diners Club card instead of his delegate admission card to pass the magnetized sentinel box, he was beaten by the ushers on duty, while the police looked on. A TV commentator trying to do a report on the situation was also beaten.

With a growing sense of incredulity, the liberal delegates saw themselves manipulated like window-dressing democrats in a police state. It was like living in Prague—or in the ghetto.

Sari Schram and Ted Bakerfield didn't go on the march to Central Police Headquarters. Instead, they went to a lunchroom near Lincoln Park. The most economical buy on the menu was the soup of the day, homemade beef barley, and they asked the counterman to bring them two bowls with crackers.

He served them quickly, and then, because it was a slack time of day, began a conversation as they ate.

"You kids going to go up against the cops in the park again tonight?" Before they could answer, he went on: "Heck, I don't blame you. If I was your age, that's where I'd be tonight. I mean it!" Ted and Sari looked at him cautiously, and he grinned. "You surprised? You think you're the first people who ever hated cops? Why, there are plenty of people in Chicago who've been hating cops since before you was a gleam in your daddies' eyes! I'm telling you!" Ted and Sari exchanged glances, wondering if they had found one of their rare allies in the over-thirty world. The counterman exposed his toothless gums in malicious glee: "Why, heck fire, you wouldn't believe what we done to cops when I was a kid. One time a bunch of us was cleaning out a warehouse over by Racine Avenue, and this cop came up behind us before we seen him, and tells us to get up against the wall. But one of my buddies was behind *him*, see? And my buddy tackles him, and the rest of us jumped him on the ground, and it's goodbye blueboy, I'm telling you!"

Ted asked what had happened to the cop. The counterman straightened his old back like a soldier on parade. "They had to retire him off the force," he said. "He was a Jew. If there's anything I hate worse than a nigger cop, it's a Jew cop. Believe me, there are plenty of places in this town where a Jew cop or a nigger cop won't go alone. We know about cops in Chicago, don't you worry. How's the soup?" Ted said it was fine. The counterman said he had just made it fresh that morning.

"How do you feel about Irish cops and Polish cops?" Sari asked. The counterman thought a moment before answering, folding his lips in until his chin almost touched his nose.

"Well, they're both mostly Catholics, and that means they got no minds of their own, they follow whatever the Pope says like sheep. And the Irish are all on the take, and the Polacks would be too, except they're too dumb. Basically, they're both no damn good, or they wouldn't be cops to begin with. But at least they're white, not like the niggers and the Jews." He watched with solicitous pride the two young people eating the food he had prepared and said magnanimously, "I got nothing against hippies. What the heck, they're just kids. If they want to talk dirty, so what? We didn't talk so clean when I was a kid, either, if you want to know. At least the guys didn't."

"You're tolerant," said Ted.

"That's it. How about a refill on the soup? I won't charge you for it." He filled their bowls again and brought them more cellophane-wrapped packages of crackers. As another customer came into the lunchroom, he leaned close and said in a hoarse whisper, "Just remember what I told you—if you go up against the cops tonight, kick the shit out of them—pardon my French, young lady." His pink-gummed, shiny smile made fellow conspirators of the three of them.

As he went to take the newcomer's order, Ted grinned at Sari. "Don't ever be a cop, babe," he said. "Jew cops are a stone drag."

"That prick," Sari said hotly. "Something's going to have to be done about garbage like him!"

"Unfortunately, that's the voice of the people. You're starting to sound like an elitist." He crumbled saltine crackers into his soup and submerged them with his spoon.

Sari looked at him levelly, her eyebrows flattened into black bars above her handsome eyes. "Watch your mouth, Sam," she said sharply.

Ted smiled, and said in a pacifying voice, "I'd rather look at yours, babe." After a moment her face relaxed, and she smiled too. They finished their soup, paid their check, and went back to Lincoln Park.

During the day, three families in what the newspapers call Chicagoland received communications from their government.

One of the families lived in a northwest suburb; the parents had planned to leave with their two younger children for a camping vacation in Wisconsin the next day, and they wondered how to tell the kids the trip was off. The second family was black; when the mother heard the news, there was no father with whom to share the grief and bitterness. The third family lived in Blue Island, where the father worked in a sheet-metal fabricating plant. Their son had been an only child, and adopted; in his agony, the father said he wished to God he had never adopted him.

Other parents were luckier. They learned that their sons were only wounded or missing, or they had no news about them at all.

9

A NIGHT ON THE TOWN

ONCE, when Mal Tolliver and Biff Maull shared an office at the old Mason-McDonald agency, they had done a beautiful thing.

The agency maintained a guest suite in the Palmer House, a block away, and one idle morning Mal had figured out which hotel windows corresponded to the M-M rooms. The next day he brought binoculars to the office to check his calculations. From then on it was possible for Mal and Biff to play voyeurs whenever agency guests occupied the suite. The novelty wore off in a few days, however, and for months the field glasses lay unused in Mal's bottom drawer.

Then one day at lunch a gossipy account man told them that the agency's mogul of moguls, Fenwick Mason, was believed to take his secretary to the hotel guest suite when it was unoccu-pied, utilizing one of the bedrooms for restorative lunch-hour workouts. Biff and Mal returned to their office and broke out the binoculars. A few days later they were rewarded by the sight of their leader and his leggy, sloe-eyed secretary entering the M-M suite.

"Mal, this is remarkable," Biff said, glasses glued to his eyes. "They're as feely as a blind kid with a braille copy of *Playboy*."

"Gimme the damn glasses!" Mal cried.

They passed the binoculars back and forth and reported to each other on the state of the liaison. Activities in the suite were moving briskly ahead when Biff had his idea. Quickly consulting the telephone directory, he called the Palmer House and asked for the M-M guest suite. Through the glasses, Mal could see Mason, naked except for black sox and garters, reacting to the ringing telephone. He disengaged his pale white body and rolled across the mattress to the bedside table, leaving his partner spraddle-legged and damp. "He's got the robust glow of uncooked lasagna," Mal told Biff.

Mason's words came through the receiver. "Hello, who's there?" squeaked the petulant elfin voice.

Biff replied in sepulchral tones, "This is God. Aren't you ashamed?"

Mason did an extended double take. Ten seconds passed before the naked tycoon's expression of baffled concentration changed to appalled understanding. Through the binoculars' lenses, he seemed to stare directly into Mal's eyes, and his lips formed a murderous obscenity as he leaped to the window and drew the curtains.

Biff and Mal looked at each other in respectful silence. Then Biff said, "If I were you, you disgusting degenerate, I'd get those field glasses out of here *tonight*. Somebody just might check all the offices on this side of the building, you know?" Mal agreed, and smuggled the glasses out in his briefcase that evening. Afterward, they told no more than forty people about the episode.

And now Biff was dead. Burned to death or asphyxiated on a couch in front of the TV set. *Does that make him a burnt offering to the god he served?* Mal asked himself. He sat alone at a table in a restaurant on Grand Avenue, a martini in his hand and an untouched steak sandwich getting cold on a plate in front of him. *I want to remember him—and after all the campaigns he wrote, all the ads and spots and jingles and brochures and copy platforms and sales meeting skits and client Christmas cards and matchbook covers and painted rocks—what I remember is the needle he gave to Fenwick Mason. Isn't that remarkable?*

His waitress, a sweet-faced woman named Betty, who did her job with the same efficient good humor with which she managed her paralyzed husband at home, stopped by the table. "Better eat your sandwich before it gets cold, Mal. Do you want your coffee now?"

His reactions were slow, and it took him a moment to respond to the question. Then he raised his martini and drained it. "Betty, you nice, wholesome, voluptuous mind-bending sex object, you—get me another martini, for Christ's sake!"

"What about your sandwich?"

"I've got to have something to wash it down with, don't I?"

He drank another martini and managed to swallow most of the sandwich and a half-dozen soggy french fries. He refused Betty's suggestion of coffee again. When he stood by the cash register to pay his check, the manager said, "Well, this is a good night to go home and watch TV with the family, right, Mal?"

Mal peered at him owlishly. "Why is that, Frank?"

"You don't want to be out on the street tonight. A cop was in here this afternoon; he said the hippies got all kinds of weapons, and maybe there might be some shooting. Stay away from Lincoln Park was his advice. Keep your nose clean and you won't get hurt."

Mal had completely forgotten the demonstrators in Lincoln Park. Now, hearing the manager's words, he determined to see the curfew scene for himself. "Oh, no, Frank," he said gravely, "you can't turn your back on history. A man has an obligation to posterity to live all the days of his years." He scooped up his change from the coin-return cup and pocketed it. "Eat the meat, and crack the bones, and suck the marrow of the times. Drink her down to the bitter lees. The truth lies at the bottom of the glass. Dig?"

Frank looked at him with an expression of modest concern. "Take care now, Mal, okay?" He watched Mal leave the restaurant, and, as the door closed behind him, gave a barely perceptible shrug.

Mal walked north on Rush Street, past the neon-splashed

night-clubs that followed one another like glass beads on a string.
He misjudged the curb at Delaware Street and fell to his knees,
tearing his hip-hugger corduroy pants. "Watch it, buddy," he
said warningly to himself. At Walton he stopped in front of a
liquor store and looked at the graceful and expensive bottles
displayed in the window. "Sure, and a man ought not to go on
an expedition into the wilds without a medicinal taste of the
creature in his pocket," he said aloud in a stage-Irish brogue.
Passers-by glanced at him. He went into the store and bought a
pint of Old Crow, tucking it into the side pocket of his denim
jacket and patting it affectionately.

He walked west to State Parkway, and north until he was in
front of Hugh Hefner's Playboy mansion. It was full dark, and
lights glowed intimately behind tightly drawn curtains. Mal
had once attended a party at the mansion when Hefner was
angling for sponsors for his "Playboy Penthouse" TV program,
and found it easy to conjure up scenes of sybaritic abandon in
the basement swimming grotto. He imagined Hefner inviting
him to enter the mansion and join the frolic, and himself
proudly refusing to be corrupted.

Oh, no, Hef, that's not the real world in there, he heard himself saying in a stern yet compassionate voice. *You foolish, de-
luded man, the world is courage, and idealism, and brotherhood
—the world is policemen's clubs and bombed villages. The
world is a hungry child crying in the dark.* Hefner's face assumed a conscience-stricken expression, and he sucked on his
pipe nervously. Mal continued the indictment, knowing that
to be kind he must first be cruel. *You live in a plastic world,
Hef. Plastic boobs and plastic pussies. Plastic people eating
plastic French food and riding around in plastic sports cars.
Face it, Hef—you're unreal.* Hefner writhed and chewed his
lips in mortification. Mal waved one arm in dismissal. *No,
thanks, I won't come in for a romp with a bunny. I have a ren-
dezvous with life, if the word is familiar to you. Ciao, Hef, old
sox, and give my regards to the Bunny of the Year!*"

He continued north on State Parkway to North Avenue. Lin-

coln Park began across the street. There were flickering lights
and movement among the trees. He had the impression of many
people just beyond the edge of invisibility. Pedestrians walked
along the sidewalks on both sides of the street, and no policemen were in sight. Mal felt a twinge of disappointment and
then realized that it was still too early for anything to happen—
it couldn't have been much after 9:30, and the curfew wasn't
until 11:00.

*Time to drop in at the FNS—the Friendly Neighborhood
Saloon.*

Mister Dooley's was crowded for so early in the evening. Mal
pushed his way to the bar and made himself heard over the
Clancy Brothers and Tommy Makem singing about the Bold
Fenian Men. Leaning against the smooth polished wood, he
sipped his draft beer and squinted through the smoke at the
Irish-American politicians on the walls. It occurred to him he
hadn't called home to tell Marilyn he would be late, and he
realized he had no intention of doing so now. He had the sen-
sation of near weightlessness; he felt he could do fifty push-ups
without undue effort. The currents of music and argument and
laughter supported him as saltwater buoys a swimmer.

He inspected his neighbors along the bar. On one side a tall,
bushy-haired man with an actory voice argued the necessity for
terrorism, while his companion, black-bearded and no less actory, held out for passive resistance. Beyond them, a fat man
with Dr. Cyclops glasses complained to friends that he could no
longer make it with his girl because she had decided she
would only ball black men. Mal could feel a buttock pressing
against his own buttocks, but couldn't tell if it was a man's or
a woman's without turning around. He looked in the other direction along the bar. A chubby woman was perched on the
barstool, heels hooked over crossbar, skirt pulled up over round
thighs. She grinned at him, wrinkling her snub nose. "Hey,
buddy," she said, "how the fuck are you?"

Mal didn't usually find it easy to talk to strangers in bars, but

it was hard for anyone to maintain reserve with Robin Goodpasture. Within a few minutes he told her a good deal about
himself. She asked him what he was doing in Mister Dooley's,
and he said he wanted to see what was going to happen in the
park. She said, "I'll show you what's going to happen, Clyde.
Take a squint at this." She pulled the loose sleeve of her blouse
up over her shoulder, revealing a large blue black bruise, puffy
and ocher-edged. "That's what's going to happen. You better
finish your beer and go back to Evanston."

He said earnestly that he couldn't go back to Evanston, because he believed that for everyone there was a time for commitment, and how did he know it wasn't his time now? She
said she gave up, how *did* he know? He said he didn't say he
knew, he said how did he know he didn't know? She said, oh
bullshit. On the juke box José Feliciano made the musical re-
quest that someone light his fire.

Other people joined them: a tall thin reporter named Finley
and a short, oily skinned reporter with an Italian name who
worked for a New York underground newspaper. Finley ordered Mexican boilermakers. Mal experienced his first blackout
of the evening; when he became aware of his surroundings
again, Goody was staring wide-eyed into his eyes, and her hand
was on his knee. "Oh, that's right—that's absolutely right!" she
said fervently. Mal had no idea what he had said.

A gray-haired man in his sixties arrived; Mal gathered he was
the owner or manager of a movie theater somewhere. Holding
his tequila glass up to the light and squinting through it, the
gray-haired man said, "One thing my generation has learned—
you can't trust anybody under thirty. Look at the mess they've
left for us to clean up." Mal headed for the bathroom, resting
his hand on Goody's hip as he squeezed around her. The bathroom floor was covered with a half inch of water. Mal splashed
cold tap water on his face and took deep breaths. He remained a
few moments, reading the graffiti on the walls, which were more
political than literary. He returned to his place at the bar, pat-

ting Goody's hip again in transit. As he picked up his glass, he
recognized a young man at a table across the room; he was a
talented writer Mal had hired two years ago and had subsequently let go because his appearance and manner had caused
A. B. Pauncefoot to refer to him disapprovingly as a "beatnik."
When Mal caught the young writer's eye he pointed his index
finger like a pistol, cocking his thumb up, then letting it fall.
The young writer waved, grinned, and shouted something Mal
couldn't make out. "You know it!" Mal yelled back.

Time blurred past, and Mal became aware he was no longer
in Mister Dooley's. He was in a crowd of people on a sidewalk
in front of an automobile showroom at the intersection of
LaSalle and Clark streets. The streets were jammed with sta-
tionary cars. Beyond the cars were police, and behind the police
was the park. Goody was beside him, with her hands cupped
around her mouth, shouting "Oink! Oink!" Mal began yelling
"Oink!" too. A voice behind him cried, "The preachers are
going back in." Mal noticed a beautiful black Morgan two-
seater immobilized in the traffic jam. He squeezed Goody's arm
to attract her attention. "Look at that goddamn sweetheart
Morgan—isn't that the prettiest thing you ever saw?"

"Come on—we're going across!" Goody announced. "If those
asshole preachers go in, *we* go in!" She grabbed his arm and
pulled him off the curb into the street. They threaded their way
between the cars, Mal patting the Morgan on its vented hood.
"You're some patter, aren't you?" Goody asked dryly.

The police let them through because it wasn't 11:00 yet, and
the park was still technically open to the public. Except for
widely separated trash fires, it was very dark. Mal remembered
the pint of Old Crow in his coat pocket, and he and Goody each
had a big swallow.

That was the last coherent, sequential memory Mal had of that
night. From then on, all he was subsequently able to dredge up
was an assortment of vignettes, lasting a few moments or a
minute or two, composed of sharply contrasting light and

shadow, like the blackout skits in a Second City review. Among them were:

A circle of cross-legged kids around a trash fire chanting "Uhhhhh-mmmm," as a fat man with a bushy black beard posed ecstatically in front of them, hands clasped before him, eyes squeezed shut behind horn-rimmed glasses. "That looks like Allen Ginsberg," Mal said. "That's because it is Allen Ginsberg," Goody said. "What's he doing?" Mal asked. "He's saying his mantra, for Christ's sake!" Goody answered. "Haven't you ever heard a mantra before?"

And . . .

A police loudspeaker called, as clear as a loon's cry over a Minnesota lake: "Anyone remaining in the park is in violation of the law. This includes the news media. Please leave the park—the park is closed." The repeated words became louder as the squad car drew nearer, then receded as the car passed and drew away from them. Even after the loudspeaker became inaudible, the memory of its authority remained to make the unamplified voices of the protesters seem puny in comparison.

And . . .

Under the glare of strobe and klieg and floodlights, fifty young people built a barricade. Acting out fantasies of Thermopylae and the Paris Commune, they piled picnic tables and trash baskets and park benches into a barrier six feet high and fifty feet wide, starting nowhere and ending nowhere. Their faces were as exalted as saints in an El Greco painting.

And . . .

As the police skirmish line advanced toward the barricade, a squad car suddenly appeared behind the demonstrators, driving slowly and without lights into the crowd. Mal stared at it wonderingly, unable to understand what the car was doing, or how it had gotten there. But the young people assumed it was a sneak attack from the rear, an attempt to break down the barricade. "Get the car! Get the cop car!" they shouted, and in one giant convulsion the crowd surged around and partly over the

blue and white Plymouth. The car came to a dead stop and
disappeared from the sight of the approaching police skirmish
line. A girl was pinned between the front bumper and the barricade. Mal could see that her mouth was open and knew she
must be screaming, but her voice was lost in the roar of a hundred other voices, "Kill the pigs! KILL THE PIGS!" Rocks
shattered the windshield and window glass; hands thrust between the gleaming shards to clutch at the men inside. The
driver, face frozen in desperation, shifted to reverse; the car
jerked backward, slowed, accelerated, began to turn. The
crowd didn't want to let it go. Mal saw one boy hang on until
his hands were cut to the bone, and black blood stained his
arms to the elbows.

And . . .

The skirmish line attacked. Some of the policemen climbed
over the barricade while others flanked it and charged it from
both sides. Tear-gas canisters fell among the crowd. One
landed near Mal's feet, and he stared at it stupidly for a moment as it spun like some malevolent toy, spitting gray smoke.
"Christ sake, let's split!" said a voice in his ear. It was Goody;
her hair was in her eyes and her lips were compressed in anger.
The police were close; two of them were clubbing a girl in a
Snoopy T-shirt only twenty feet away. Mal and Goody trotted
toward Clark Street.

And . . .

"Walk, don't run!" cautioned a slender, blond seminarian, one
of the contingent of preachers. But the crowd ran anyway, and
the seminarian found himself between the retreating protesters
and the advancing police. He began to walk faster, and then it
was too late. A wooden club smashed against the back of his
head, and he fell to his knees, stunned. As he knelt in involun-
tary and insensible prayer, an officer clubbed him on the side
of the head, and he rolled sideways on the grass. The officer
struck him twice more, once over the kidney and once at the
point of the hipbone. The seminarian lay without movement.

Mal felt so crammed full of fear and loathing he had to vomit some of it out. He stood flat-footed, facing the advancing police. "You killed a priest—you dirty goddamned mother-fuckers killed a priest!" he shouted. Goody pulled at his arm, and after a moment he let her draw him away.

And . . .

On Clark Street the police began their attack on the Press. Mal saw them spray one reporter with Mace, smash a photographer's lights and camera, pursue another reporter up onto the porch of a house and club him unconscious. Goody kept worrying about Frank Finley: "They clobbered him yesterday—if he catches another one on the head, it could blow his brain for good," she told Mal anxiously. A cop raised his club and started toward them, and they ran into the street and ducked between the stalled cars. Mal saw the beautiful black Morgan two-seater again. It was empty, and its windshield was smashed.

And . . .

Tear gas drifted out of the park, and the crowd moved south and west to stay in front of it. The east side of Clark Street was deserted except for a handful of police moving among the parked cars at the curb. Mal watched them deliberately slashing the tires of the Volkswagens with McCarthy bumper stickers or flower decals on the windows.

And . . .

Mal had swallowed a mouthful of tear gas and stood hanging on to a lamppost, retching. Goody pulled at his arm impatiently. "He may have gone into the Lincoln Hotel—come on!" she said. He tried to answer her, but could only cough and gag. At that moment a teen-age street gang suddenly appeared from a nearby alley. Mal watched their wavering figures through a blur of tears as they swarmed into the street and attacked a slow-moving squad car with rocks and flattened tin cans. In seconds all the windows were starred with cracks; the young guerrillas had hit and run before the cops could stop the car and climb out. "Hey, man—dig the greasers!" said Goody excitedly. "It's the first time in their lives the little bastards have ever been on the right side of anything!" Frustrated, the two cops started toward Mal and Goody, and they hurried into the Lincoln Hotel.

And . . .

Frank wasn't there. Mal and Goody stood with twenty or thirty other people under the hotel marquee, watching the dwindling violence. There were famous people in the group—writers from New York and Hollywood and overseas, TV personalities, a nationally known civil rights lawyer—but nobody had much to say.

Goody asked Mal if he still had his bottle, and to his surprise he found it was intact. He offered her a drink. She drank three big swallows, eyes closed, hair straggling, skin dead white under the neon glare. Mal was suddenly aware of her as a woman, as flesh. The TV commentator asked if he could have a drink. Mal estimated how much whiskey was left, drank half of it, and handed the TV man the bottle. "Finish it, buddy." He put his hand on Goodys arm, just above the elbow, and squeezed gently. "Don't you think it's time we took ourselves out of harm's way?" he asked. "Hell, I want some more to drink!" she replied. They went to Oxford's saloon, a half block north, where they found the door locked; they had to identify themselves before they were allowed in. The room was crowded with a mixture of neighborhood and Movement people. Everyone was edgy, expecting a police raid at any time. Goody recognized a tableful of acquaintances and insisted on joining them. Mal ordered two beers and two shots of tequila at the bar. The juke box thudded, bass notes amplified, trebles blotted up by the voices and bodies crowding the room.

Sometime later Mal found himself talking to the people at the table. He had intended to talk about the police in the park, but when the words came out they were about Biff Maull. "He didn't ever wake up, that's the hell of it. He crapped out drunk on the sofa and just slid into death like a fireman down a greased pole. He didn't get a chance to regret things. It's terrible, to live for thirty-eight years and then die without having a chance to regret things!" The people around the table frowned at him. He could feel moisture around his eyes. He raised his voice and shouted, because it was important that everyone should hear and understand what he was saying. "I've got some regret coming, too—they better not try to take it away from me! Goddamn their dirty little souls, they better not try!" The people looked a him curiously for a moment, then went on talking to one another. He sat slumped in his chair, drained.

And . . .

Mal and Goody started for her apartment. It was almost two in the morning, but there were still many police on the streets, looking for people in groups and attacking them. From Division to Diversey, and west as far as Halsted Street, they clubbed on sight. Mal saw a squad of twenty cops sweep Lincoln Park West. They formed a line under the streetlights at Lincoln Avenue, twenty beefy, helmeted men abreast, extending across sidewalk, street, and further sidewalk. Then they started down the old street, past houses and apartment buildings built in the ashes of the Chicago fire—past the Wacker house like a Swiss chalet built of milk chocolate and marshmallows; past the understated Louis Sullivan row houses that taught young Frank Lloyd Wright most of the things he needed to know; past the white farmhouse with the picket fence where the Director of the Chicago Historical Society lived—the police line moved like a ponderous, multiarmed machine, colored baby-blue above, navy blue below, counting cadence for itself by chanting, "Kill! Kill! Kill!"

Mal saw the police begin their sweep of the street and pulled Goody under the steps of a house halfway down the block. The police line passed less than ten feet from them. To Mal, looking out through a crack in a wooden riser, the sight of the policemen's helmets gleaming under the streetlights, shielding faces made invisible by shadow, was the most frightening thing he

had ever seen. For the first time in his life he realized what it
meant to be powerless, and in the dark, and hated. *My God,
what in the world am I doing here?* he thought. The chanting
of the police diminished as they turned into Menomonee Street
and disappeared. Mal and Goody returned to the sidewalk. The
only movement on the street was the gentle swaying of the
trees, whose upper leaves gleamed silver under the streetlights.

They reached Goody's apartment without further incident.

To Mal's surprise, the apartment was crowded. People were
sitting on the floor and sleeping on the bed and the sofa, eating,
drinking beer, smoking dope, and listening to Frank Zappa on
the stereo. He recognized the underground newspaper reporter
from New York and the copywriter who had once worked for
Pauncefoot Associates. The copywriter's face showed traces of
dried blood from a small scar on his forehead. He grinned at
Mal and said, "Hey, Cowabunga, man!"

"All right, you bastards," Goody shouted angrily, "get that
goddamned pot out of here! You may want to go to jail for
possession, but I sure as hell don't! NOW! I mean it! With
cops crawling out of the woodwork, I don't want one lousy roach
in this house! NOW! MOVE!" She stood glaring around the
room until a girl with red hair that reached her hips began picking up butts and flushing them down the toilet, and two men
took their supplies and left. Then she turned to Mal with an
apologetic smile and put her small, soft hand on his wrist. "I
think you and I deserve a beer," she said, opening her eyes very
wide and blinking them twice.

They drank two quarts of beer, and talked about the war, and
exploitation of minorities, and Women's Lib, while the people
around them dropped off to sleep by ones and twos. After a
while they were the only ones still awake. Goody hung on
Mal's words eagerly, and Mal thought with surprise that she had
a remarkably good mind. "You know, you're a hell of a broad,
Goody," he said gravely. Goody said she wanted to dance, and
they took the Frank Zappa album off the turntable and substi-

tuted an old Jimmy Lunceford swing album. They danced together on the rug in the middle of the living room, with sleepers snoring around them. Mal was intensely aware of Goody's breasts and belly, and the firm thigh pressing between his legs.

"I'm gonna tell you, baby, gonna move away from here," she sang huskily, her warm breath tickling his cheek. "I don't want no ice man, I'm gonna buy a Frigidaire— When we move way out on the outskirts of town." Their feet stopped moving, and they kept the rhythm of the music with their bodies. Goody's eyes were closed and her lips were open. Mal kissed her, and her tongue thrust stiffly and insistently into his mouth. They clung together for a minute or two, exploring each other with their mouths and hands and the pressure of their limbs. Then Goody sank down on the rug, drawing Mal to the floor on top of her. "Oh, Christ, my clit feels like a prickly pear," she gasped. Her body arched and twisted a moment, as she tugged down her panties and freed one leg. Then her white thighs rose to bracket him like two trained porpoises breaking out of dark water.

They made love in the lamplight, to the sound of sleep-breathing and the scraping of a phonograph needle in the last grooves of the forgotten record. For Mal it was incredibly good, better than anything he had done or even remembered for years. But looking back at it later, he wouldn't be sure that Goody had ever reached a climax, in spite of her passionate groaning, trembling, and panting. It would occur to him that perhaps she never did, which no doubt explained a lot of things.

After half an hour, Mal tumbled blindly into sleep.

10

CITYSCAPE
That Toddlin' Town

THERE IS A CERTAIN SPECIAL MIXTURE of awe, outrage, disbelief, and cocky pride with which Chicagoans regard their city, which is not found outside of Cook County, Illinois. Not that the inhabitants of other great cities don't view their hometowns with attitudes that are also unique: only the New Yorker is so sure that his city, with faults that render it unlivable to everyone else in the republic, is nevertheless "the only wheel in town"; only the San Franciscan believes so certainly that his city is his loving mistress, desired by all the world, but faithful to him because only he understands her. Citizens of Boston and New Orleans and St. Louis and Los Angeles have their unique attitudes too, and so, no doubt, do citizens of Chillicothe and Akron and Flint. But nobody, nowhere, feels the way Chicagoans feel about Chicago.

When a Chicagoan reads the report of still another local crime or disaster—the Haymarket Massacre or Memorial Day Massacre, Loeb-Leopold's Bobby Franks or Richard Speck's nurses, Dion O'Banion gunned down in his flower shop, or the ward heeler most recently packed away in his his own automobile trunk—the Chicagoan thinks, "What a terrible thing! I must be one tough son-of-a-bitch to live in a town like this!" All Chicagoans are akin to the young dentist who found it exciting to pal around with gangsters, and so had his own cavities filled by Al Capone's soldiers on St. Valentine's Day.

People who live "back of the yards" regret the emigration of the meat packers from Chicago not so much because of the lost jobs, one suspects, as because of the lost smell; in the old days, on a hot summer night when the wind was right, they could tell themselves that nobody else in the world could live with a stink like that.

Chicago is a spectacularly beautiful city—at least part of it is —with miles of beaches and parks, and the most dramatic sky-line in the world. Not every native is privileged to live near the lakefront, but everyone is proud of its sweep and grandeur. In its beauty Chicago is like a handsome stallion with a killer in-stinct; his owner knows nobody else can ride him, and he wouldn't have it any other way.

On Tuesday the population of Chicago woke up once more to the comforting conclusion that they were indeed tough sons-of-bitches. The story of the previous night's battle in Lincoln Park was featured on TV and radio and splashed across the front page of the morning newspapers. It was apparent that something important was happening in the park—possibly some-thing as important as what was happening in the Amphitheatre, certainly something that would add a new page to Chicago's rich history of excess. It was enough to make a million people say smugly, "My God, what a town we live in!"

In Lincoln Park the police and the protesters looked at each other in a new way. They weren't the same people they had been twenty-four hours before; the catharsis of violence had purged both sides of any self-doubts or hopes of compromise. The police knew that ahead of them lay force and more force; it was something they were good at, and for the most part they welcomed the opportunity to demonstrate their skill. The Yippies and Mobe kids knew that the acceptance and even solicitation, even provocation, of brutality had become the reason for their presence in Chicago. Each side had begun to feel respect for the willingness of the other side to play its necessary role; under the piled feather beds of hatred in their minds, they may even have felt a single pea of gratitude.

Tuesday morning it was hard for a convention delegate to get his eyes open. The session the night before had lasted until almost three in the morning, due to trouble over the seating of the Georgia delegates. The convention leadership had delayed past TV prime time and then tried to slip in the Lester Maddox delegation, hoping the viewing public would be shielded from any resulting unpleasantness by the lateness of the hour. Enraged liberals, rallying to the support of the Julian Bond delegation, paralyzed the parliamentary process, shouting and booing the chair until Mayor Daley stood up and moved his hand like a puppet master, gesturing to Chairman Carl Albert to adjourn the session.

But get out of bed the delegates must, even to the nauseating stench of chemical stink-bomb pellets dropped on the lobby rugs and ground in beneath some anonymous sneaker- or sandal-shod foot—a half-vomit, half-excrement reek that had mysteriously made its way into the air-conditioning system and now permeated every part of the Conrad Hilton Hotel.

Heigh-ho, rise and shine! This morning the candidates themselves were meeting the uncommitted delegations, and each delegate felt Destiny perching on his shoulder as fiercely taloned as a bald eagle!

The Californians met with Humphrey, McCarthy, and Mc-Govern. Humphrey used his mouth as a spawning salmon uses its tail, in automatic and indefatigable struggle. McCarthy chose to punish his audience for their devotion to Robert Kennedy by refusing to talk to them. McGovern charmed them with his boyish sincerity, and they applauded him vigorously, as much to pay back McCarthy as to reward McGovern. The session, which was completely meaningless, was treated by the media as though it were only slightly less momentous than Yalta.

Outside the convention hotels other people were also having meetings. A group of neighborhood residents formed themselves into the Lincoln Park Emergency Citizens Committee and drafted a statement asking the police to end the curfew in the park and allow the demonstrators to sleep on the ground there. They requested a meeting with the Commander of the 18th Police District to present their statement in person. Clergymen in the group also announced that a prayer vigil would be held in the park at 11:00 that night.

Tuesday was the birthday of the President of the United States. The Democratic leadership planned to give him a birthday party at Soldier's Field, so the Mobe and the Yippies organized an Un-Birthday Party at the Coliseum. Posters announcing the festivities appeared on trees and lampposts in Lincoln Park that morning. The appearance of Norman Mailer and Allen Ginsberg was promised. The artwork, which was out of register, seemed to depict a Hieronymus Bosch–type orgy of maids and monsters.

The sour-smelling taverns on Skid Row were open by 8:00 A.M., and televised news commentators discussed the events in the park and at the Amphitheatre. But few of the men and women bellied up to the bar paid any attention. For people on West Madison Street, the news is what's happening outside, not on TV. And what was happening outside was this: all of a sudden there didn't seem to be any cops around. Citizens weren't being hassled, or busted into the drunk tank; chicks weren't being shaken down or run in; kids weren't being pushed up against the wall. For the last two or three days, it had been easier to breathe than anyone could remember.

Nobody loses all the time.

11

A QUESTION OF GERONTOLOGY

MIKE ROGOFF awoke with a well-earned headache on Tuesday morning. Lying on his back in bed, he opened his mind to a rush of troubles. He thought about the strike at the theater for a while, and then about his girl Mary Cvetla, and wondered whether Johnny the guitar player was getting in yet. He turned to larger problems and thought about Cossacks clubbing and gassing people at home and bombardiers blowing up people across the Pacific. He returned to smaller problems, wondering how long his bank account would keep him if he didn't get some revenue from the theater soon. He breathed deeply and checked his chest for pains, and felt over his neck, stomach, and groin for growths. He found something that might be a small cyst behind his right ear and fingered it uncertainly a moment, before deciding it was too small to warrant worry. *I couldn't afford a biopsy anyway*, he thought with gloomy satisfaction.

He couldn't face the prospect of a day's work in his cramped, stuffy office at the cinéma vérité, not if he had to cross a Wobbly picket line to get there. Instead, he decided to pay a visit to his sister, Ruth, something he had put off doing for three months.

Ruth Myerson lived in a comfortable retirement home in Rogers Park, which she had selected for herself after the death of her husband. She was seventy-one and in good health. Her clothes came from Saks and Bonwit Teller, and she had her hair done once a week. Like most of the other residents of the glass-and-fieldstone tower on Sheridan Road, she played a good deal of bridge, drank a cocktail before lunch and a couple before dinner, and was discreetly aware of any interest shown by members of the opposite sex. She was worth more than $200,000, which would be divided between her two children on her death.

Mike was fond of his sister, although he found that two or three visits a year discharged his affectionate feelings. She was a clever woman, and sometimes refreshingly outspoken, even though her life as an upper-middle-class Hadassah matron hadn't placed a premium on either originality or candor.

As Mike waited for her in the lounge, feeling shabby in a Barcelona chair, he reflected on the two roads they had chosen to escape the West Side ghetto of their youth. For Ruth it had been the business college, the secretarial job on LaSalle Street, the careful cultivation of her huntress' skills, and the marriage to her boss. For him it had been the party: Harlan County, Kentucky, and the horror of a Falangist prison after Teruel; doubt and disillusionment and ultimate repudiation and a hole that nothing ever filled again. *I agreed with old Debs, that I would rise with the ranks, not from them,* he thought dryly. *Only somehow the ranks got ahead of me.*

His sister entered the room and he rose to greet her. She shook hands briskly, and her large, dark eyes took in his appearance with affectionate malice. They sat down at a table, and when the waitress came they both ordered Rhine wine spritzers. "Shalom," said Ruth perfunctorily. "Mike, you look terrible. That suit looks like you slept in it, and your face doesn't have any muscle tone. When are you going to start living and acting like a sixty-five-year-old man?"

"When I'm seventy-five? Look, Ruth, growing old gracefully isn't so easy for proletarians. Very few of us patronize Helena Rubenstein regularly, for example."

"Because you're too busy getting hit on the head in Lincoln Park. Don't tell me. Mike, you've been there with those hippies, haven't you? Playing Bolshevik when you should be sitting back in an easy chair and adding your life up. Hippies!" Her nostrils flared. "They don't even know how to talk like real radicals!"

They continued their conversation, probing and teasing each other in vulnerable areas. As they talked, he thought to himself, *She's hit it on the button, of course. It's uncanny how she does that. The question is, is it time for me to slip into old age like a suicide into a warm bath, or do I keep struggling against the gross weight of the accumulating years? She points out that I am undignified—I can accept that. She also points out I am ineffective. That's not so easy to accept. Finally, she suggests I am comic. I have lived through too much pain in my life to tolerate that.*

She asked a question that cut through his inner soliloquy and captured his attention. "Mike—the radicalism, the fighting, the trouble—where did it ever get you? Why is it so important to hold on to it?" He looked at her sharply and saw that she was sincerely asking for information. He was silent a moment and then gave her an oddly boyish grin.

"It was my life, Ruth—it was my vigor, it was my joy. It brought me whatever love I've known, and whatever comradeship. It filled my lungs and made me stand like a man. It was the element I lived in, like a fish lives in water and a bird lives in air. Can you understand that?"

"But when does it *end*, Mike?" she asked quietly.

"I suppose on the day when I wake up in the morning and say to myself, 'Relax, old fella, take it easy, have a glass of seltzer, think about old times, stop swimming, tread water, float—enjoy the days you have left.'"

"Don't you ever feel that way now, even a little?"

"Not even a little, Ruth. Not for a single moment."

She looked at him quizzically, with a half smile on her handsome, hawklike face. "I envy you, and I wouldn't live like you do for a million dollars," she said.

He shrugged. "With your money, you wouldn't be eligible anyway."

They played a rubber of bridge with an old man named Samuels and his middle-aged son, who was a furniture dealer. As Ruth was dealing the cards, the younger Samuels commented on the events surrounding the convention. "A plague on both their houses, is what I say." He picked up each card as it was dealt and fitted it into his hand. "The Democrats have nobody to blame but themselves. Truman, Kennedy, The Great Society, all that permissiveness, where was it supposed to lead? New math, high school kids don't even know their multiplication tables!" He grabbed for a card and accidentally turned it over. It was a face card. He quickly slipped it into the fan of cards in his hand, grinned at his father, and said jovially, "You didn't see that, Papa!" Ruth finished dealing the hand, and as the other three players arranged their cards, the furniture dealer addressed Mike: "No, but isn't that right, Mr. Rogoff? Isn't it the chickens coming home to roost? The Democrats opened the way for the Communists to take over, and now the Communists want their pound of flesh. Am I right?"

"Well, *I* would—wouldn't you?" asked Mike pleasantly. "Who's the bidder?"

"I bid a conventional club," said the older Samuels firmly.

Riding home on the el later, Mike realized he hadn't been honest with his sister. He was a good deal closer to the moment of accepting old age than he had admitted—so close sometimes that all it would take to put him over would be a wish, and a sigh, and a loosening of certain muscles. He felt that if he ever relaxed his guard he might slip over whether he wanted to or not. The question wasn't only whether he desired the alleged serenity of old age—it was also how much longer he would be able to choose before the decision would be made for him.

He tightened his hands into fists and looked at them. They were knobby and corded and brown-spotted, but it was still possible to imagine them striking with effect. *These aren't an old man's hands,* he thought. *They don't have to be. Not unless I think they are.*

It was almost suppertime when he got home. He turned on the television and watched films and still pictures of the clubbings in Lincoln Park the night before. *Worse than Sunday!* he thought. *I'm glad I didn't go to the park last night!*

He fixed himself chicken soup and crackers and a cup of Sanka, and sat eating in front of the TV set. The soup tasted unusually pungent and flavorful, and he drew comfort from it. He thought he would spend the evening at home and go to bed early. He took a mouthful of soup, then held the empty spoon in front of him. It seemed to tremble in his fingers. *What's wrong with going to bed early once in a while?* he asked himself. *At my age?*

What was wrong with going to bed early once in a while, age notwithstanding, was that he couldn't sleep. At a quarter of ten he got dressed and left the apartment. He went to a neighborhood saloon called Little Al's, a block away. It was a place where he had often brought Mary Cvetla, and when he sat down on a stool the barman said, "Hi, Mike—where's Mary?" He replied gruffly that he had no idea and ordered a shot and a beer.

There were few customers in the room, the juke box was quiet, and the bartender, after an unsuccessful attempt at conversation, subsided into a silent inspection of his fingernails. Mike was able to listen to thoughts that rustled in his brain like dry leaves stirred by a fall wind. Ideas and images followed one another in no particular sequence, and he experienced them passively, not troubling to impose any continuity or significance upon them. He drank four shots and four beer washes.

Mary Cvetla and Johnny the guitar player came in and took

a booth against the wall. Neither noticed Mike, but he watched them in the mirror behind the bar. There was a row of bottles below the mirror, and Mary's face appeared directly above the Cutty Sark. Mary and Johnny leaned across the table toward each other, and talked intimately, and smiled. Mike watched them for two or three minutes, until Johnny put his hand over Mary's. Then he rose from his stool and walked to their booth.

"Well, hello, Mary—hello, Johnny," he said heartily. "Buy you a drink?"

Mary's eyes widened. "Oh, Mike, hi! Gee, I don't know—" She glanced nervously at Johnny. The guitar player shrugged his broad shoulders. "Why not, man?" he said carelessly. He had a tough baby face like Jimmy Cagney's, incongruously wimpled by shoulder-length red hair. He didn't bother to remove his hand from Mary's, as Mike slid into the booth beside her.

Mike ordered drinks and drove the balky conversation forward until they arrived. He asked Mary about her son Stash ("Stanley," she corrected automatically) and about her job, and Johnny about the rock group he played with. Mary answered awkwardly, and Johnny lowered his eyelids as though he were on the nod and hardly bothered to answer at all.

The drinks came, and Mike threw down yet another shot of whiskey and chased it with half a glass of draft beer. He closed his eyes and ears for a moment so that the sensations of sight and sound wouldn't seduce any of his attention from the alcohol entering his system. When he became aware of his surroundings again, he was surprised to discover that Johnny was speaking.

". . . ignorant assholes. I hope they get everything they're asking for. If I was a cop, man, I'd really get my jollies this week. I mean it, man!"

Mike noticed that Johnny's small, lipless mouth sucked in and blew out as he talked, like the gills on fish. "Why do you say that, Johnny?" he asked politely.

"They make everybody look bad, that's why. People see a cat with long hair, you know, or sharp clothes, bell bottoms, fringe jackets, stuff like that, and they think he's some kind of Yippie freak, man, some kind of unpatriotic Commie revolutionary, you know? So everybody gets uptight, all the stuff dries up, you can't get gigs, it's all bad news, just because these assholes have to come on with all that peace shit!"

Mike drew a deep breath. "It'd be better to forget all the peace shit, right, Johnny? Before it screws up the important things?" He spoke slowly, as though savoring the words. Mary started to interrupt, but Mike silenced her with a gesture.

"Well, you know, man, don't mess up the other guy's bed, okay? I mean, how do you know where you'll be sleeping tonight?" Johnny grinned at Mary and patted her hand, as if to call attention to his words. Mary's face was stiff.

"I think you better take your hand off her before you give her a disease," said Mike. He tried to speak levelly, but his voice trembled. "Filth like you could rub off and be contagious."

Johnny stared at the gray-haired man incredulously. "Hey, that's not a nice way to talk, man. You keep that up and somebody's liable to forget you paid for the drinks and ram your goddamn teeth down your throat."

"Johnny, for heaven's sake—" Mary said placatingly.

"The hand, you lump of Fascist garbage," said Mike, pointing. "Remove it." He rose from his seat and leaned toward the other man. "Use your fingers for playing dirty songs on your guitar—somewhere else!"

"You crazy old fruitcake!" Johnny yelled. He sprang to his feet and pushed Mike out of the booth. Mike stumbled backward three steps and sat down heavily in the middle of the floor. Johnny took a step after him, and Mary seized his arm. "Johnny, for Heaven's sake, he's an old man!"

"He wasn't too old for you!" Johnny threw off her arm and took another step toward Mike. The bartender shouted for them to cool it, and the other patrons shifted their positions for a better view. Mike started to rise to his feet, but while he was still off balance, Johnny pushed him down again.

"You *momser*, let me up!" Mike shouted. "Storm trooper! Hophead! Degenerate!" He scrambled backward and regained his feet. For a moment he stood, red-faced, panting, and disheveled, his eyes hot with humiliation and rage. Suddenly he grabbed a beer bottle from a table, and, raising it above his head, threw himself at Johnny. He brought the bottle down on the guitar player's left ear. Johnny roared wordlessly and hit Rogoff a powerful blow over the heart, which set him down on the floor again.

The barman rounded the end of the bar, calling for an end to hostilities and picking up his own beer bottle en route. Mike struggled to his feet a third time, while Johnny stood in a boxer's bent-kneed stance, swaying and bobbing in front of him. "Scab! Vigilante! Ku Kluxer!" Mike called hoarsely, and swung his beer bottle again. It missed, and Johnny hit him on the cheekbone. He started to fall and was caught from behind by the bartender.

"Enough, goddamnit!" the barman snarled at Johnny. "Mike —Mike, listen, you crazy bastard, are you all right?" Mike looked over his shoulder in surprise. "All right? Of course I'm all right!" He spat a little blood. "It's a question of human decency," he explained, trying to pull himself loose from the barman's grasp.

"Human decency, shit!" Johnny protested. "The crazy son-of-a-bitch tried to brain me with a bottle!" He turned to Mary for confirmation. "You saw it—he clipped me on the ear! Well, didn't he?" Mary didn't answer. She was watching Mike as, freeing himself from the barman's hands, he squared his shoulders and brushed his coarse gray hair back from his forehead. His eyes met hers, and he inclined his head toward her in a formal little nod that might have meant anything.

Kindly but firmly the barman explained to Mike that it was

time for him to leave. Mike nodded. He picked up his change
from the table in the booth and started for the door. Then he
turned and said to Johnny, "You know, you're right about one
thing. Sometimes you can really get your jollies hitting a person on the head."

He walked back to his apartment. His cheekbone hurt, he
had a pain in his chest, and the first quivering of approaching
regurgitation tickled the back of his throat. He was also aware
that it was a splendid night—warm, but fresh, with enough air
movement to keep the skin dry. Soft light from streetlights
filtered down through leafy trees and shimmered on the sidewalk. From many blocks away, in the direction of the park,
various human and mechanical sounds combined into a gentle
ululation, which formed a background for his thoughts.

I said these hands aren't an old man's hands, he told himself.
*Not unless I think they are. And I don't think they are—and I
bet Johnny doesn't think they are either.*

At the vestibule door of his apartment building he stopped
and filled his lungs with the sweet night air. *Hoo-boy,* he
thought, enjoying the soreness in parts of his body that made
him conscious of his flesh and nerves and muscles; *what I need
is a night with a woman!*

Then he went upstairs and threw up.

12

STATIC ON THE LEFT

THE RULES OF THE GAME being played in Lincoln Park were simple, and the participants understood them perfectly: the police were to beat, and the protesters were to be beaten. There were some who wanted to change the rules, however.

Ted and Sari interrupted their own argument about the morality of violence to join a friendly but unaroused crowd listening to Bobby Seale. The Black Panther leader, who had only been in Chicago a few hours, cried for bloodshed: "Black people know what police brutality is, and you whites who've been asking whether it's real found out last night! Take care of the pigs! Get your shotguns and your three fifty-seven magnums! If a pig starts swinging a club, then put it over his head and lay him on the ground! If the pigs treat us unjustly tonight, we'll just have to barbecue us some of that pork!" Many people in the audience thought the most interesting thing in his speech was the way he pronounced the word "pigs"; he broke it into two syllables—"pih-yigs"—with the second syllable flatted, like a blue note.

A black motorcycle gang appeared in the park shortly after Seale finished his speech. Since the almost complete absence of blacks from previous marches and demonstrations had been a source of disappointment to the protesters, the denim-jacketed Harley and BMW riders were immediately surrounded by crowds of friendly white youths. Ted and Sari joined a cluster around a slim, caramel-colored biker with a carefully trimmed imperial beard.

The biker told them to prepare for an uprising in the black community. According to the intelligence he bore, Negro activists were ready to launch an attack on South and West Side police stations, where garrisons had been weakened to provide for the Lincoln Park task force. All that was required to start the rising was for the Yippies and Mobe people to follow Bobby Seale's advice and "barbecue some pork." "You got to show us you mean it, see? Then we'll all come in—the Disciples and the Rangers, the Cobras, the Vice Lords—"

"And the Panthers too?" asked an eager Yippie.

"Why sure, man, the Panthers too. I wouldn't shit you, baby."

"But you won't start till we do?"

The brown face behind the beard and dark glasses was as smilingly inscrutable as a hip Bronzeville Buddha. "Well, you know, man, it's your turn now, right? You just do your thing—don't you worry about the brothers."

When he and his fellow bikers departed in a roar of engines and a stink of burned rubber, Sari looked earnestly at Ted, and asked, "What do you think?"

"B.S.," Ted answered flatly.

"Is that what you really think, or what you'd like to think?"

"Look—it's a chance to get whitey to mess over whitey, maybe radicalize a few white kids to kill a few white cops, while they sit it out and enjoy the show. If you were black, you'd probably feel the same way."

Sari chewed a loose splinter of skin at the corner of a fingernail with strong white teeth. "But what if they mean it, Ted? What if they *would* come in like he said, take over the police stations, really let it loose! Man, it could be the beginning of everything!" She clapped her hands eagerly, and her fine eyes flashed. "It could be the day the balloon went up—the day we changed the world!"

"It could also be the day we destroyed the Movement and got ourselves killed in the process," Ted answered flatly. "Don't be dumb. Our job here is to bear witness, not to try to out-pig the pigs."

She looked at him angrily. "Don't you ever get tired of coming on like the voice of sweet reason? Boy, you would have been hell on wheels at Lexington and Concord! I can see you now, bearing witness while everybody else was shooting redcoats!"

"Well, I haven't gotten my orders from General Washington yet," he said with heavy irony. He felt the first twinges of his familiar reaction to violence: his head felt light, his skin numb, his mouth dry. "Let's just let it lay, all right?"

But Sari didn't want to let it lay, so they argued. It was an argument that had been in preparation for a week, and its time had come. To Sari, the violence of Sunday and Monday night was valuable both as justification and preparation for counterviolence. We have borne witness enough, she insisted; we have proved with our bodies who the aggressors are, and now it's time for self-defense. Bobby Seale was right: if a pig starts swinging a club, then put it over his head and lay him on the ground! And if they start shooting? Ted asked. Then take their guns away from them and shoot them back! Ted could taste his stomach juices in the back of his mouth. "Oh, Sari, that's rhetoric!" he argued impatiently. "Nobody's going to disarm the Chicago Police Department. The only thing you're going to do is maybe get five or ten freaks killed!"

"All right—maybe that's what it takes!" Sari snapped. "Maybe we've been trying to buy liberation too cheap—maybe that's been the trouble all along!"

Ted's face was as pale as writing paper. "Tell me about breaking eggs to make omelets," he said in a low, unsteady voice.

She looked at him for a moment. The anger disappeared from her face, and her expression became judicious and sad. "What's the point? You already know. Look, Ted, I'm splitting. Stay loose, okay?"

"Just like that?"

"Just like that. We've said it all. Anything more would just be summer reruns. So, later, friend." She turned and strode rapidly away across the grass. He watched her slim dancer's body, clad in a sleeveless shirt, worn, rope-belted blue jeans, and huaraches on her slender feet, until she disappeared in the crowd.

He shivered. *Now comes lonely-time,* he thought. He walked slowly to a nearby bench and sat down, thrusting his legs straight out in front and hanging his head back so he could stare up into the sky. He thought, *My God, but I'm going to miss her!* He leafed back over his memories of the month they had been lovers. *We didn't fight enough, that was the trouble. It couldn't last with somebody like Sari, not unless we fought sometimes. But, Christ, how I hate fighting!*

After a few minutes he thought he better build up his blood sugar. He walked out of the park and bought a pint of ice cream at a drug store on Wells Street and brought it back to eat on his park bench. It was fudge ripple, and he ate it with a pink plastic spoon. He was down near the bottom of the carton when a little-girl voice beside him said, "Can I have a lick?"

The girl looked as unlike Sari as it was possible for an attractive young woman to look. She was plump and blond and pug-nosed, and stood barely five feet tall in her Italian sandals. Her skin was golden brown and sprinkled with freckles, and her bouncy round breasts were unconfined beneath her Brooks Brothers shirt. Ted looked at her in pleased surprise and offered her a spoonful of ice cream. She licked it clean with a quick, catlike tongue.

When she was finished, she told him her name was Monkey Morrison. "I'm a Pol Sci major at Northwestern. Who are you?"

He told her, and they continued to get acquainted as they finished off the ice cream. Monkey's family lived in Barrington, Illinois, and her father worked on LaSalle Street; he was, she said happily, loaded. Her parents had no conception whatever of the drives and ambitions that motivated her, but they were good cats and never bugged her or put her down because of their differing value judgments. She had been liberated since she was a sophomore in high school. She believed in the Age of Aquarius.

She was as irresistibly pettable as a puppy, and Ted felt much the same delight with her he had felt when he received his beagle, Max, as a present on his eighth birthday. *But Max never had what she has,* he thought randily. Sari was suddenly far away.

Monkey had a transistor radio. During the early evening they listened to news from the convention. The report came that the delegates at the Amphitheatre had passed a compromise motion to seat half of Julian Bond's Georgia delegation and deny seating to half of Lester Maddox's delegates. "Oh, wow!" said Monkey. She put her soft, cool little hand on Ted's and squeezed it excitedly.

Around them in the gathering darkness, people began to cheer. Their accents were varied: dude-ranch western, Hyannisport-eastern, midwest suburban, and college-quota Jewish; but they blended into the homogenous sound of middle-class young America, reared in an income bracket that could afford a conscience.

13

IT DOESN'T MATTER
HOW MUCH YOU LOSE

WHEN MAL WOKE UP in Goody's apartment Tuesday morning, Goody had left for work, but almost everyone else who had been in the apartment the night before was still there. He was aware of a sense of sudden panic, as though awakening on the edge of a cliff. For the first few moments of consciousness, all he could say to himself was, *Oh shit, you've blown it this time.* He became conscious of the smell in the room, which was both stale and gamy. Opening his eyes without moving his head, he saw a limp arm dangling from a sofa on his right and a girl in shorts asleep in an armchair on his left. He could hear at least three people nearby snoring in different keys.

Very carefully he rolled his head to the right. He was now able to see a man and a woman asleep on the shag rug three feet away; their position, if not literally coital, only lacked fulfillment by an inch or two, and their clothing offered no impediment. He rolled his head slowly to the left and discovered his friend the young copywriter sitting cross-legged against the wall and drumming a complex rhythm on his knees with dancing fingers. The copywriter grinned at him. "Whoo-ee, man, too much!" he said softly. "I'll flip you to see who goes out for the beer."

Mal sat up and put his hands to his temples. "What time is it?" he asked in a voice that sounded as though it was filtered through phlegm.

"Nine, ten, eleven, some time like that. Scooby-doo. You look awful, man. What you need is a beer, no lie."

Mal got to his feet and went into the bathroom. He splashed cold water on his face and looked at himself in the mirror. He was pale, and his eyes were bloodshot; his shirt was grimy, his coat wrinkled and stained, his pants shapeless. There was nothing he could do about any of that. He rubbed the tip of a finger across a bar of soap, and then across his teeth and gums, generating a mouthful of bitter soapsuds. Gagging, he rinsed out his mouth with cold water. It tasted worse than before, but he hoped it smelled better.

He found a telephone in the kitchen, and, closing the door behind him, dialed the number of Pauncefoot Associates. The telephone operator with the expensive English accent answered, and he asked for his secretary. When she came on, he said, "Hey, Linda, this is Mal. Look, I'm not going to be able to get in today. Marilyn and Lisa are both down with some damn virus or something, and I've got to do the Florence Nightingale bit." He paused, but she didn't say anything. "So what's happening along the Left Bank? Mimi die of consumption yet?"

"Well, one thing that happened," Linda replied in a low, expressionless voice, "was that Marilyn called up to see if you were at work or not. She didn't sound too far gone with the damn virus—I couldn't say about Lisa."

"Oh." Mal thought a moment. "Yeah, well, I'm sorry—that was dumb. The point is, I'm not about to get into the office today. I was in the park last night, and I haven't gotten over it yet. Only don't tell Toby Tobin that."

"Oh, Mal, you didn't get hurt, did you?" she asked, with the instant forgiveness that made her more valuable to Mal than her typing or shorthand.

"Sniffed some tear gas is all," he answered brusquely. "Probably won't be able to remember it tomorrow."

"Maybe you ought to have a doctor look you over anyway. Oh, and Mal—about Toby Tobin. He was in the office waiting

to see you when Marilyn called. He heard my end of the conversation, so I think he knows you didn't spend last night at
home."

Mal cursed. "It would have to be Tobin, wouldn't it? Ahh,
the hell with it. If anybody asks, tell them there's sickness at
home, but I'll try to make it this afternoon. I won't, but by the
time they realize it the day will be over. Okay?"

"Okay." Her voice became maternal: "Mal, what in the world
were you doing in the park? You could have gotten yourself
killed, you goof."

"Linda, love, there are more things in heaven and hell than
are dreamt of in your philosophy. Why, I understand there are
even people in this country who don't use a HydroDent appliance, or start off their morning with Brek-first. How does that
grab you? Shakes the goddamn pillars, doesn't it?"

"Mal, I think you're still drunk from last night," she said in a
tone of affectionate disapproval; she was more comfortable with
alcohol than tear gas.

"Is it morning already? Look, hang in there, Linda. See you
tomorrow." He hung up the phone and went back into the living room. People were starting to move around; Janis Joplin
was shouting on the stereo; the young copywriter was still trying to find someone to flip with to get beer. Mal passed through
the room and left the apartment by the front door, descended
two flights of dark stairs, and emerged from the vestibule into
bright sunlight. He looked around, blinking, searching for familiar landmarks. St. Michael's Church was only a half block
away. He walked toward it and then past it, heading east toward Lake Michigan.

Ten minutes later he stood by the outdoor chess pavilion at
the water's edge, kibitzing two old men locked in a savage,
sanguinary game. He watched as Black, with a two-pawn advantage, forced White to trade knights, bishops, and finally
queens. In a matter of minutes the board looked as if the Four
Horsemen of the Apocalypse had used it as a bridle path. *It*

*doesn't matter how much you lose, as long as the other guy
loses more,* Mal thought. But then White began to play for stalemate, and after a few moves it became obvious that Black had
overextended himself and no longer had the strength to administer the coup de grâce. White, a hairless little man whose features were defined solely by three parallel horizontal creases,
chuckled and lit his pipe; Black, as righteously indignant as a
Fundamentalist preacher at a topless discotheque, declared yet
another impotent check. Mal watched for a few moments more,
as Black charged and White danced away, until Black forgot
himself and left White with no alternative but to place himself
in check next time. "Stalemate!" cried White, in the voice of a
boy soprano. "I'd be switched if I'd play a prissy, picayune
game like that!" answered Black bitterly. Mal laughed, and
retreated under Black's outraged glare.

He thought about the game as he walked along the breakwater toward the point, thrust out a quarter mile into the lake.
*Stalemate means nobody wins, nobody loses—but when you've
been losing before, doesn't not-losing constitute a victory of
sorts? And when the bully-boy jock with the unbroken win record comes out with a split decision for once, will he ever believe
in his own superiority with such unquestioning smugness again?*

White gulls fished off the pilings, and as he moved out farther
over the water, a thirty-mile vista of steel and concrete opened
to both sides. He could see the smoke-smudge over Gary, the
hotels and high-rises of Hyde Park, the stately parade of sky-
scrapers in downtown Chicago, and Navy Pier pushing its
mosque-and-minarets into the lake. To his left, the shoreline
stretched north toward Evanston, fronted first by green parkland, then by luxury apartment buildings. Hull-down on the
horizon, an ore boat headed for the Upper Peninsula. If he had
been a few feet higher, he could have seen the Michigan shore.
The sky was cloudless, and the breeze was brisk and just a touch
fishy. *This is some prize to play for,* he thought. *But who gets
the prize if there's a stalemate?*

He could see the building where Pauncefoot Associates had its offices. He retasted the tequila of the night before and shivered momentarily with the chill a man feels when he confronts his own life half gone. What was it Henry Miller said at the beginning of *Capricorn*—that he was still a failure at thirty-three, the age of Christ when he was crucified? *I'm three years older than that,* Mal thought somberly.

He reached the very tip of the breakwater and sat down on the edge, with his feet dangling above the choppy waves. He thought about his work, and his family, and what, to use another simple word, he called his soul. The first unavoidable fact to be faced was the role he played, and the stake he held, in the system. In midtwentieth century America, capitalism depended on mass consumption. The motivation and manipulation of consumers had become the *sine qua non* of the American Way of Life. To achieve it, marketers and their advertising agents had spun a vast web of overt and covert persuasion around all aspects of national experience. Near the center of this web labored a small, well-fed, nonpoisonous spider named Mal Tolliver.

Look, if the system is okay, you're okay—and if the system's full of shit, you're full of shit. Will you accept that?

Maybe not. Maybe it's so oversimplified as to be meaningless. Isn't it possible to be a private person, doing your own job professionally and well, cherishing your wife and your kids, supporting the symphony and the ACLU and the Chicago Cubs, paying your bar bill regularly, reading books about breakthroughs in genetics and psychedelics, voting for nonmachine Democrats?

Sure it is, but how does that change anything? You're still part of the system.

Mal shifted uncomfortably. Sourness rose from his stomach, reminding him he had eaten nothing today. *Well, how can you be all that sure the system's bad?*

I didn't say it was bad—you said it was bad!

The hell I did! You did!

And just who do you think I am, dummy?

Mal groaned and stared down at desert boots, speckled with drops of spray from the slapping waves. *All right, then, what's the alternative? LSD in Lake Michigan and balling in the bushes? Dirty feet? Rhetoric as brainless and brutal as a rabid dog? The clear conviction that everything gracious, temperate, or sympathetic is a copout?*

Sorry you had such an unrewarding time last night, Mal.

That was an episode, for God's sake—you don't build a life-style on it!

What do you build a life-style on? The virtues of the Hydro-Dent appliance? Now there's a rock, baby!

Oh, get off my back, will you? Mal willed the dialogue to end, and put his mind to practical questions. He realized he would have to call his wife and considered various stories he could tell her. He decided to say he had gotten drunk, blacked out, and awakened on the floor of an Old Town apartment be-longing to an art director he knew. He would tell her not to expect him home that night, because he believed it was impor-tant for him to see what was happening in the park. She wouldn't understand that, but it would stop her from reporting him missing to the police.

With a sigh he got to his feet and began walking toward shore. He wondered what to do with the rest of the day. He considered and rejected going to work, visiting the Art Institute, the Field Museum, the Aquarium, or the Bird House at the zoo, drinking beer and eating peanuts on Wells Street, browsing in a secondhand bookstore. It wasn't until he had eaten breakfast and called his wife that he reached a conclusion: he would ride buses through as many different neighborhoods as he could reach before dinnertime.

Transferring from one bus line to another, and sometimes walking a few blocks and paying a new fare, he visited Italian, Polish, and Puerto Rican neighborhoods on the West Side,

Chinatown, the Greek and Mexican districts on Halsted Street, Bronzeville, and Hyde Park. He looked into people's faces, and people looked back at him with curiosity, hostility, friendliness, or unconcern. All afternoon he felt a freedom that reminded him of skinny dipping in Lake Michigan at midnight on a summer night.

At 7:00 he returned to Old Town, ate dinner, and walked over to the park to listen to the speeches.

14

WHEN TRUE SIMPLICITY IS GAINED

AT 11:30, as the police loudspeakers ordered everyone out of the park, Mal stood across the street, in front of the Georgian Court Apartments. He could hear the prayer meeting off to his left, although it was hidden from his sight by trees.

A busful of police reinforcements was held up by traffic directly in front of him, and he heard them singing. A chill ran up his spine as he recognized the song. It was from *Snow White and the Seven Dwarfs:*

> "Heigh-ho, heigh-ho,
> It's off to work we go—"

Time moved slowly, and the air was charged with menace. The crowd on the sidewalk across from the park grew larger. People fidgeted, bored with the waiting, but unwilling to leave until they had seen something dramatic enough to repay them for the time they had invested.

A little after midnight a voice behind Mal's shoulder said, "Hey, I know you. You're Mal Tolliver—you're married to Marilyn Beeman." He turned to face the woman who had spoken. She was tall, with broad shoulders and full breasts, wind-blown hair streaked with gray, and a wide smile that involved her whole face. As he groped for her name, she saved him the embarrassment of failure: "I'm Helen Haggarty—I

knew Marilyn before you were married. I worked on some commercials with her when she was at J. Walter."

"Of course." Mal thought he remembered meeting her at a
cocktail party two or three years before. "How've you been,
Helen? What in the world are you doing here?"

"I live here." She gestured toward the Georgian Court building. "All you people are right spang in the middle of my dog-
walking route." For the first time he noticed she was holding
a leash; attached to the other end was a German shepherd,
fine-boned and intelligent-looking. The dog was wearing an
arrangement of steel and leather braces over its hips and upper
back legs and moved with the painful economy of a cripple.

"Hi, boy," said Mal. "What's he wearing the corset for?"

"Dislocation of the hip. It's fairly common among dogs that
have been overbred. The hip socket is so shallow the ball of
the thighbone won't stay in place. Without the brace, the poor
old guy can't even get up and down the front stairs. What's
happening in the park?"

Mal told her the police had ordered everyone out forty-five
minutes before, but nobody had come out yet, so something
should be happening soon.

"Damn them anyway," Helen said angrily. "The thing I
can't forgive them for is enjoying it so much!" Mal glanced at
her in surprise. "The police?" he asked. "Of course, the police," she replied. "Who did you think?"

"I'm just surprised at a friend of my wife's thinking hostile
thoughts about the police, that's all."

"I have all kind of friends who think all kind of ways," Helen
said firmly. "It has no effect on my evaluation of things I see
with my own eyes." She frowned at Mal, as if expecting him
to disagree; when he smiled instead, so did she.

They talked for ten minutes, waiting for something to happen
across the street. Then they heard the first warning of the
police attack—a complex sound that blended cries of fear and
shouts of anger in a dense harmony like oboes and trombones

in octave intervals. Moments later the first protesters appeared through the trees and bushes. They trotted toward the street, stopping every few steps to look back, a few helping others who were injured. They were silhouetted against the glare of flood-lights behind them. Many more appeared, until the east side of Clark Street was crowded with them. A few dashed across the street, but most stayed on the walk, technically outside the park.

The police line appeared, moving through a gray mist of tear gas that hung between the trees like torn mosquito netting. The officers were insect-eyed in their gas masks. In the center of the skirmish line a Sanitation Department truck rumbled slowly forward. It had been specially equipped for spraying tear gas, and two cops operated the nozzle that swayed over the roof of the cab like a hunting snake.

As the first policemen reached the sidewalk, they charged the protesters standing there, driving them between parked cars and into the street. One boy of fifteen or sixteen dashed toward Mal and Helen. As he gained the safety of the curb, he stopped beside them, panting. "Get off the street, man!" he said hoarsely. "They're *killing* us tonight!" He was wearing goggles edged with vaseline, and blood from a cut in his scalp trickled over one lens. He turned to Helen. "I mean it, lady—you better get that dog home fast!" He hesitated a moment, then disappeared in the crowd that jammed the sidewalk.

The first acrid wave of tear gas billowed across the street, and Mal felt its barbs in his nose and throat, and the scene suddenly blurred behind acid tears. Helen grabbed his arm, the dog whined, people around them coughed and swore. Across the street the shouts of the attackers and the attacked swelled to a roar.

"Mal, come on—we've got to get out of here!" Helen shouted in his ear. Pulling the dog after her with one hand, dragging Mal with the other, she shouldered her way toward the entrance of the Georgian Court Apartments. They ran along the sidewalk toward the lighted vestibule in the middle of the U-shaped building. "Hurry up, Boots," Helen ordered the German shepherd, whining in protest behind them. Other tenants of the building were hurrying to their apartments; nobody wanted to be caught in a police sweep of the court. Helen unlocked the inner vestibule door, and they clattered up two flights of stairs to her apartment. Slamming and locking the hall door behind them, she gestured toward the kitchen and bedroom. "Close all the windows at that end of the apartment," she ordered, as she began to pull down the living room windows. "If gas gets into the drapes, I'll never get it out!"

They shut every window in the five-room apartment and then stood looking out into the courtyard and the street beyond. After a moment Helen sighed, and her body lost its rigidity. "Lordy, Lordy," she said, with the deliberation of one who swears infrequently, "now there's an item for your memory book!"

"Incredible!" Mal said. He found he was trembling. "My God, but you feel helpless! Last night when I was out there, I was too drunk to know what was going on. But tonight—" He hesitated, unable to find the words he sought.

"I know. It's like some terrible natural disaster, like a tornado or a tidal wave—something that will wipe you out with no more compunction than swatting a fly." She paused, then added, "Only tornadoes and tidal waves don't love their work so much."

"When the cops came by in their bus tonight," Mal said, "they were singing 'Heigh-ho, heigh-ho, it's off to work we go,' like Happy and Dopey and Doc on their way to the diamond mine! You're right—they do enjoy it. Those bastards!" They looked out the window in silence, watching figures on the sidewalk surge back and forth, back-lit by floodlights and flash bulbs, and blurred by a scrim of tear gas. Some people fell and rose again, a few remained where they had fallen.

"Of course there's another possibility," Mal said reflectively.

"They may be scared witless, and whistling to keep up their courage. It would be nice to think they were."

Helen turned to him, her eyes bright. "Oh, yes! Oh, you've got to be right! They're scared to death—that's why they're acting this way!"

Mal shrugged. "Well, whether they are or not, it doesn't make any difference in the way they come on." They watched in silence again. Boots, sensing the charged emotions in the room and the violence outside, whined and pawed the rug. "Here, boy, it's all right, it's okay now," Mal said. The dog came to him in stiff-legged discomfort, and Mal scratched him behind the ears.

"Fix you a drink?" Helen asked abruptly. "I've got Scotch or vodka—or coffee, if you'd rather."

Mal said he'd have whatever she was having. While she was out of the room he patted the dog, and looked out the window, and thought that nothing he had done since Monday afternoon had any relationship to anything else in his life. He felt the way he had felt one summer afternoon years before, when he was fishing alone on a lake in Minnesota. The outboard motor had run out of gas, and he had used a canoe paddle to work his way back to shore. But then the sky had suddenly darkened, and a chilling wind sprang up, and the boat began skidding across the choppy, foam-edged waves toward the middle of the lake faster than he could paddle toward land. The helplessness he felt had stayed with him since that day; he was a speck on a heedless gun-metal expanse, alone and forgotten, and there was nothing he could do but drown.

Helen came back with coffee, apologizing that it was instant. They sat with the coffee table between them, Helen on the sofa, Mal in a comfortable wingback chair, and began a conversation that required a good deal of concentration from both of them, in view of the performance taking place outside.

They began with their jobs and their marital states. Mal learned that Helen had graduated from Northwestern School

of Speech, and been in dramatic productions at Goodman
Theatre and Hull House, and had studied under Cordelia
Spaulding, the fountainhead of improvisational theater. During
these years she had earned her living as a TV producer rather
than an actress, which had allowed her to keep a touch of
innocence toward her avocation, a luxury few professionals can
afford. This innocence stood her in good stead when she
changed jobs and became the Director of the Uptown Theater
Arts Program, an activity of the Department of Urban De-
velopment. Anyone without a high innocence quotient who
worked for the D.U.D. found himself poisoned by cynicism
in a month.

Helen was divorced. She had been thirty-three when she
married. "You'd think anybody who waited that long would
be able to use a little judgment, wouldn't you? Well, you
couldn't be wronger." She grimaced; it was a self-mocking
smile that involved her whole face. "I could hardly wait to dig
under that handsome façade to discover what I'd bought myself, and you know what? The façade was all there was! Inside, he was as hollow as a chocolate Easter bunny! Oh, boy,
what a great awakening!" She paused, as if remembering some
private detail of disillusionment. Then she shook her head
vigorously, sending her hair flying. "Well, so much for life's
little losers. Tell me about you and Marilyn. You have a little
girl, and you live in Evanston, right?"

Mal talked for a while about his family. He felt the temptation to begin laying the groundwork for a "my-wife-doesn't-
understand-me-in-the-ticky-tacky-suburbs" approach, but rejected the ploy. *No games tonight,* he thought. *Whatever happens, let it be straight.*

Outside there was a crackle of pistol shots. The clock on the
mantel said 1:25.

"I don't know about you, but I'm ready for a drink," Helen
said. She rose, and he noticed the efficient and graceful way
her body moved. "How about some Scotch and water?"

"You're on." While she was in the kitchen this time, he inspected her phonograph records and was pleasantly surprised to find a number of modern classical discs. He clicked on the amplifier and stacked up Aaron Copland, Roy Harris, and *The Age of Anxiety* on the spindle. *Appalachian Spring* fell first, and he lifted the player arm with his finger and set the needle down in the middle of the record. Helen brought their drinks just as the Shaker hymn section began. She stopped in the doorway, head cocked to one side, listening to the familiar melody. The second time it came around, she sang in a clear, true voice:

> " 'Tis the gift to be simple, 'tis the gift to be free,
> 'Tis the gift to come down where we ought to be—"

Mal looked into her eyes and saw they were dove gray, with flecks of black and copper, and crinkled at the outer edges. They sang the next verse together:

> "When true simplicity is gained,
> To bow and to bend we will not be ashamed;
> To turn, to turn, 'twill be our delight,
> Till by turning, turning, we come out right."

She brought him his drink. "Good for you," she said lightly. "It's that kind of night." She sat down on the sofa again, and they listened to the coda until it ended on its note of quiet affirmation. Outside noises were inaudible under the music, although the smell of tear gas was faintly pervasive.

Then, as though their relationship was an elevator that had suddenly reached a new level, Mal began to talk. In one uninterrupted twenty-minute monologue, he threw everything in his mind at her—Marilyn and Lisa and the Beer-beque, the work he was doing and not doing at Pauncefoot Associates, the death of his friend Biff Maull, the mixed attraction and repulsion he had felt toward the protesters in the park, his dive into drunkenness, his imaginary dialogue with Hugh Hefner, and his kaleidoscopic memories of the violence the night before.

"I didn't go into the office today," he concluded. "I rode around town on buses, visiting different neighborhoods. I haven't got the faintest idea why. A great discontinuity seems to have come into my life. You know that menopause of the middle-aged man the women's magazines are always talking about? I wonder if that's got anything to do with it." He shook his glass gently, and the ice cubes tinkled.

"Oh, I wouldn't think so," Helen said. "You're not middle-aged yet. You've just come to the dog-leg in the road."

"The dog-leg?" He glanced at the dog lying on the floor, its back legs held in position by a metal brace. "You mean a leg like Boots has—the kind that won't stay where it's supposed to stay?"

"I didn't mean that, but maybe it's not so far off either. Look, when Ralph and I split, I knew I had to go back to work, but I couldn't stand the idea of twenty more years as an agency TV producer, with a clipboard and a ten-second stopwatch. It was as if the road had come to a dead end, and I was looking at brick walls. But after a while I noticed this little street running off to the side, and a few hundred yards along it, the main road started up again, going the way I wanted to go, straight as a string. I was at a dog-leg in the road, that was all." She took a swallow from her glass, emptying it. "Deciding to go back into the theater, that was what the dog-leg was. I decided I wouldn't need to be afraid of failing, as I had been when I got out of college, because I wouldn't limit my options to acting this time; I would do anything I could make a living at, just as long as it was connected with theater. In a way, it was being prepared to settle for less so I could ask for more. I'll never be a great actress, but I've got a good chance to work in some branch of theater all my life. Which seems like a pretty fair deal, at this point."

Mal reached out his hand for her empty glass. "Let me make us two refills, and then you tell me about the theater program you're doing." He went to the kitchen and mixed Scotch, water, and ice. The kitchen walls were lemon yellow, with a montage of theatrical posters on one wall and a happily insane Miró reproduction on another. There was a round oak table, a vinyl floor that looked like Mexican tiles, and copper-bottomed pots and pans. He thought it was a room in which he would like to dawdle over coffee.

When he came back into the living room, Helen was standing in front of the phonograph, turning the records over. There was a blending of angularity and curvature in her posture—of self-reliance and dependency was the way he translated it—that flushed him with desire. He suddenly wanted to feel her erect body relax against him, the firm muscles soften, the cool, dry skin become warm and moistly adhesive. He stood stock-still with a glass in each hand, thinking that if he could put them down quietly, he could step up behind her, slip his hands under her arms, cup her breasts, and kiss her on the back of the neck.

She turned, and, seeing him, reached out for her glass. He handed it to her. She looked down at it a moment, a half smile on her lips. He stood flat-footed, unable to decide what to do. She looked up, her gray eyes wide under raised eyebrows. "Cheers," she said, raising the glass to her lips and turning away from him in one easy movement. She sat back on the sofa and tucked her feet under her. "Well, you said the magic word—you asked about the D.U.D. Theater Arts Program, you lucky man."

He sat in the wingback chair. "That I did, that I did," he said. He felt relief, as if he had safely passed a point of peril, and frustration, because his desire remained.

She told him about the program—how it was organized, who had the political clout, how much money was involved, and what the goals were. Then she began to talk in specifics. She described some of the hillbillies and blacks she was working with, the time-serving bureaucrats that threatened her from the right, and the SDS militants who hoped to wreck the program from the left. Finally, a little diffidently, she talked of the pride she was beginning to feel. "These people have been losers all their lives! Most of them have never done one single thing that didn't turn to crud in their hands. Now they're working together to create something good, something that's here now that wasn't here before! And when they do, they'll never be quite the same again!" Embarrassed by her enthusiasm, she grinned ruefully. "I get carried away so often I feel like Mehitabel. But, gosh, I think something great could come out of this, if we don't strangle it in the cradle!"

"You know something, Helen? I envy the hell out of you!"

She looked at him with an expression both grateful and mocking. "Why? Because I'm around the dog-leg and you aren't? Think of it this way: you may be on a healthier dog."

He grinned. "That's what's known as looking at things from a flea's-eye view."

"Don't knock it if you haven't tried it." The record on the turntable ended, and in the brief interval of silence before the next record fell, they could hear shouts outside. Mal went to the window. Three or four running figures passed the front of the building, and a police siren shrieked in the distance. Mal looked at the clock. "Jesus Christ, it's almost two-thirty, and they're still beating up people out there!"

"It must be like this in Prague tonight," Helen said. "Only worse, because the Russians shoot demonstrators, and we only hit them and gas them."

Mal turned to face her. "You know why I said I envy you a minute ago? Not because you're around the dog-leg at all. It's because you're doing work that just possibly may have some validity for you after all this business out there is over—and what I'm doing has about as much meaning as collecting baseball cards! I don't know how I can keep on doing what I'm doing, and I don't know what else I can do!"

"What else do you want to do?" she asked him quietly.

"God, I don't know! Write articles for the *National Geographic*—do a documentary on the Melungeons in Tennessee— once I talked to a guy about collecting seaweed and selling it for iodine. I'd like to learn to be a really good photographer, I think. Maybe I could write a book and illustrate it myself, if I had anything to say. Maybe! The thing I'm afraid of is, maybe there isn't anything else I want to do enough!"

"How does Marilyn feel about it? As I remember, she was always a pretty practical gal."

"Oh, Marilyn—" Mal began irritably, and then caught himself, hesitated, and said, "I don't think it's really Marilyn's problem. Marilyn has other things to worry about." He teased the two ends of his mustache with his thumb and forefinger. "Let's not talk about Marilyn." He looked at her levelly, and she returned his gaze. "I don't want to go out into the street tonight. I want to stay here, with you. Can I?" His mouth was dry, and his heart pounded.

"Yes, you can stay here. But you'll have to sleep on the couch." One corner of her mouth turned up, and her eyes gleamed in the lamplight. "It makes up into a full bed, and it's very comfortable. Here, help me pull it out." She stood up and began to lift a cushion. He jumped to his feet and moved to embrace her. She interposed the cushion between their bodies.

"I didn't mean I wanted to sleep on the couch," he whispered, his lips brushing her temple.

"I know you didn't, my dear." She drew her head back until she could look into his eyes. "But that's where you are going to sleep—unless you want to take your chances with *them*." She nodded toward the window.

"Helen, oh, God, don't you know how much I want you?" He tried to reach her lips with his own, but she turned her face aside. The sofa cushion between their bodies felt ludicrous. He tugged at it, and it moved a few inches.

Suddenly, surprisingly, Helen was free of his grasp, standing three feet away, with the cushion held in front of her more like a weapon than a shield.

"I mean it, Mal," she said evenly. "Not tonight. Maybe never, but certainly not tonight." She stood motionless except for the deep rise and fall of her breathing. "You can either accept it, or leave."

He felt his hands flexing. Desire and embarrassment bubbled together in his brain, and he wished he could crawl off somewhere, by himself. "Helen—I'm sorry. I feel like an asshole. Really. I won't do it again."

She regarded him gravely. "Don't," she said. "All right, let's get that bed of yours made up."

He opened up the sofa while she brought bed sheets and two feather pillows. "I don't think you'll need a blanket, because you sure won't want to open any windows," she said briskly. "I'll use the bathroom first and get out of your way. Mix yourself a nightcap if you want to—I'm going to bed." She turned off the phonograph and started out of the room, then turned to look at him again. " 'And indeed there will be time,' " she said gently. " 'Time for you and time for me—' good night, Mal."

"Good night, Helen. Sleep well." She went into the bathroom, and five minutes later he heard her come out and, calling the dog to follow her, go into her bedroom and close the door.

He lay on his back on the sofa bed, waiting for sleep. After a while he began to believe his senses were sharpening, rather than dulling as he expected them to. He heard street sounds clearly, and could taste the tear gas in the room, and feel its abrasive touch on his eyeballs under his closed lids. He could hear Boots's heavy breathing through the closed bedroom door, and once or twice he thought he heard Helen shifting her position in bed.

I bet she's wearing a nightgown, he thought. *Light blue, and smooth and silky, and warm with the warmth of her body.*

"Oh, hell!" he groaned aloud.

It was nearly 4:00 when he looked at the luminous dial of the mantel clock for the last time. Outside, there was only the sound of an occasional truck or el train in the distance. His lids felt heavy, and languor flowed gently through his body.

Sleep, he thought drowsily. *Everybody sleep, so we can get ready for tomorrow..*

He slept.

15

THE KNOCK ON THE DOOR

WEDNESDAY BEGAN in Robin Goodpasture's apartment at about the same time Tuesday was ending at Helen Haggarty's.

Ted Bakerfield and his new friend Monkey Morrison needed a place to crash. A friend of a friend of Monkey's had given her Goody's address, and at 1:00 A.M. the young couple rang the doorbell of Goody's Old Town apartment. Goody opened the door and peered at them belligerently through sleep-swollen eyelids. She was wearing a pink shortie nightgown. "They're not here," she said.

"Who?" Ted asked automatically.

"Anybody." Goody began to close the door, but Ted held it open until he could mention the name of Monkey's friend of a friend and ask if they could spend the night. Grudgingly, Goody let them in. "You can have the couch, there. I'm dead. G'night." She went into her bedroom and shut the door.

Ted was so keyed up he felt as if he had been rubbed down all over with liniment. The police attack in the park had put his metabolism in high gear, and two close calls in the streets had kept it racing. His blood sugar level was high from two Mars bars he had eaten, his emotions were raw from the violence he had witnessed, and the desirability and apparent willingness of the girl beside him made him sharply aware of the tightness of his jeans at the crotch.

"Well, all right," he said, dropping onto the couch, with his arms spread wide. "Come here and relax in relative safety, and we'll pass the night away constructively." He hoped for a confident tone, but his voice trembled like a reed. Monkey sat beside him, her back upright and her eyes shining. She was a talker, and she wanted to talk about their evening in the park and on the streets.

Each time he pulled her to a semihorizontal position, she thought of an incident she wanted to reexperience or an idea she wanted to test, and pulled herself upright again. Her lips were soft, her breasts were round and her voice never stopped for a moment. It was enough to drive a man up the wall.

Sirens wailed in the distance, and once there were pistol shots not far away. About 2:00 Ted managed to close Monkey's mouth with his own for twenty seconds, which was long enough to interest her in other related activities. He was unbuttoning her Brooks Brothers shirt as her swift little fingers assisted, when there was a sudden great pounding on the door, and a theatrical voice outside shouted, "Sanctuary! Sanctuary for the People's Freedom Fighters!"

Goody stumbled out of her bedroom and opened the door, moving like a deep-sea diver climbing over a submerged derelict. "Wha'? Who?" she asked, wiping her eyes with her hand. Then, recognizing the man in the doorway, "Aaronstein, you stupid jag-off, go away!"

"Hear that, Lyle?" the tall actor said to the black boy who followed him into the apartment. "It was ever thus. Never expect gratitude from the people you're fighting for. 'Oh, it's Tommy This, and Tommy That, and Tommy, 'ow's your soul? But it's "Make way for Mister Atkins," when the drums begin to roll!' Right, Lyle? This hardly comes as a news flash to us, does it, Lyle?"

"Shee-it," said the boy, staring unblinkingly at Goody.

"Look, you've got to have a place to crash, you can crash here," she said crossly. "There are a couple of kids here already, you can fight with them about who sleeps where. Only please try to keep your voices down. I've got to go to work tomorrow, okay?"

"You're all right in my books, Goody!" Aaronstein said in a resonant, sales-manager-type voice. "Four-Oh, if you get my drift. A real brick, right, Lyle?"

Goody went back to her bedroom. Aaronstein bowed formally to Ted and Monkey and pantomimed his desire that they stay on the sofa and allow him and the black boy to occupy two easy chairs. Ted nodded agreement. Aaronstein, a gentle smile softening his Lincolnesque features, turned off the overhead light, and the two newcomers made themselves comfortable in their chairs.

Stealthily, Ted slipped Monkey's shirt away from her breast, and lowered his lips to her nipple. It stood out as stiff and round as the eraser on a new pencil. She gave a welcoming sigh and pulled his head closer.

The hall door opened, and in the cascade of light from the bulb outside, six people filed into the living room. First came Goody's ex-husband, Frank Finley. Behind him were three young men and two young women. One of the men had a strip of cloth tied over his eyes, and another had a huge bruise on one side of his mouth. One of the girls had a lump on her forehead that was partly covered by her hair.

As Ted raised his head and blinked into the light, Finley walked to the door of Goody's bedroom, opened it, and went in. A moment later a bedroom light snapped on, and then Finley's voice said, "Goody, you have a few guests." The young people in the living room stood silent and waiting.

Goody's head appeared in the bedroom door. She stared wide-eyed at the five kids. "Jesus, Mary, and Joseph, what are all these people doing in my house?" she cried. "It's the middle of the damn night!"

"Well, they've got to go somewhere, and I couldn't think of any place else," Finley said apologetically. "Honest, now, Goody, you wouldn't want them out in the street tonight, if you could see what's happening out there."

Goody gave an assenting groan. "All right, tell them to sleep in the living room, with everybody else. Good night!" She closed the bedroom door. Finley turned on the floor lamp in the living room, the new arrivals dropped into corners or onto chairs, Monkey swiftly buttoned her shirt, and Ted couldn't make up his mind whether to curse, or laugh, or cry.

Somebody put Bob Dylan's record of "The Times They Are A-Changin'" on the phonograph.

In her frilly canopied bed, Goody slept the sleep of the just for an hour. Then the bedroom door opened, and a dim figure slipped into the bed beside her. She awoke to a voice in her ear whispering, "I thought you might like a little company, sweetie," as an arm snaked around her waist, and a long, bony body adjusted itself to her rear.

"OH, SHIT!" Goody shouted at the top of her lungs. She sat upright and swung one arm wide, feeling a satisfying shock as it encountered some part of the person beside her. "I don't even know who you are, you asshole! Get out of my bed!" She struck out again, this time hitting something she was certain was a head. "Out! *Out!* OUT!" The person beside her hastily pulled away and jumped out of the bed. Goody rolled after him, swinging her fists through the empty air. "I'll kill you, you rapist, you moron, you male chauvinist pig!" The man ran out of the bedroom door, slamming it behind him. All his silhouette told her was that he was tall and skinny.

A few seconds passed before she followed him, pausing in the doorway to survey the scene before her. Ten people crowded the small living room. Some were asleep on chairs and on the floor. Ted and Monkey looked up at her from the sofa; Frank Finley sat cross-legged in a corner with a quart of beer in front of him; Aaronstein was dancing by himself, with his eyes closed, his head thrown back, and his Adam's apple bobbing.

"All right, which one of you drinks of water is the sex fiend?" she shouted above Bob Dylan's nasal twang. "Finley, you bastard, did you try to rape me while my back was turned?" Her ex-husband looked at her with an expression of bewildered innocence, making a gesture with his large hands as if he were blessing a multitude. "Aaronstein, you crazy hambone, did you sneak into my room to betray my hospitality?" The actor continued his gyrations. "Aaronstein, did you attack me?" she bawled. Aaronstein's eyes opened briefly. "The way you talk!" he answered with chilly dignity and continued his dance with lowered lids. "You, there, on the couch," she demanded, pointing a finger at Ted. "Did you try to diddle me in the damn darkness?" Ted opened his mouth to answer, but Monkey, grinning impudently, forestalled him; stretching as sensuously as a cat, she asked in her little-girl voice, "Do you really think that's very likely, under the circumstances?"

"Ah, the hell with it," Goody sighed. "I guess I might as well have a beer." She sat down on the floor beside Finley and tilted up his quart bottle.

"Watch that nightgown!" he told her severely. "No wonder you're always being attacked, when you wear clothes like that!" The shortie nightgown was riding above her hips. She tugged it down until it provided her with precarious and temporary modesty.

"Try not to think about it," she said, raising the bottle to her lips again.

The sky outside the window was bluish-gray. It was after 5:30 in the morning, an hour that is healthy only when it's the beginning of one's day, not the end. Goody knew it was too late to go back to bed if she expected to be at work by nine. The best thing for her to do now would be to drink a lot of coffee. Or, she amended, drink a little beer and *then* a lot of coffee.

Like it or not, her Wednesday had begun.

Then, as Frank Finley treacherously began to nod, as Ted and Monkey slipped off to sleep on the couch, and as Aaronstein snored in a corner, knees and elbows bonily akimbo, the last knock of the night came at the door.

Goody rose to answer it, but before she could reach the knob, the heavy knocking was repeated, and a voice outside said loudly, "Open this door! Police!"

Her reaction was to tell them that if they weren't more quiet, they would wake everybody. "Don't you know it's not even six o'clock yet?" she said to the police lieutenant standing outside. "There are people asleep in here!"

"I bet there are," the lieutenant said. He had a bright-red, pockmarked face that bore witness to a vicious skin disease during adolescence. "Step aside, please." He started to shoulder past her, and the three policemen standing behind him moved to follow.

Goody shifted to block his way. "What do you think you're doing, Charlie? This is my home here!"

"We have information that a hippie shooting gallery is being operated in this apartment." He spoke in a flat voice and didn't look at her. "Now please step aside." He moved forward again, and his shoulder struck Goody and pushed her out of the doorway. The four policemen entered the apartment. Two of the patrolmen had their hands on the butts of their pistols.

"All right, everybody up on your feet," the lieutenant commanded. "Now! Move! Everybody!" He stepped over to the sofa and began kicking it. "On your feet, junkies! On your feet!" Ted opened his eyes in startled surprise, and the sight of the blue uniform instinctively brought him to his feet. Beside him, Monkey looked vulnerable and frightened.

Goody followed the lieutenant, demanding answers. "Have you got a warrant to break in here? Who told you this was a shooting gallery? What are you going to do to these people? Answer me, goddamnit!"

He ignored her, and he and his three subordinates jostled and punched all the sleepers to their feet. "Up against the wall, there. Face the wall, put your arms over your head, palms against the wall. Hurry it up, let's see you move!" Prodded by billy clubs and still only half awake, the nine men and women and the black boy lined up with their arms up and their backs to the police. The lieutenant looked expressionlessly at Goody. "You too, lady."

"Me?" cried Goody incredulously. "You want to search *me?*" She raised her arms, and her diaphanous shortie nightgown shot up to reveal three inches of crisp pubic hair. "What the hell for—crabs?"

"I said, you too, lady. Up against the wall. I mean it. Don't make me use force."

"Get over here, Goody, for Christ's sake!" Frank Finley called over his shoulder. "Don't give them any reason to work you over, or they will!"

Glaring at the lieutenant, she stalked to the wall and took her place between Finley and the young man with the bruised mouth. The policemen began frisking everyone for narcotics and weapons. She bit her lips in silent fury as a pair of hands ran over her breasts and belly, and a finger poked between her thighs.

One of the cops found a switchblade knife in the pocket of Lyle, the black boy. "Hey, Lieutenant, look what the little jiga-boo was holding," he said excitedly.

"You mother-fuck," the boy said clearly.

"What did you say?" asked the cop in surprise. The boy re-peated the epithet, and the cop struck him at the base of the neck and knocked him to the floor.

Aaronstein turned to face the club-wielder, who immediately pointed his pistol at him. "It's people like you who shake our confidence in our police force," the actor said gravely. He low-ered his hands to shoulder height and moved a step away from the wall. The cop raised his pistol and sighted it at Aaronstein. "Now you stop right there," he warned.

Behind the actor, the lieutenant took a baton from a patrol-man, and, taking deliberate aim, brought it down across Aaron-stein's right kidney. It was a powerful blow, and the tall man fell whimpering to his knees. "Now, just stand there, people, and nobody will get hurt," the lieutenant said. "Burnett, you

keep them covered. Reiss, Ockermann, shake down the apartment. Check the bedroom, the kitchen, the bathroom, see what
you can find."

One of them went through the knapsack and bedrolls in the
living room. He found Ted's syringes, and was very excited
about them for a few moments, until Ted showed him the insulin and the doctor's prescription he always carried with him.
Disappointed, the cop dropped the syringes on the floor.

For five minutes the line of people facing the living room wall
stood silent, listening to the sound of the searchers going
through the apartment. Frank Finley's tall body swayed toward
Goody. "You're clean here, aren't you?" he whispered.

"Of course I'm clean," Goody hissed back. The lieutenant
poked her with his finger and warned her to shut up.

The two patrolmen reported the results of their search to the
lieutenant. "Nothing, not even grass." "Okay," the lieutenant
acknowledged, then raised his voice: "All right, you lucked out
today, but don't think you're out of the woods. We know who
you are, and if you as much as pick your nose from now on,
we'll throw you in the slammer so fast it'll make your head
swim! Okay, men, let's go!" The four patrolmen left the apartment; when they were outside the hall door, the officer said,
"You can turn around and lower your hands now." He looked
into Goody's eyes, red-flecked with rage. The lines at one side
of his mouth altered, as though the muscles were trying to form
a smile and had forgotten how. "We are all judged by the company we keep, lady," he said ambiguously. Then he followed
his companions from the apartment, closing the door behind
him.

For a moment everyone in the apartment remained motionless, listening to the descending footsteps on the stairs. Then
Goody let her breath out explosively. She bent over Lyle on the
floor and felt his collarbone. Finding no indication of a break,
she called Frank and Ted to help her get him into bed. They
moved him into the bedroom, put a pillow under his head, and

pulled a sheet over him. He was conscious, and his eyes rolled from Goody, to Ted, to Frank. Goody touched him gently on the neck, where the club had struck, and asked him if it hurt. He nodded silently. "Oooh, boy, are you going to have a bad old bruise before long, you know that? And boy, is it going to be sore!" she said cheerfully. "That cop, he sure didn't want you to forget him, did he?" She turned to Frank. "Go see how Aaronstein is, will you? Help him into the john, if he needs it." She turned back to Lyle. "You think you could stand a big glass of milk, or would it hurt to swallow?"

"I could stand it," answered a small voice.

She went to the kitchen and poured out a glass of milk. The five overnight guests who had arrived with Finley hurried past her and out the back door, without a word. "You're welcome!" Goody shouted after them. She carried the milk to the bedroom, passing Frank and Aaronstein on the way to the bathroom. Aaronstein was bent almost double, and under his mop of snarled hair, his face was gray.

Goody held the milk glass while Lyle drank from it. A few drops dribbled down his chin and onto his T-shirt, which bore the words, "Dracula sucks." Goody looked at the boy with tenderness and touched his forehead lightly with her fingers. "You're going to be all right, tiger," she said softly. He drank half the glass and then lowered his head to the pillow, smiling up at her with white teeth under a milk mustache.

In the living room, Ted sat on the edge of the sofa, rubbing his hands together and moving his eyes restlessly around the room. He spoke to Monkey Morrison without awareness of her as an individual, simply because she was nearest to him. He talked about a film he had once seen of hunters killing seals in the Pribilof Islands. "The cubs have the finest fur, so they pull them away from their mothers and brain them. But if they're too little, they kill the mother instead, and leave the cubs to starve," he said. "I guess if you want to live in a fur coat world, you've got to brain a seal or two."

"The pigs can't get away with this, Ted!" Monkey said excitedly. "We're not nobodies they can push around! My daddy's in *Who's Who in the Midwest!*"

Ted started to talk about a terrible scene in a movie called *Mondo Cane*, but his mouth was suddenly full of bile, and he could only gag and swallow. *I can't live in this world,* he thought wretchedly. He closed his eyes and lay back on the sofa, shuddering.

In the bedroom, as Goody turned away from the bedside, her eye fell upon her purse, lying open on the dresser. A corner of her red billfold was sticking out. "Oh, no!" she whispered, grabbing the billfold and opening it. There had been more than forty dollars in it; now there was nothing but a few small coins.

She strode to the bathroom door and pounded on it. Frank opened it; behind him Aaronstein sat slumped on the toilet with his pants around his ankles. "All right, Finley, you're supposed to be a reporter—I've got a story for you to print!" She thrust the billfold under his nose.

"Oh, sweet Jesus, don't call me that word!" Frank groaned. "Do you want to get me killed?"

"Just the same, it's your job to tell the truth in that lousy rag of yours—and the truth is that those bastards stole forty bucks worth from me while they were shaking down my bedroom!"

Finley made an elaborate gesture denoting helplessness. "Goody, cops stealing from citizens isn't news in Chicago—"

"They didn't even leave me carfare! They stood me up against the wall at gunpoint, and felt me up while they calmly took my purse and stole all my money! Frank, that's terrible! You've got to do something!"

"Oh, Goody, Goody, what do you want from me? I'll turn in the story if you say so, but you know what good it'll do? In case it gets printed, which it almost certainly won't, it'll tell every cop in Chicago what your name and address is, and that you've made scurrilous and unprovable charges against police officers in the execution of their duty. You think you've got troubles now, just wait!"

Aaronstein gave a groan that had at least as much agony in it as histrionics, and Goody began to cry. She didn't cry easily or often; when she did, she breathed as though she had hiccups, and the tears burned her eyes. "I don't know how I'm going to get to work!" she gasped. "They didn't even leave me busfare!"

Frank knew how important it was to her to be able to get to work each morning, no matter what had happened the night before. In some way it seemed to wipe the slate clean for her. "I'll put you on the bus, honey," he said, wrapping his arms gently around her and drawing her to him. "Don't worry, you'll get to work just as sure as if you lived in Highland Park." Her sobs increased in intensity. He stood holding her, feeling her body as warm and smooth through the gossamer nightgown as if she were naked. Awkwardly he put one hand on the back of her neck and pressed her face against his shoulder. She nestled against him, and gradually she stopped crying and her breath became deep and regular.

16

CITYSCAPE
Tuning up at the Band Shell

WEDNESDAY MORNING Lester Maddox of Georgia, famous for his backhand form with an ax handle, withdrew his unlikely candidacy for the presidential nomination. At a news conference he branded the Democratic Party as the party of looting, killing, and draft-card burning. "I denounce them all!" he said. This was amusing to the people in Lincoln Park.

Not so amusing was Eugene McCarthy's comment, published in the morning newspapers, that he had no hope of winning the nomination. With the debate on the Vietnam plank of the platform scheduled for the afternoon, and the balloting for the presidential candidate in the evening, the peace faction inside and outside the Amphitheatre felt he had cut them off at the knees.

The grass and shrubbery in Lincoln Park smelled acridly of Tuesday night's tear gas, and the protesters were glad to leave it for ungassed Grant Park, where a rally was scheduled for 1:00 P.M. The Mobilization to End the War in Vietnam had secured a permit from the city to hold the rally, but had been refused permission for a march after the program.

Shortly after noon the first demonstrators began arriving at the Grant Park band shell; before the afternoon was over, there would be nearly 10,000 people present. It was a clear, bright, sunshiny day, with the bracing edge Lake Michigan supplies to the best Chicago weather. Most people arrived from the north, entering the park at Monroe or Jackson and walking over the gently rolling ground, past softball diamonds and soccer fields, past Buckingham Fountain with its plume of silvery spray, until their paths converged with the paths of hundreds of other, like spring freshets swelling a creek, and they found themselves part of the crowd around the band shell and were strengthened by a sudden conviction of solidarity.

Policemen circulated through the crowd distributing hand-bills, offering one to each new arrival and leaving one on every unfilled seat. The flyer announced that a legal permit had been granted for the rally, but not for a march afterward, and warned that any persons attempting to march would be subject to arrest. Only black policemen were assigned this duty, a clever move on someone's part; their dark skins helped make their baby-blue shirts more tolerable. A few even exchanged jokes with the protesters.

Fred Moler watched them from the Columbus Drive side-walk, west of the band shell. He and his partner, Charlie Horine, were part of a reserve contingent inconspicuously posted on the left flank of the rally audience.

"I don't think there's going to be any trouble today, do you, Charlie?" Moler said. "They don't seem to mind them colored officers walking right in among them."

"They like them better than if they was their own color." Horine's eyes were a shade lighter blue than his helmet, and at least as hard. "They like anybody better than a plain, decent, hardworking American white man."

Moler wrinkled his brow perplexedly. "It's hard to figure what gets into kids nowadays, you know? I got a long-distance call from my stepbrother Emil—he says his kid, Bobbie, run away from home for the third time." He looked at Horine, await-ing a reaction. When none came, he went on: "You remember me telling you about Emil, Charlie. When he got back from Korea, Emil didn't just jump into the first job that come along. He figured out that plastics was the industry of the future, so he wrote letters to a bunch of businesses saying he was willing to start at the bottom, doing anything, so long as he could get Into Plastics." He said "into plastics" as if the words deserved capitalization, like "The Church." "He got a job with the Fabry Corporation in Appleton, Wisconsin, and he's been there ever since."

"I remember you telling me," Horine said grudgingly.

"Yeah, well, he's really got it made. He's in middle management, and they've got a house on Lake Winnebago, three kids, two cars, and a boat—a really nice home, Charlie, with sliding glass doors that open on the patio, and a big outside brick oven for cookouts. Everything you can think of, they got. Bobbie's the oldest kid, and up to this year he's been making nothing but As and Bs in school. Emil says he would have got a scholarship to college if he'd wanted one. Nice-looking kid, good manners, a natural athlete, a star in the school play—and what do you think he does?"

"Runs away from home?" Horine was bored and made no attempt to hide it, but Moler's concern kept him from noticing.

"That's right! He came here to Chicago, and it took them three weeks to find him, and he was living in some crazy hippie commune, with girls, and drug addicts, and all like that! Well, they took him home, and gave him a bath, and told him they wouldn't hold it against him as long as he straightened out. And Charlie, it wasn't three months till he went and did it again!"

"No shit." Horine masked a yawn.

"That's right! Only this time he headed west, and the first word they got on him was from a jail in Las Vegas, Nevada! So Emil flew out and brought him home, and gave him a real tough talking-to. Well, Bobbie seemed to settle down after that, and they figured he'd learned his lesson, you know? And then Emil called long distance yesterday and said he took off again. He wanted me to know, in case Bobbie decided to come to Chicago again." He shook his head in resignation. "How can you figure a kid doing something like that?"

Horine's eyes slitted as he remembered the thrashings he had received from a drunken father almost every week of his boyhood. "No discipline when he was growing up—that's the trouble with all these kids. Their fathers didn't kick their ass for them, so now we got to do it."

"If he was going to get drafted, I could see it," Moler mused. "But he was supposed to go to college next year, and college guys don't get drafted. He could have stayed in school till the war was over, or Emil could have got him in the National Guard if he wanted to drop out. Either way, he didn't have to worry."

"Just too lazy to crack the books. Wants to screw around smoking dope and let society take care of him. All these hippie queers are alike." Horine picked a lump of mucus from one nostril, rolled it into a ball between thumb and forefinger, and flipped it away. From the band shell came the sound of a voice testing the loudspeaker system. A bus drove up Columbus Drive, stopped near them, and disgorged thirty more policemen.

Moler was silent a few moments, thinking. Then he asked his friend the question that had been bothering him more and more during the past few days. "What makes them come here and cause all this trouble, Charlie? Most of them don't have to worry about the war any more than Bobbie does."

"I told you—no discipline. They think they know what's good for the country better than the President."

"Yeah. They don't realize the President's got all kinds of Secret Sources of Information." Moler's voice capitalized "secret sources of information." "Well, I sure hope they go home after the convention. I don't like these twelve-hour days, Charlie. You know I haven't bowled a line in two weeks?"

Speeches started on the band-shell platform. David Dellinger introduced Rennie Davis, Jean Genet, William Burroughs, Allen Ginsberg, and other notables. The audience shouted and applauded good-naturedly. The aisles were crowded, as young people strolled up and down looking for friends in the crowd.

Poster and button salesmen peddled their wares. Except for the number of four-letter words employed by the speakers, the program had much the flavor of an old-fashioned Fourth of July picnic.

It was broad daylight, the rally was legally authorized, thousands and thousands of people were assembled in peaceful and constitutional protest.

For the first hour, Grant Park was a happy place to be.

17

RALLY 'ROUND THE FLAG

WHEN MAL WOKE UP Wednesday morning, Helen was dressed for work. They breakfasted together in the cheerful kitchen, under the Miró print. Helen asked him what his plans were for the day, and he said he hadn't made any yet. She said, "Whatever you do, buy yourself a new shirt first." He knew she was right and realized to his surprise that he enjoyed her telling him. After she left the apartment, he took a shower, shaved his face with the razor he supposed she shaved her legs with, and turned his attention to his clothes. He was able to sponge the denim jacket semiclean with a washrag, but the red-checked shirt was definitely over the hill. He sloshed his armpits with deodorant, hoping it would neutralize the sour sweat-and-booze smell that was bound to follow him until he could find a new shirt.

He thought about calling his office and his wife on Helen's phone, but decided to make the calls later on a pay phone somewhere. It didn't seem fair to talk to Marilyn from Helen's apartment, but he wasn't sure whether it wasn't fair to Marilyn, to Helen, or to himself.

On an impulse, he found a pencil and a sheet of paper, and wrote Helen a note. "Dear Good-Samaritan-Lady—Am on way to purchase garb less olfactorily offensive, as per your delicate hint. Unable to face day at office, so plan to swell multitude at Grant Park. Plans go no further. Will be in touch when I have more to say. Mal."

He frowned at the letter, aware of its ambiguity and yet unable to express his emotions more clearly. He tried other sentences in his mind, but they either said too little or too much. "Well, it'll have to do," he said. He folded the paper and left it propped up on the hall table, and let himself out of the apartment.

At a men's clothing store on the corner of State and Division he bought himself a shirt with a button-down collar, and a striped tie. He put them on in the fitting room and left his red-checked shirt in the wastebasket. His self-confidence increased, he went to a drugstore and dialed his office. Carefully not identifying himself to the operator with the Mayfair accent, he asked to speak to his secretary.

"Linda, this is Mal. Look, is anybody in the office with you?"

"No, but there are people in the hall outside."

"Well, don't let them know you're talking to me, okay?"

"Okay. Are you still drunk?" Her voice was carefully noncommittal; he had the impression of a cat making up its mind which way to jump.

"No, I'm not drunk. Things are happening, is all. I don't see how I can make it in today."

"Swell."

"What's going on down there? Many people been looking for me."

"You could say that," she replied dryly. "Everybody from Mr. Pauncefoot to the mail boy. Toby Tobin's been in three times today, and each time his grin gets a little bigger." A note of concern entered her voice: "Look, Mal, we've got troubles. I don't know what you think you're doing, but whatever it is, it's not raising your stock around here."

"I know that, Linda." He hesitated a moment, wondering how much pressure her loyalty could stand. *She must know it's back to the secretarial pool for her if they nail me*, he decided. "Run interference for me, will you, sweetie pie? Get that HydroDent Marketing Plan run off and distributed—it's in a manila folder on my desk. Check it over first—the pages are out of order, and there are corrections to some of the figures." He continued with instructions for other rush jobs awaiting his attention, some to be reassigned, some to be redated, some to be simply shuffled to the bottom of the pile. "The main thing is, don't show the white feather. Anybody who'll believe it, tell them I'm sick; anybody who won't, just say you don't know where I am."

"Mal, if you don't get in tomorrow, they'll tear you apart." Her voice suddenly changed and became pointedly unconcerned. "All right, Mother, have it your way. You make the reservation for Saturday night."

"Bye-bye, luv," Mal said, and hung up the receiver. The phone booth was stuffy, and he pushed the folding door back and forth to create a draft. After a few seconds he realized he was stalling. He closed the door again and dialed his home in Evanston. His wife answered almost immediately. Her voice was cool and low, but he thought he could detect a ragged edge of emotion under it.

"Hello, Marilyn, this is Mal. I'm reporting in from the trenches," he said perkily.

"Oh, hello. It's nice of you to call. Your daughter and I have been wondering whether you were still alive."

"Oh, I'm alive. I'm not at the office, though, so I'd just as soon you didn't try to call me there, in case you were thinking about it."

"Where are you, if that's a permissible question? Still at whatever *pad* you shacked up in last night? I don't hear a juke box, so you can't be in a saloon."

He sighed. "I'm in a drugstore on North State Street. From here I'm going to a rally in Grant Park. I think it's very unlikely I will lay any chicks there, although in times like these anything is possible."

"With you, I'm sure it is." She was silent a moment, and when she spoke again, her voice was high and tremulous. "Oh,

Mal, come home! Please come home! Lisa and I need you!"

He drew a deep breath. "I can't do it, Marilyn. This is something I have to see through. Tomorrow or the next day it'll all be over, but now it's here, and it's too important to miss."

"What's important? Getting drunk, getting your head split open, getting in trouble at work, maybe losing your job? I don't understand, Mal! All I know is, you're lying down on your responsibilities!" He tried to answer that men have many different responsibilities, but she rushed on without pausing: "You're not a kid in college anymore. You're a man with a family and a mortgage! What do you expect us to do if you ruin your life? Move into a commune somewhere and eat turnips and practice plural marriage?" Her voice kept rising in pitch until it was almost a squeal: "I want you to come home, Mal! Right now! Do you hear me?"

In a tired monotone he told her again why he had to stay in town. When she interrupted, she had regained her self-possession, and her voice was low and deliberate. "Mal, if your juvenile foolishness harms our child or our home, I'll never forgive you. As long as I live. I mean it. You better understand that."

"Goodbye, Marilyn," he said heavily, and hung up. His new shirt was damp under the arms and stuck to the small of his back. He opened his collar and turned up his sleeves, and, carrying his denim jacket over his shoulder, began walking slowly down State Street toward Grant Park.

Wednesday morning Mike Rogoff applied himself to the trade publications and business correspondence he had neglected for almost a week. He told himself he would work diligently and unreflectively until noon, after which he would allow himself a half-hour's indulgence in introspection.

He had accomplished a good deal by the time he stacked the magazines in a neat pile and slipped a small packet of envelopes to be mailed into his breast pocket. He rose from the table where he was working and put his hands gently on his lower back, searching for centers of pain. *He never laid a glove on me,* he thought, exploring the three sore areas where Johnny the guitar player had, in truth, laid not a glove but his bare knuckles on Mike Rogoff. *I'll bet his head is ringing like a gong today. That schmuck.*

Mike planned to attend the Grant Park rally, but the clock told him he had forty-five minutes before it was time to leave, and he decided to read something. He hesitated between Montaigne and de Tocqueville and then rejected both in favor of a little group of paperbacks sitting together on the shelf, dingy and dog-eared and smelling of old paper and glue. They were books published by International Publishers in the late thirties—*The Soviet Power, Hope in America, The Labor Spy Racket, From Spanish Trenches*—books that presented the Communist Party's viewpoint with an innocent simplicity that made them seem more remote than Montaigne's *Essays* or *Democracy in America.* As he turned the pages, smiling nostalgically, he remembered how he had felt about these books once—that they were weapons in the class war, bombs of paper and ink, capable of blasting the pillars of capitalism and bringing the roof down on the exploiters of humanity. *We really felt like that then!* he marveled. *My God, what a mixture of cynicism and naiveté we were!*

He set the books in his lap and leaned his head against the back of the chair. He thought of his first years in the party, the sense of adventure, the welcome discipline, the fullness of the days. He remembered again how the first doubts came, which he had refused to recognize as doubts, insisting to himself that they were simply the shadings of the artist's brush, the grays that would add depth to a black-and-white poster world. The doubts had nibbled away much of the faith before he was willing to acknowledge them. But in those days it was possible to live as a Communist on the basis of what you were against, rather than what you were for. Rogoff was against Fascism,

against gun-thugs, against scabs, against poverty, against prejudice, against cruelty in any form. By the time he went to
Spain with the Lincoln Battalion, he was no longer sure what
he believed in. But while the Civil War lasted, being *against*
was enough.

But it ceased being enough when Hitler and Stalin agreed
to the dismemberment of Poland. Suddenly he discovered that
the people who were against what he was against were not his
fellow party members at all. Apparently the party could coexist
amicably with Nazism when no liberals and very few conserva-
tives could stomach it.

So he quit the party. He paid a high price for his freedom
of conscience.

Besides the loss of his ideology, he forfeited his friends, his
profession, and his sense of purpose. The only family he had
was his sister Ruth; he had never married or fathered children;
the women he slept with were either party members, fellow-
travelers, or casual pickups; his close male friends were all Communist activists. With the exception of Ruth, his world became
instantly composed of strangers. Women he had once delighted
looked at him with disgust, and men he had faced death with
cut him dead on the street.

He tried to enlist in the armed services in World War II, but
the FBI labeled him a "premature anti-Fascist" and blackballed
him. He worked in a defense plant until 1945, then found a
job selling college textbooks at a store on Michigan Avenue.
He saved his money and, when he thought he had enough,
started his own hole-in-the-wall bookstore. He stayed open
until ten at night six days a week, read most of the books in his
stock, and barely made expenses.

The Justice Department asked him to become a professional
witness in the witch trials of the early fifties, as did a Senate
committee. He refused both and soon found himself appear-
ing on various official and unofficial lists of subversives. The
Chicago Police Department began to take an interest in the

books he sold, and in 1952 he was arrested, fined, and briefly jailed for filling an order for *Lady Chatterley's Lover*. The Catholic War Veterans picketed his store, and he received a number of threatening phone calls.

It had been, he reflected, turning the yellow-edged pages of John Strachey's *Hope in America*, a dim, dull, depressing life. Later, as he had moved out of the book business and into the art film business, it had not improved. Today he was hardly better off than when he had started—and older, and just as lonely.

All right, he told himself sardonically, *you can think about the girls you've had. I'll give you ten minutes.*

He began with the first one, on the roof of his apartment house when he was thirteen years old. He remembered girls on el platforms, on beaches, on back staircases, in empty garages, and even one in his mother and father's bed. He had struggled under a king-sized load of guilt for months over that. There were girls on dusty car seats, and in furnished rooms, with neon lights flashing outside the drawn shades. There were girls who were Comrades, who acted as though making love were a way of bringing about the classless society. There were whores. There was a Spanish girl, a peasant, colored honey and crimson and black, who kissed like an angel, tasted of garlic, and smelled of manure.

He stirred restlessly. *You've got about thirty seconds left,* he told himself.

Surprisingly, then, he remembered a girl he hadn't slept with, a mountain girl in Harlan County, Kentucky, a slight, drawn little thing with a withered leg and a timid bud of a mouth, and the biggest, deepest eyes he had ever seen.

Why, hello, Phoebe Hord. Did you find a man to love you, and to value your courage and your patience? Did you find any justice in those hopeless hills? You must be pushing sixty by now—do you have any grandchildren who can fight like you fought? Or has the breed died out?

Remembering the struggle to organize the Eastern Kentucky coal fields, the exaltation that accompanied each step forward and the despair that shrouded each setback, he thought, *I'll never go back there again—but there are people in Grant Park who are against the things I am against. I don't know what they are for, and I'm not sure they do either. Maybe I can join them.*

He slipped the old paperbacks into their place in the bookcase and left the apartment. The clean air, washed by the lake breeze, invited deep breathing, and he filled his lungs. *It's a beautiful day in Chicago!* he thought, and walked with elastic steps to the bus stop.

Sitting on a bench listening to Phil Ochs singing "Call it peace or call it treason/ Call it love or call it reason/ But I ain't a-marching anymore," cheering and applauding as Pigasus, the Yippies' porcine presidential candidate, oinked into the microphone, Mal's spirits were lifted by a sense of euphoria. For the first time in years, he felt as if the muscles of his will were relaxed, and he was moving and thinking without programmed volition. He was prepared to view everything around him in the most favorable possible light: obscenity was healthy sexuality, rudeness was candor, inexperience was originality, and faddish eccentricity was a new tribal life-style. Under the cloudless sky, surrounded by enthusiasts who hoped to stop a juggernaut with their bare hands, he felt he was participating in the birth of a new America.

And yet, underneath it all, a voice warned, *Don't be a dummy!*

A Good Humor vendor pushed down the crowded aisle, and Mal tossed him a quarter, receiving an ice cream bar in return. A kid selling peace buttons came hawking his wares, and Mal bought a pin almost as large as a saucer, showing a graceful white dove with a laurel branch in its beak. Then came a poster man, handing out free copies of a poster showing a young man burning his draft card and bearing the words, "FUCK THE DRAFT," in letters four inches high. Mal took one, thinking, *I'll put it on the bedroom wall—Marilyn will have a hemorrhage.*

Assuming Marilyn and I ever share a bedroom again, he amended, ruefully, but without any deep feeling of concern.

He paid more attention to the traffic in the aisle than to the introduction of speakers and performers on stage. He saw a few people he knew: an erstwhile research analyst who sang folksongs in Old Town; a kooky girl illustrator who specialized in dogs and cats; a copywriter from Leo Burnett, who looked as surprised to see Mal as Mal was to see him. He greeted each of them with a V gesture, and called "Peace!" The folksinger and the copywriter returned the gesture, and the illustrator raised her charcoal-smudged fist in the Black Power salute.

A gray-haired man in his sixties pushed apologetically past half-a-dozen pairs of knees and seated himself in the empty seat next to Mal. "This isn't taken, I hope," he said politely. Mal gave him a perfunctory glance and then looked back more carefully. The man's face, with its candid-seeming brown eyes, long, crooked nose fuzzed with gray hairs in the nostrils, and wide, ironical mouth, was very familiar, but it took Mal a moment to place it. While he was searching his memory, the man extended his hand and said, "You're right. In Mister Dooley's, on Monday night. My name's Mike Rogoff, and you are no longer the oldest man in Grant Park."

Mal shook the dry, sinewy hand and assured Rogoff he remembered him. They exchanged comments on the police, the convention, the war, and the weather. After a few minutes, Mal realized he was sitting beside one of the few people in Chicago he could talk to. It was as if Rogoff might have the answers he needed, if only he could find the questions to ask.

"I've never been big on mass meetings," Mal said. "I never wanted to submerge myself in this much emotion. I always felt I owed it to my own individuality to stay on the outside, where I could think clearly. Hell, I never even liked to go to football games, for fear I'd get carried away. So here I am cheering a goddamn pig who's running for President!" He shook his head in wonder.

Rogoff had bought himself an ice cream bar, which he had eaten with relish; he licked the last bit of ice cream off the stick before he answered: "Being carried away isn't always bad. Sometimes it means being taken to a place you couldn't get to under your own power. And as for owing something to your own individuality, it could be the other way around. Maybe your own individuality owes *you*, for keeping you set aside like something special all these years." Rogoff grinned to take any possible sting out of his words. "I'll tell you my experience with individuality: Tender loving care it doesn't need. You couldn't kill it with a stick."

The crowd around the band shell began to sing "Where Have All the Flowers Gone?" Mal was forced to wait until the song was over before he could pick up the conversation. "Mike, what's happened this week, in Lincoln Park, and now here— is it important? I mean, really important?" What he was actually asking, Mike knew, was *Am I a damn fool romantic for being here instead of at the office?*

"I don't know if it's important," the ex-Communist answered. "But there's one thing I'm sure of. It's irreversible."

"How do you figure?" Nervously, Mal smoothed the ends of his mustache with thumb and forefinger. His eyes were bright with hope and worry.

"When I was a kid in school we used to study geography, and one of the things we had to learn was the important rivers, where they were, and which way they ran, you know? One time there was a big flood in the newspapers, and the teacher asked me what was the next town downstream that was going to be in danger—Cairo, Memphis, Natchez, one of those. Well, I got confused, and told her the name of some town that was *upstream*. 'You mean to say you don't know the difference between downstream and upstream?' she asks me. 'Not on a map I don't,' I told her. '*Oi gevult!* Look here and I'll show you,' she says. 'Rivers run together, they never separate. Whenever you see two rivers join up to make one, you know that's the way the water is moving. See how the Ohio runs into the Mississippi, and then the Missouri from the other side, and it all becomes one big river running to the sea? Well, it's always that way. Many little ones forming one big one, never one big one splitting up into many little ones. It's a fact of nature.' "

Rogoff fell silent, a smile on his lips. On the band-shell stage, a speaker was describing the horrors of the Vietnam war. Mal asked quizzically: "Are you sure you're not oversimplifying things, Mike?"

"No, I'm undercomplicating them, which is something else again. Figure *that* out, and you'll be an expert on dialectics!"

Just then they both noticed a disturbance near the flagpole on the left of the band shell. Rogoff craned his neck, and Mal rose from his seat to get a better look.

Ted Bakerfield was thirty or forty yards nearer the flagpole than Mal and Rogoff. He was sitting with Monkey and a group of her friends from Northwestern, who were cheering and booing and having a fine time. Ted didn't share their mood. Oblivious both to the speakers on the platform and the crowd around him, he was reliving the predawn raid at Goody's apartment.

This time it was different from the park, he thought sickly. *This time I couldn't run from the violence—this time my hands were flat against the wall. And I was scared to death. I was so scared I would have done anything they asked me, signed any paper, sold out any friend. Face it, man,* he charged himself, *you don't hate violence, you're just afraid of it.*

He felt a wave of disgust radiate outward from the pit of his stomach to the tips of his fingers and toes. Like many New Left radicals, Ted was highly puritanical in nonsexual matters and was unprepared to admit to himself that he was a coward. For all his diligent study of economics, sociology, and psychology, his ideal of masculine behavior hadn't changed much since he formed it fifteen years before, while reading Edgar Rice Burroughs' tales of John Carter, Warlord of Mars.

Sari would despise me if she knew. It's better that we split up when we did. Now she can find somebody with balls. He shook his head numbly and cracked all the knuckles of one hand with the other hand.

Monkey grabbed his wrist suddenly. "Look, Ted, the flagpole," she said in her breathless little voice. "Somebody's climbing it."

Ted raised his eyes and looked where she was pointing. He saw a teen-age boy in an army helmet shinnying up the lower part of the flagpole, reaching for the halyards. Hundreds of other spectators noticed him at the same moment and began shouting advice: "Pull it down!" "Burn it!" "Piss on it!" and also: "Don't touch that flag!" and "Leave it the hell alone!" In a moment the small figure squirming up the metal pole had become the focus of the crowd's attention. The police along Columbus Drive, nearest the pole, moved restlessly and flexed their muscles, like athletes waiting for their event to be called.

On the platform, David Dellinger took the microphone, and, a worried expression on his placid face, urged the pole-climber not to pull the flag completely down, but leave it at half-mast in honor of demonstrators wounded and jailed. The crowd took up the suggestion. Ted, his inner dialogue forgotten, was one of thousands who shouted, "Leave it at half-mast!" The boy on the pole lowered the flag halfway, and secured it again. The crowd cheered, and the boy climbed down the pole.

The police were waiting for him. Their clubs rose and fell, and the boy sprawled writhing at their feet. In the moment before the crowd realized what had happened, the policemen lifted their victim and half-carried, half-dragged him toward a waiting paddy wagon.

Then, belatedly, members of the crowd nearest the flagpole attempted a rescue. They surged around the police squad, throwing soft drink cans, newspapers, rocks, peace buttons, small change, match folders, bus transfers, anything they had in their hands or pockets, and shouting "PIG! PIG! PIG!" in rhythmic fury. But the police reached the safety of their lines. Mobilization marshals urged angry crowd members back to their seats, and Dellinger's voice over the loudspeakers cautioned patience. "Remember, this is a legal meeting! Don't let them push you into illegal behavior—don't let them incite to riot!"

The people in the crowd sat down again. Monkey squeezed Ted's arm with both her hands and pressed it tight against her breast. "Oh, wow, did you see those pigs? Did you see the way they messed over that cat?" she asked breathlessly. "You don't think they're going to bust us today, do you?"

Ted, his heart pounding, spoke with feigned confidence. "Not here in Grant Park in broad daylight, not after passing out handbills saying this is a legal rally. No way. We'll have to wait till tonight for that." He disengaged his arm. "Let's hear what our peerless nonleaders are saying."

But before the crowd could settle down again, a half-dozen burly young men surrounded the base of the flagpole, untied the halyard, and dropped the flag to the ground. It was done so swiftly and efficiently it seemed like a military operation. A gasp rose from the crowd, and voices began shouting, "No! No!" Ted felt as if he were an unwilling party to a profanation. "Why did they do that?" he said—and then, as the answer flashed into his mind, he shouted, "They're spies! They're cops in plain clothes!" He pushed out of his seat and into the crowded aisle, with Monkey Morrison trailing behind him. He was furious, certain that agents provocateurs were operating on orders to give the uniformed police an excuse to attack the crowd. His anger was so intense it obliterated all other emotions.

Hundreds of others felt the same way, and they all jammed together in an immovable mass around the flagpole. At the center, one of the burly men attached a yard of red fabric to the halyard and ran it up the pole. For a moment a super-stitious hush fell over the crowd, as nearly 10,000 people saw whatever-it-was—a scarf or union suit? a Vietcong flag? the red banner of revolution?—usurp the place that even the most radical instinctively felt (until they corrected themselves) be-longed to the American flag.

Then a squad of police charged into the crowd, and a second squad followed on their heels. From the band shell Rennie Davis shouted into the microphone, "Here come the bluebon-nets!" He jumped off the platform and pushed toward the flag-pole, shouting instructions to cool it. The police, however, had no intention of letting it be cooled. They struck savagely with their clubs, forcing a path toward the pole. In a few moments they reached it, and one of them lowered the "flag," while the others surrounded the men who had raised it. None of them was harmed, but when Rennie Davis reached the spot, he was clubbed to his knees, and blood covered his face and shirt.

Ted was in the middle of the crowd, unable to move except with the surge of the massed bodies around him. The police were only ten feet away. Their faces were distorted by ex-pressions of hatred, fear, and joy. Many were shouting, but their voices were inaudible. Ted felt a flash of panic claustro-phobia; what would happen if he stumbled and fell? He shifted his weight to push backward, and felt Monkey Morri-son's soft body flattened against his back. For half a minute he, and the people around him, and the police in front of him hung in a terrifying stasis of thrust and counterthrust; then the pressure broke, as the police withdrew toward Columbus Drive. Mobe marshals moved into the space between the antagonists, linking arms to hold the crowd back. From the platform Del-linger called, "Sit down! Sit down! There's a lot more of the

program to come," there was breathing room around Ted, and
he took advantage of it by filling his lungs.

"My God," he said to Monkey, "I didn't know if we were
going to get out of that or not!"

There were still many hours left in the day.

When the incident at the flagpole ended, Mike and Mal
resumed their seats. Above their heads two police helicopters
crisscrossed the sky, their roaring engines sometimes drowning
out the public address system. Police reserves were posted to
their left and right, and behind them, as Mike pointed out to
Mal, the silhouetted figures of National Guardsmen could be
seen on the roof of the Field Museum.

"They've got us in a box here. If they want to close the lid,
we've got no place to go," Rogoff said.

A worm of disquiet crawled up Mal's spine. "What about the
leaflets, though? If they planned to break up the rally, they
wouldn't have passed out leaflets saying it was legal, would
they?"

The ex-Communist shrugged. "Who knows? I've seen times
when the cops authorized a meeting or a march, and then
engineered a pretext to break it up. The idea is to Teach Them
a Lesson."

"You think that's what they plan for today?"

"My friend, if I could predict what the Chicago police are
going to do, I would never have gone to jail for selling dirty
books."

It was hard to hear the speakers on the platform, and Mike
found himself watching the restless movement in the aisles
instead. "The wonders of nutrition in modern America," he
said reflectively. "They all look like basketball players. Who-
ever heard of socially conscious basketball players?"

His eyes met the eyes of someone he knew. It was Dagmar
Correlli, pushing a path for herself by the side of Mark Phillips.
She was wearing the green shirt of a Marine Corps NCO, and

Rogoff thought she must own as many enlisted men's shirts as old-fashioned college girls owned sweaters. She stopped dead when she saw him, and her face assumed a wary expression. Rogoff grinned at her, letting his eyes move from her swarthy face and blond ponytail, down her body to her slim brown ankles and dirty sneakers, then up to her face again. "Ciao, comrade!" he called, and raised his fist, not in the Black Power salute, but in the "¡No pasarán!" salute of thirty years earlier. She looked back expressionlessly. Phillips, hot-eyed and taut, followed her gaze; when he saw Rogoff, his handsome mouth twisted into a sneer. He raised one hand a few inches and moved it outward in a short arc—as patronizing a gesture as rubbing the gray poll of an old Negro.

Rogoff watched them until they disappeared in the crowd, then turned his attention back to the platform. He had barely begun to separate the speaker's meaning from his rhetoric, however, when sounds and movements around him broke his concentration. He became aware that the crowd's focus had shifted from the band shell to the area near the flagpole, and as he looked in that direction he saw a cloud of gray smoke rising.

The police had begun hurling tear-gas grenades into the crowd.

Beside him, Mal's voice cried shrilly, "They can't do that! It's like the Cocoanut Grove fire—people will be trampled to death!" But they *were* doing it; more tear-gas grenades exploded, and a police skirmish line advanced into the gray fog. They wore gas masks and swung clubs, and the crowd recoiled in front of them in sudden panic. Unable to move quickly enough between the rows of seats, people began climbing over them; benches upended and collapsed; men and women fell on the ground, to struggle first under the feet of their fellows, then under the batons of the police.

This was more than a brief sortie, Rogoff realized. This was a deliberate charge. The police were rolling back wave after wave of the audience onto the people behind them, attempting to cause a stampede that would sweep 10,000 protesters out of their seats. Standing where they were, Rogoff and Mal both concluded their chances would be better if they stayed put rather than trying to push their way to safety.

Most of the other people in the crowd made the same decision, and the police tactic failed. The sheer *incompressibility* of the massed bodies in front of them stopped the police before they had penetrated more than a quarter of the way into the seating area. The impetus of the charge died as the resistance increased, until the thrust reversed itself and the police found themselves falling back through the rows of overturned chairs and benches, gas, and injured young men and women.

"Marshals to the point! Marshals to the point!" cried the public address system belatedly, but the crisis was past; the crowd had protected itself well enough, and the police line pulled back from the band-shell area, resuming its original position near Columbus Avenue. People moved back into the disputed space, setting up their seats again, fanning the air to dissipate the gas; medics with white armbands began giving first aid treatment to the scores of injured. Allen Ginsberg took the microphone and began to intone his mantra, "Uhhhh-mmmmm," with an expression of tranquillity on his round face, and some of the crowd responded. Mal and Rogoff exchanged glances. "Son of a gun!" Mal said, with the shaky but proud grin of a small boy getting off a roller coaster. "They almost got us, didn't they?" Rogoff nodded, and, taking a deep breath, intoned the mystic nonsense syllable along with the poet: "Uhhhh-mmmmm." To his surprise, his pounding heart seemed to quiet a little.

The program resumed. The police seemed content to maintain their position on the sidewalk and observe, as did the National Guardsmen to the south. On the platform, the black nightclub comic Dick Gregory drew heavy applause when he said, "Don't blame the cops, man, the cops aren't responsible. The cops are the new niggers. The real blame goes to Mayor

Daley and the crooks downtown. Mayor Daley is a prick and a snake, and, worst of all, he ain't got no soul!"

"Right on, brother!" called a young black with a goatee and an Eldridge Cleaver button. Mal had never heard the phrase before. He looked inquiringly at Rogoff. "Right on?" he repeated.

"The Black Panthers say it," Rogoff explained. He cupped his hands around his mouth and shouted, "Right on, brother! Salud!"

More speakers followed, and at 4:30 David Dellinger took the microphone again and announced he would lead a march to the Amphitheatre, lack of a police permit notwithstanding. It would be a nonviolent march, he cautioned; anybody not prepared to abide by the rule of nonviolence could go into the streets of the Loop and do his thing but was to stay away from the march. "If you're looking for trouble, stay out of the area —we don't want you," he warned.

"Feel like stretching your legs?" Mal asked Mike.

"Somebody's got to chaperone these kids," Rogoff replied gruffly. They moved with the largest part of the crowd toward the Columbus statue, near the band shell, where the march was forming. Dellinger began negotiations with the police for permission to march, and police loudspeakers announced that anyone remaining on the east side of Columbus Drive—the bandshell side—was now in violation of the law. Obediently about 2000 people crossed to the west side of the street. They were now on a narrow strip of parkland between Columbus and the sunken tracks of the Illinois Central railroad, which ran on a slant to the west and south. The National Guard formed the cork in the bottle: they took up a position along Balbo Drive to the north, standing at Parade Rest, with fixed bayonets on their rifles.

Sari Schram stood with Lucky Lindy, waiting for Dellinger to conclude his discussion. She was in a nervy mood—angry at the police, a little frightened, resentful of Ted for not being with her, and irritated with Lindy for being in Ted's place. She had also seen as much as she cared to of the Yippies at close range. They tended to bound about, grabbing at one another, laughing wildly, and shouting scatological comments. With many of them, their approach to personal hygiene was more than a negative feeling toward cleanliness—it was a positive enthusiasm for dirt. They smelled; Lucky Lindy, for instance, had his own special odor compounded of stale sweat, navel lint, and Juicy Fruit Gum.

They were sharing a roach. Sari took a deep drag and then ground the butt beneath the heel of her huarache. "They're going to keep us penned in here till dark, so nobody can see them when they work us over. Let's find us a bridge and get over to Michigan Avenue."

Lindy shrugged agreeably, and they walked north. The National Guardsmen at Balbo let them through, but when they reached Congress, they found the bridge to Michigan Avenue closed by another Guard company. "Those chickenshit draft dodgers!" Sari exploded. "They just can't wait to use those bayonets on us!"

"Well, man, you know, different strokes for different folks," Lindy said vaguely.

"What's that supposed to mean?" Sari snapped.

"Like, stay loose, you know?" Lindy frowned. "How the hell should *I* know what it's supposed to mean?"

They walked in silence toward Jackson Street. Sari felt the frustrations and irritations within her coalescing into a single hot ball of rage. It seemed to her that the city itself, with its great passive buildings, its heedless cars and buses, its uncommitted population, was allied with the police, the Guard, and the omnipotent Establishment. *If they're not part of the solution, they're part of the problem,* she quoted bitterly to herself. *They deserve to be smashed.*

The sidewalk was crowded with young people looking for a way out of the park. Mostly they seemed to be Yippies, although here and there were straight-looking Mobe kids and older men and women.

At Jackson Street they found the bridge closed. Sari's pulse quickened; she glanced at Lindy and saw that he looked bothered too. She laughed nervously. "Sort of gives you the idea they don't want us to get out, doesn't it?"

"Bad scene, man," Lindy said reflectively.

They walked on north, past the rear of the Art Institute. The first unguarded bridge they came to was at Monroe Street, almost a mile from the band shell. "Thank God," said Sari. "I thought we were going to spend the rest of our lives in Grant Park. Those bastards!"

They crossed over the I.C. tracks and approached Michigan Avenue. Suddenly Lindy stopped dead. "Hey, am I tripping out, baby?" he asked unbelievingly. "Do you see what I see?"

A mule train was slowly crossing the intersection.

18

HAYMARKET

AT THE AMPHITHEATRE, the debate over the peace plank ended. Hale Boggs and Ed Muskie had been among the speakers supporting the majority (or Hawk) plank; Wayne Morse, Ted Sorensen, and Albert Gore were some of those speaking for the minority (Dove) plank. When the vote was taken, the majority plank won, three to two. The chairman then tried for a quick recess, but the dovish New York and California delegations began to sing "We Shall Overcome." The convention managers tried to drown them out by turning off their microphones and ordering the band to play "Happy Days Are Here Again."

A battle of music began, as hawkish delegates stamped off the floor angrily. The band switched to "I'm Looking Over a Four Leaf Clover"; the doves countered with a spirited "Battle Hymn of the Republic." The band tried again, with "If You Knew Susie," and then gave up, packing away their instruments and leaving the near empty hall to the singing victors.

It was the only victory they won in Chicago.

Helen Haggarty dismissed the Theater Arts group at the D.U.D. building in Uptown a few minutes early and was at her apartment by 5:15. She read Mal's note, was disappointed by its brevity, and annoyed with herself for being disappointed. Boots, the German shepherd, whined his welcome. She snapped on his leash and took him for a brief walk in Lincoln Park, which seemed unnaturally empty.

She returned to the apartment and riffled through her phonograph records. Smiling slightly, she selected Copland's *Appalachian Spring* and placed it on the spindle. *They're playing our song*, she thought mockingly. She started her dinner in the double boiler and mixed a tall Scotch highball. Then she sat down, closed her eyes, and sank into the music.

For a while it held her completely, blocking everything but melody, harmony, and rhythm from her mind. About the middle of the third section her concentration broke down, and she began to think about Mal and the strange evening they had shared. *He's the most attractive man I've met since I doused the torch for Ralph. He's younger than I am—but not so much. I wonder what he thinks of me. That I'm frigid? I wouldn't be surprised.* Something cold pressed into her hand. It was Boots's nose. She scratched him behind the ears and looked at the cumbersome harness that held his thighbones in their sockets. "It's hell to be overbred, isn't it, Boots?" she asked gently. "The difference between dogs and people is that people can forget their breeding if they feel like it. Right?" The dog closed his eyes and flattened his ears and leaned against her fingers to increase their pressure.

That Marilyn, I wonder why he ever married her. She's so small-minded—not the open, curious kind of a person a man like Mal should live with. She used to read book reviews instead of books. She was a dumdum.

Helen snorted. *You're the dumdum!* she told herself harshly. *Up to yesterday, you always liked Marilyn. What's the matter with you?* She knew what the matter was and therefore avoided answering herself. Instead, she turned her thoughts to the day's rehearsal of *Dark of the Moon*, which was to be the Theater Arts Group's major production and would, she hoped, serve as proof of the program's value to the community. It had been a disaster. She began to tap her fingernail against her strong white front teeth as she ran through all the characters who appeared in the first act, seaching for flaws she could correct by direction.

The Shaker hymn section of the suite began, and the familiar melody disarranged her thoughts. As she had the night before, she sang along with the music:

> " 'Tis the gift to be simple, 'tis the gift to be free,
> 'Tis the gift to come down where we ought to be—"

The calm determination of the verse heartened her. The hymn section was followed by the coda, and the music ended. She felt that something in her own life was about to be affirmed. *I am as strong as I need be,* she thought.

She turned off the phonograph and turned on the TV. As the picture swam into view, it took her a few seconds to recognize the scene as the Grant Park band shell, where she had attended a number of free concerts that summer. There were policemen with clubs, and clouds of tear gas, and faces so full of hatred they startled her. Her first feeling was shock at the inappropriateness of the scene to the action: *Grant Park is for music, not mayhem!* Then the picture changed, and she was looking at a line of National Guardsmen, bayonet-barbed rifles in their hands, faces monstrous in gas masks. A young protester appeared in front of them, his mouth forming inaudible phrases, his right arm extended in the Nazi salute. One of the Guardsmen leaned toward him, pushing the point of his bayonet at the boy's chest. The figures jumped, as though the camera had been struck, and abruptly a new picture filled the screen.

My God, those are soldiers! They've called out the soldiers! The police weren't enough—now they're using soldiers against us! The pronoun "us" passed by the monitor that scanned her stream-of-consciousness unnoticed; the night before, the attackers and the attacked had both been "them." For Helen,

as for thousands of other watchers that night, the change was
significant.

*Soldiers mean war, like the Russians in Prague! And that
idiot Mal is down there in the middle of it!* Helen was a woman
of both thought and action, but when she thought a lot, she
usually didn't act, and when she acted, it was often without
much thought. She turned off the TV, put the lobster New-
burg away in the refrigerator, and left the apartment. Five
minutes later she was on a State Street bus, heading downtown.
Rush hour traffic was tapering off, and she made good time.
Wabash and Van Buren was as far south as the bus went, and
when she got off there, it was 7:15, and she was four blocks
from the Conrad Hilton Hotel.

The mule train that had caused Lucky Lindy to doubt the
evidence of his senses was a miniparade of three wagons pulled
by real mules, and bearing signs that read "Jobs and Food for
All." The Poor People's Mule Train had been organized by the
Southern Christian Leadership Conference and was endowed
with a precious permit to parade in the Loop and on Michigan
Avenue. The Reverend Ralph Abernathy was there, along with
a number of blacks dressed rather unconvincingly in bib overalls and wide straw hats. "Join us, brothers, join us!" they called
to the protesters on the sidewalks, and within minutes the mule
wagons were flanked by hundreds of shouting, cheering young
people. Sari Schram and Lucky Lindy were among the first to
join the wagons, and Ted and Monkey followed soon after.

For a few important minutes the police couldn't decide what
to do. In the first place, the mule train had a legal right to
parade. In the second place, it was a black group; so far, the
blacks had held aloof from the protest meetings in the parks,
and the police wanted very much to keep it that way. In the
third place, the bigwigs from the Democratic Convention were
returning to their hotels; Vice President Humphrey was already
at the Conrad Hilton, and the streets outside bristled with tele-

vision cameras. It was not a time for a career police officer
to act rashly.

While the police hesitated, the mass of demonstrators engulfed the mule train and bore it south like a surfer on the
ninth wave. With each block the crowd grew. By the time the
first mules reached the intersection of Balbo Drive and Michigan Avenue, more than 4000 persons were crammed behind
them in the street. There they were checked by a police line
hastily drawn from one side of Michigan to the other.

Ted and Monkey were in the middle of the street, a few
feet from the second mule wagon, fifty feet from the police
line. Bodies pressed against them from all sides, and the air
above danced with waves of escaping 98.6° heat. "Dump the
Hump! Dump the Hump and Hump the Dump!" roared the
voices around him. "The streets belong to the people!"

Ted felt the return of that afternoon's panic claustrophobia
and instinctively began to push against the bodies on his right.
His shoulder jammed into the chest of a tall Yippie with a droop-
ing mustache and glasses so thick his irises looked like buck-
eyes. "Hey, man, what the fuck you doing?" the other said
angrily, driving an elbow into Ted's ribs. Ted pushed back,
white-lipped. "Let me by!" he demanded. "Don't be an asshole!" the other snarled, and lunged against him, his knee
striking Ted's thigh. Ted swayed backward, bumping people
behind him, who began shouting, "Watch it, you guys! Christ
sake!" Monkey Morrison seized his left hand in both of hers,
crying, "Ted! What are you doing?" Realizing the futility of
any individual attempt to withdraw from the crowd, Ted
stopped struggling and stood still. Desperate signals ran up
and down his nerves like ants.

"What do we want? PEACE! When do we want it?
NOW!" chanted the voices around him. Accepting the solidarity he couldn't escape, Ted raised his voice to join them.
"PEACE . . . NOW! . . . PEACE . . . NOW!" he yelled, his
voice as dry and grainy as old corn husks.

A few feet nearer the police line, Sari Schram shouted the same words. She was filled with excitement and anticipation; she knew that danger threatened and that if it developed her position in the crowd made it inescapable for her. When danger, like rape, is inevitable, lie back and enjoy it! "PEACE . . . NOW! . . . PEACE . . . NOW!" she screamed. Eyes shining, lips parted, she had never looked more beautiful.

Mal was near the leading mule wagon, alone in the crowd and troubled with misgivings. He and Mike Rogoff had been separated by the rush of young bodies; now Mal was anxious to work his way off the street and into the Conrad Hilton Hotel, if that was possible. He remembered the police attack that afternoon too well and sensed that the confrontation now shaping up on Michigan Avenue could make the earlier one look like warming-up exercises. There was a congenial bar in the hotel, with large windows overlooking the avenue. It would be pleasant to perch on a padded bar stool, sip a chilly martini, and watch the drama outside.

I should have left an hour ago, when I could, he thought. *I should have known that dumb march was never going to get off the ground. Before Daley would let us march to the Amphitheatre, he'd endorse birth control.*

He maneuvered between close-pressed bodies with more finesse than Ted had shown and was able to move a few feet closer to the hotel's entrance. He was edging between a clean-shaven college student with a McCarthy button and an enormously fat Yippie with "F*U*C*K*" written on his forehead with lipstick, when he saw one of the blacks from the S.C.L.C. Mule Train pass through the police line and begin an animated discussion with a senior police officer. They were too far away for him to hear their voices, but from the black man's expression and gestures he could guess what the man was saying: that he and his people were in the middle of all this by accident, and they wanted no part of it, and would the police escort them out of the crowd? The police would, and did; wedges of

helmeted officers pressed the crowd back and led the wagons
into the safety of their lines. The black who had made the
arrangements climbed up on a wagon and began to speak
through a police bullhorn. The burden of his remarks was that,
although the Poor People's Coalition sympathized with the
peace movement, each group had its own row to hoe.

"Bye, bye, blackbird!" shouted a girl near Mal. "Oink, oink,
you-all," called other voices derisively. The black spokesman
shrugged and handed the bullhorn to a policeman. In a few
moments the three wagons began to move, escorted by police,
heading south down Michigan Avenue.

Mal began to work more determinedly toward the hotel
entrance. If the presence of the S.C.L.C. Mule Train among
the demonstrators had caused the police any qualms, he realized, there was no reason for them to entertain them any
longer.

Robin Goodpasture didn't get out of the office until after
6:00. Her natural conscientiousness kept her working to correct another girl's mistakes. As she worked, she listened to her
transistor radio and learned about the growing confrontation
outside the Hilton hotel. "Shithouse mouse, the balloon's going
up, and here I am pounding a goddamned typewriter!" she
complained to the empty office. Finishing the page, she ripped
it from the machine, thrust one carbon into her top drawer for
filing, routed another copy into distribution, and put the original on her boss's desk. Then she snapped off the office light
and ran for the elevator.

When she got to Michigan Avenue, the sidewalks were filled
with rally-goers headed home: long-haired kids in groups of
two and three and middle-aged men and women in ties and
girdles, anticipating a meaningful dialogue over cocktails.
There were vendors of protest buttons and underground newspapers with names like *Rat* and *Screw*. It reminded Goody
of the parking lot of Wrigley Field after a Cubs game, and she
was afraid she had missed all the excitement.

But beyond Randolph Street, the scene changed. The young people weren't in twos and threes, but tens and twenties, and they weren't walking north, they were standing on the curb jeering at the police cars and three-wheelers that now made up a large and increasing part of the street traffic. When she reached Congress, she found both the street and the sidewalks packed solid with demonstrators. She decided to withdraw from the crowd, swing around to Wabash Avenue, a block to the west, and follow Wabash until she was beyond the Hilton. Then she could get back on Michigan and approach the hotel from the south. She would be in a position to tell every passing Humphrey-Daley delegate exactly what she thought of him.

For this was basically what the Convention Week disturbances meant to Goody—an opportunity to tell the other side what she thought of them. The issues were simple: good things were peace, freedom, opportunity, noncomformity, and soul; bad things were war, oppression, censorship, and white middle-class morality. People were divided the same way: good people were Mike Royko, Justice Douglas, Ernie Banks, Ralph Nader, Ho Chi Minh, Walt Kelly, Paul Newman, Huey Newton, and Golda Meir; bad people were Richard Nixon, Al Capp, Richard J. Daley, Arthur Rubloff, Ari and Jackie Onassis, all of Dow Chemical, General Motors and the CIA, and any Pope except John XXIII. For some reason William Buckley was on both lists.

Goody found she was free to move down Wabash, but each successive cross street was blocked by a police line. She went all the way to Roosevelt Road before she could make her way back to Michigan Avenue. There she found she was in National Guard territory. Soldiers in formation were lined up east of the street, and there were odd-looking vehicles along the curb —olive-drab jeeps with wooden frames strung with barbed wire jutting in front of them.

She cupped her mouth and shouted, "Sieg Heil! Sieg Heil, you storm troopers!" The Guardsmen who heard her looked back in anger or embarrassment. She gave the Nazi salute with her index finger extended and began walking toward the jammed intersection three blocks away. Except for the soldiers across the street, there were very few people near her. The shouts and chanting from the crowd ahead sounded tinny, like music from a juke box across the lake on a summer night.

A block from the hotel the S.C.L.C. Mule Train passed by, escorted by motorcycle police and squad cars. "Hey, man," Goody called, "aren't you cats going the wrong way?" One of the black men in the lead wagon made a gesture of rejection or disgust. Goody watched the brief procession until it reached 11th Street and turned right.

As she neared the Hilton, she saw that something was happening to the crowd of demonstrators beyond the police line. It took her a moment to realize what it was. *Why, they're sitting down in the street! Oh, damn! I had to pick today to wear my pink linen sheath from Bonwit's!*

She hurried on in her high heels.

Rogoff stood near the intersection of Balbo and Michigan, outside the Hilton hotel entrance. He felt strangely remote from the excited young people around him, unfrightened and curious in an almost impersonal way. He was quite sure that violence would erupt within a few moments, and he expected it to be murderous. Yet he felt no desire to leave. *It's not predestination that binds a man—it's free will,* he thought. *Only the free can know how bound they are.* He experienced a sudden chill of déjà vu and wondered if he had made the same observation some previous time or heard it made by another. He realized he needed to go to the bathroom.

The police bullhorns began the familiar demand to disperse that had heralded most previous attacks that week. As a countermove, demonstrators started sitting down where they were, chanting, "Hell, no, we won't go!" Mike remained standing as the people around him squatted, and found himself looking once again into the eyes of Dagmar Correlli, standing with Mark Phillips thirty feet away. There was a startled expression on her face, as though she had been caught unexpectedly in the open. She stared at Rogoff a moment, wideeyed, then suddenly disappeared in the crowd of seated bodies.

Fifty yards farther on, a skirmish line of police advanced toward the intersection.

It was 7:57 P.M.

During a strike at the McCormick Reaper Works in May 1886, a peaceful meeting of strikers at Haymarket Square was interrupted by a large force of police demanding its immediate dispersal. Someone—it has never been established who—hurled a bomb into the police ranks. In the carnage that resulted, caused both by the explosion and the indiscriminate firing that followed it, sixty-seven policemen were wounded and seven of them died. Casualties among the strikers were twice as heavy. In the subsequent trial, eight leaders of the strike were tried, not for their actions, but for their beliefs, for they were anarchists. Four of them were hanged, and a fifth committed suicide in prison.

For reasons that defy rational explanation, the management of the Conrad Hilton Hotel chose the name "Haymarket" for their luxurious ground-floor cocktail lounge on the southwest corner of Balbo and Michigan. The room was decorated in a bogus but expensive Gay Nineties style, and advertising in local newspapers described it as follows: "A place where good guys take good girls to dine in the lusty, rollicking atmosphere of fabulous Old Chicago."

Sari was sitting on the sidewalk a few feet from the large plate-glass windows of the Haymarket when Ted saw her. His sudden glimpse of her made him forget his apprehension, and he pushed toward her, towing Monkey Morrison in his wake. He threaded his way rapidly among the demonstrators seated on the sidewalk, ignoring the curses that followed him, and reached her in a few seconds. "Hi, there," he said, squatting down next to her. "How are you?"

Sari's eyes widened in surprise, then crinkled at the corners. "Ted! Oh, wow, have I missed you!" She put her hand on his arm and squeezed.

Lucky Lindy, sitting beside Sari, gave Ted a casual wave. "Hey, man, what's happening? Your chick here is a stone drag, you know that? I mean, nowhere, you know?" His eyes flicked from Ted to Monkey, and brightened with sudden interest. "Hey, who's the fox? Hey, hello, fox."

Ted gave Sari a rueful half smile. "I missed you, too. I was worried about you, last night in the park."

She tilted her chin with a touch of defiance. "I got along."

"So did I."

"So I see."

"So *I* see."

They looked at each other with wary affection, wondering how much annoyance it was safe to show one another. Lucky Lindy reached his hand to Monkey and began to draw her down to the pavement beside him. Inside the Haymarket, comfortable people sipped cocktails and watched the spectacle outside the window, as uninvolved as sightseers at an aquarium.

Then the protesters on the sidewalk became aware of the police advance down Balbo toward them. They struggled to their feet and began to move around the corner into Michigan Avenue, only to find that the increasing density of the crowd brought them to a halt after a few steps. Crushed together in an immovable mass, they were slowly and relentlessly forced back toward the walls of the Hilton and the plate-glass window of the Haymarket Lounge.

A second line of police advanced down Michigan Avenue from the north, driving the demonstrators in front of them into the pocket formed between the Balbo line and the original police defense line across Michigan.

It had finally happened—the demonstrators had no place to

run. Unlike the past three nights in Lincoln Park, there was no open escape route; unlike the afternoon's melee in Grant Park, there were no longer 10,000 bodies to defeat the police by sheer weight of numbers. Here in front of the Hilton, there was a crowd the cops could handle, perhaps 2000, with their backs to the wall. The cops knew it, and a fierce exaltation swept through them like fire in a dry forest. "Kill! Kill! Kill!" they chanted. "Kill the cocksuckers! Kill the cunts! Kill the Commie queers!"

Sari and Ted clung to each other as the tide swept them against the Haymarket's window. Sari's face was pressed against the glass, her nose flattened, her mouth open in an inaudible scream. Ted, facing the crowd, had his back against the pane. His shoulders rose and fell as he pushed futilely against the inexorable pressure. Other terror-filled faces crowded in against them from both sides. For a moment the plate glass held, against apparent logic, as if it were bound by surface tension, like water rising above the top of a tumbler and still not overflowing. Then it exploded inward with a noise like a cannon, and gleaming blades of glass flew fifteen feet into the room.

Ted fell backward across a table, upsetting it and crashing to the floor in a welter of glasses and furniture. He hit on the back of his neck, and for a few seconds lay dazed, as others stumbled or jumped across his body.

As Sari burst through the glass, a jagged shard entered her face below the right cheekbone and slashed downward almost to her chin. For a moment before they were obscured by blood, her upper and lower molars gleamed through the open flesh.

Twelve or fifteen people were forced through the window, and the police were behind them, clubbing demonstrators and customers of the cocktail lounge impartially. An elderly businessman at the bar saw a policeman charge toward him, club raised; he cried, "No, no—I'm staying here at the hotel!" and cupped his hands over his eyes to protect his glasses. The policeman's club broke his fingers. An out-of-town reporter reached into his pocket for his credentials; before he could produce them, his eyes were filled with blinding Mace and a knee drove into his groin. A demonstrator whose leg had been deeply cut by broken glass lay in a pool of blood. A policeman seized his arm and attempted to pull him to his feet. "My God, I can't walk—can't you see?" the boy cried. "I'll show you how to walk!" the policeman answered, dragging the injured youth toward the lobby door with one hand and striking him across the neck and shoulders with the other.

Ted returned to consciousness to hear Sari's voice pleading, "Ted, Ted, get up! We've got to get out of here!" His eyes focused on a face he only half recognized. Her black hair was matted with blood, and blood had gushed over her shoulder and down her arm to the ends of her fingers. Her face was somehow asymmetrical, as though the right side was pulled down by the weight of the dreadful gash on her cheek. "Ted, please!" she cried in an oddly thick voice, tugging at his inert weight. "They'll kill us in here!"

He struggled to his feet and started for the lobby door. It was jammed with people fighting to get through. Lucky Lindy and Monkey Morrison were there; Lindy's eyes streaming water, temporarily sightless from Mace, and blood covering one of his ears; Monkey whimpering in mindless panic, her Brooks Brothers shirt torn open from collar to waist.

The police charged into them from the rear, clubbing, as an officer urged: "Get 'em out of here—clear the area! Move 'em, now—lay it on 'em!" A nightstick cracked against the back of Ted's head, and he was dizzy with sudden pain. Miraculously, the bottleneck in the doorway broke, and he felt himself stumbling out of the Haymarket into the wide lobby of the hotel. He took a half-dozen steps and fell to his knees, pulling Sari down with him.

Once past the doorway, the demonstrators and customers spread out like an exploding Roman candle, dashing across the crowded lobby with the police in hot pursuit. The clubbing continued, before the unbelieving eyes of hotel guests, reporters, and Democratic campaign workers. Lindy went down under the clubs of three policemen, who worked him over with almost graceful efficiency. Monkey Morrison threw herself on a startled middle-aged matron with blue gray hair, begging for protection. A policeman began dragging the girl toward the Michigan Avenue entrance. "Leave her alone!" the matron ordered imperiously. The policeman cursed the older woman and pushed her roughly back into her chair. He jerked Monkey after him, and Monkey fell down. "Stop it, you animal!" the matron cried, jumping to her feet again. With a deft backhand blow, the policeman laid his club across her breasts. The woman sprawled back in her chair, white-faced with pain and shock; her mouth moved, but no sound came out.

A young McCarthy worker saw the gash on Sari's face and tried to help her toward an elevator, intending to take her to the McCarthy suite on the fifteenth floor for medical attention. A stocky policeman with wild eyes blocked their way. "Outside, outside, goddamnit!" he snapped. "This girl's badly hurt. She needs a doctor," the McCarthy worker answered. "Fuck that, she goes into the wagon," the policeman said, pushing Sari with his nightstick. "My God, do you want her to bleed to death?" "Into the wagon, I said! Into the wagon, whore!"

Ted hit the policeman from behind, in a clumsy tackle that made him stumble but not fall. The policeman twisted around and clubbed Ted on the back of the head. Ted sprawled on the rug, unconscious, but the blows continued. The McCarthy worker took advantage of the interruption to hurry Sari into an elevator.

Outside the hotel, the police lines cut into the trapped crowd like a comb through a crew cut. One line would attack, then another, each officer selecting his own targets, choosing which demonstrators he would drag back to the waiting paddy wagons and which he would leave sprawled on the pavement. People were not clubbed to be arrested, for not one out of ten who were beaten ever saw the inside of a van—people were clubbed to be clubbed.

This was quite clear from the overview of the fifteenth floor. Frank Finley leaned out of an open window in the McCarthy suite, watching the police attack at the intersection below and not quite believing what he was seeing. It was like the old newsreels of student riots in foreign countries—Japan, or Mexico, or Egypt—that had always seemed unreal to him because nothing like that ever happened in Chicago. Gang murders, sure—police scandals, ghetto shootouts, drug raids, vice roundups, even an occasional labor massacre like the one at Republic Steel—but a student riot? *Students should stay piled up in telephone booths where they belong,* he thought, as he watched a police line advance once more down Balbo Drive, the helmets looking as neatly machined as a row of baby-blue bb's.

"Oh my God in Heaven," breathed a fat young McCarthy worker from Minnesota, who shared his window, "how long are they going to keep it up?"

"Either they've gone on too long already, or else they've barely begun," Finley answered. "Either way, it's a bummer. Are you sure you guys don't have something to drink up here?"

Behind them a door opened, and a number of people entered the room. Some of them were the walking wounded from the Haymarket and the lobby, and others were medics to administer first aid. Finley and the fat Minnesotan watched as the medics helped the injured to chairs and onto tables, or propped them gently up in corners. Finley's eyes were drawn to a girl with a long and bloody gash the length of her cheek. *So beautiful,* he thought, *so beautiful once.*

Trained reporter that he was, he moved toward her, drawing his pencil and pad from his pocket. Even as he formed his first question, his thoughts spun off to Goody. *That nutty broad, I hope she has sense enough to stay home. With her looks to start with, she can't afford a scar like that.*

✻   ✻   ✻

When the police began their attack, Mike Rogoff knew, with an old tactician's certainty, just how bad it was going to be. He realized two things simultaneously. One was that his best chance of escape lay to the east, into Grant Park. The other was that he had seen Dagmar Corelli a few moments before near the center of the police pocket. Unhesitatingly, he pushed toward the place where he had seen her. His sense of irony disappeared in the fear and excitement of the moment; he didn't ask himself why he should care what happened to a foul-mouthed little bitch of a troublemaker who was probably a thief as well. She was somebody he knew, somebody who worked for him, somebody he had eyed with an amiable and uncalculating lechery once. *That kid could get hurt,* he said to himself.

As he neared the corner of the hotel, the crowd thinned out, allowing him to move more rapidly. The scene around him resembled the Brownian movement of suspended particles under a microscope: police dashed in and out, clubbing, making arrests, dragging struggling bodies behind them; trapped protesters tried to feint their way around the police; injured people struggled to regain their feet or crawl to safety on their hands and knees.

He saw her on the sidewalk, near the Haymarket's broken plate-glass window. She was trying to get up; her weight was resting on one elbow, and she was attempting to pull her feet under her, without success. Her sneakers scuffed aimlessly on the concrete, and her eyes were unfocused.

Rogoff took her arm and began to help her up. "Dagmar, it's all right. Upsy-daisy, now." Quickly but gently he drew her to her feet. "Come on, kid, let's get out of here." She stood flat-footed, unmoving. "Dagmar, come on! Can you hear me? Come on!" She shook her head slowly from side to side and raised a hand to brush a strand of hair from her face. Her face was completely expressionless.

A policeman was coming toward them.

"Jesus, kid, move!" Rogoff dragged her after him into Michi-

gan Avenue. Her weight pulled against him, sluggish but unre-
sisting. He stumbled over a boy with a silky golden beard, who
groaned at the contact. He pulled Dagmar to one side so she
wouldn't step on the boy. Suddenly the policeman was in front
of him, shouting at him to stay where he was. Releasing the
girl's arm, Mike faked a movement to the left, sidestepped to
the right, thrust his right leg forward, past the cop's knee, and
hit him with all his strength on the side of the head. The cop
lurched sideways and fell over Mike's knee, hitting the street
with a thud. Mike grabbed Dagmar's arm and jerked her toward the far curb, but before she was past the downed policeman, he clutched her ankle and began to pull her back toward
him. Without hesitation, Mike pivoted and kicked him in the
temple, just below his cocked helmet.

Other policemen saw it, and Mike heard simultaneous roars
of anger from three different directions. *Oh, that did it—they'll
kill me now!* he thought, as he began running again, with Dagmar's inertia pulling against him. Ahead of him the density
increased; he began to weave and twist between people like a
broken-field runner, with the pounding feet of the pursuing police growing louder in his ears.

Fortunately for Rogoff, the crowd on the sidewalk east of
Michigan had seen him kick the policeman too and moved to
open a passage for him and to impede his pursuers. In another
second he was deep in a mass of young bodies, while the police
behind him were pushing against the outer edge of the crowd,
baffled and furious. Helping hands touched him, supporting
him, patting him, and voices cried excitedly, "Cool, Dad!" "You
really messed over him, man!" "That pig won't see straight for
a week!"

More slowly, now that he was safely out of the street, he
guided Dagmar into Grant Park. As soon as they got to grass,
he sat them both down. "Dagmar, listen, kid, it's okay, we're
out of there now. You hear?" He put his hand on her cheek and
pinched it lightly. "You hear me? Nobody's going to hurt you
now."

She raised her head slowly and looked at him, and Rogoff saw that the whites of her eyes were pink from broken capillaries. She opened her mouth to speak, but it was two or three seconds before any words came out. Then she asked, "Where's M-Mark Phil-lips?"

Rogoff shrugged. "You were alone when I found you," he said. "Maybe your friend had pressing business elsewhere."

"No, he was with me—he was with me when the police started hitting people! He was right there with me—didn't you see him?"

"Look, take it easy, all right? Lie back down there and close your eyes. I think you've had one hell of a bonkus on the conkus. Come on now, lie back on the grass."

Dagmar stared at him, as if she were seeing him for the first time. "Mike Rogoff," she said wonderingly. "Mike—why?" He smiled crookedly and didn't answer. After a moment she sighed, closed her eyes, and lay back on the soft grass.

Mike sat beside her and watched her breathing grow regular as she slipped into a doze. Then, gradually, he became conscious of a new sound. He listened: it was a chant, and it seemed to be coming from all around him. Thousands of voices joined to create it, and, when Mike understood the words, he lent his voice to it too.

"The . . . whole . . . world's . . . watching!" he intoned. "The . . . whole . . . world's . . . watching! The . . . whole . . . world's . . . watching!" Beside him, Dagmar stirred and groaned in her sleep.

Whether it was the chanting of the crowd, the helplessness of the victims, or a simple surfeit of blood and brutality, some policemen began to show a distaste for their work. Not that there was any refusal to obey orders—there was none of that, ever. It was rather that a few of the attackers found other options, other alternatives to club-swinging. One officer spent five minutes at the peak of the battle escorting an elderly couple out of the area; a middle-aged sergeant occupied himself unsnarling traffic a block north of the Hilton; there were half-a-dozen men help-

ing wounded demonstrators to paddy wagons and even apply-
ing a little rough first aid where they could. One lieutenant
intervened a number of times to protect injured or unconscious
persons from further harm, and another prevented the arrest of
newsmen and McCarthy delegates.

But if a few policemen sought alternatives to head-cracking,
the great majority did not.

Fred Moler was near Michigan and Congress when the chanting began. He couldn't make out the words. "What are they
saying?" he asked Charlie Horine. Horine told him, bitterly.
"Oh, because it's all going to be on television?" Moler asked.
"That's right, because those television cocksuckers want to show
the city in a bad light, and they don't care who they hurt, as
long as they make the mayor and the police look lousy," Horine
answered. "They're the bastards I'd really like to work over."

The two policemen remained north of the bloody intersection of Michigan and Balbo and at 8:20 had still taken no part
in the action. Then four empty paddy wagons pulled up at the
curb, and the lieutenant ordered his men to fill them up. Moler
and Horine began walking purposefully toward the Conrad
Hilton. The first person they encountered was a woman in a
torn pink sheath dress, limping awkwardly on high heels, her
hair in her eyes, and one hand pressed tenderly to her side.
"All right, sister, into the wagon," Horine ordered, pushing her
roughly toward the curb.

"Oh, no. No way." Goody was angry and tired and lonely;
she felt old, and her good dress was ruined, and she was in pain
from a blow across the rib cage that made it hurt to breathe.
She had no intention of being stuffed into a police van. She felt
no terror of the officers, only an overpowering disgust. "Get
your rotten fucking hand off my arm," she said.

Horine slapped her across the mouth, and she staggered backward toward the curb. "Oh, you bastard!" she gasped, and then
she began to curse him with every obscenity she had heard since
the Yippies had come to town. She told him that his mother

performed fellatio with Negroes, that his father was an oral-anal sodomite, that his sister enjoyed animal contact. Horine hit her a second time, this time with his fist. She stumbled back again, coming to rest against an iron railing built to prevent pedestrians from falling off the sidewalk into a lower-level ramp leading to the Grant Park underground garage. "Pig, pig!" she screamed, her face a distorted mask. "Hit! That's all you can do, pig! Hit!" Swiftly, rhythmically, like a boxer punching a bag, Horine struck that mask, pushing Goody backward with each punch, until she was bent across the iron fence like a bow, prevented from falling only by the pressure of her thighs against the railing.

Moler tried to stop it. He grabbed his partner's shoulder, shouting, "Charlie—she's going to go over!" But Horine struck again, and with startling suddenness Goody pivoted over the railing, her knees flying upward as her upper body disappeared. She turned through half a somersault before she passed below the sidewalk. She hit the ramp below with a clearly audible sound, like the smack of raw meat hitting a counter in a butcher shop.

Moler pushed past Horine and looked over the railing. Twelve feet below him, Goody was lying jackknifed on the pavement, head and torso below, buttocks and thighs above. She was wearing nylon panties over pantyhose, and in the semi-darkness of the lower level, what Moler saw at first glance looked like the bottom half of a broken doll, once loved, now discarded. He stared down at the grotesque sight, waiting for some movement that would be an indication of life. Long seconds passed before the body moved; then slowly one leg bent and kicked, the body's weight shifted, and the buttocks slipped sideways to reveal the head and shoulders below it.

Horine jogged Moler's elbow. "Come on, Fred, you going to stand there all night? Let's roll!"

"Look at her down there," Moler said in an awed voice. "Did you hear her hit? Jeez, I bet her back's broke!"

Horine glanced down. "Look, she's wiggling her legs like a fucking upside-down beetle!" His voice sounded a little high and breathless. "Come on, Fred, let's go make some arrests."

Moler followed him away from the railing, with a picture in his mind he would never forget.

Night was falling over Chicago. Illuminated by streetlights and floodlights, the police occupied the intersection outside the Conrad Hilton. The only demonstrators still in the street were those, mostly too badly hurt to walk, whom the police hadn't yet loaded into paddy wagons and taken to jail. All that remained of the crowd—about 1000 or 1500 persons—had been herded into Grant Park and penned in the strip between Michigan Avenue and the Illinois Central tracks, and now the National Guard moved in to line the sidewalks.

But there were other demonstrators who had left the area, and some, in groups of ten or twenty, made their way north and west into the Loop. A few of them, convinced that the revolution had begun, smashed shop windows, crying "Pig property!", threw firecrackers and cherry bombs at passing cars, talked wildly of occupying the Civic Center. The police followed them; three-wheelers, squad cars, and paddy wagons careened along State, Clark, and LaSalle; police lines were formed ahead of the marauders to contain the infection, but again and again, the sprinting, shouting youths got by.

It was 9:38 by the clock outside the State and Randolph entrance to Marshall Field's when Mal caught up with Helen. He had been searching for her more than an hour, ever since he had glimpsed her in the crowd outside the Hilton. For a split second their eyes had met across thirty yards of struggling bodies, and Mal had seen the flash of recognition in Helen's eyes. Then the crowd had shifted to conceal them from each other again.

Mal had worked his way toward her, but she remained as hidden as a swimmer in the trough of a wave. As the crowd began to break up under the police attack and people ran blindly down the side streets away from the battle, he felt panic rise. For dangerous as it had been in the middle of the crowd, it was just as dangerous to be alone in the Loop with the police looking for people to club.

He ran north on Wabash. There was a cluster a block ahead. It was a squad of police surrounding a group of Yippies. A van was at the curb, and the officers were pushing and dragging the Yippies into it. All of them appeared to have been beaten, and one or two were bleeding heavily. Helen wasn't in the group.

A police siren whooped along State Street, and he sprinted down a dark side street until he reached the corner. Another squad of police, another van, another mass arrest—no Helen.

West to Dearborn, where a cop almost catches him, North on Dearborn to Jackson. Waiting in a dark doorway while a gang of demonstrators marches past in the middle of the street—no Helen. East on Jackson to State. In front of a restaurant in the middle of the block two cops beat a skinny kid in a fringed Indian jacket. A man in a black suit and clerical collar tries to intervene, and one of the cops hammers him to his knees. No sign of Helen. North on State, moving from one shadowy entrance to another as the squadrols scream by. Suddenly a girl rounds the corner ahead of him, a cop close behind her. Mal presses against the wall as they pound toward and past him. The cop catches her beneath a streetlight fifty feet away. Not Helen—Mal moves furtively north, avoiding lighted areas.

A subway entrance ahead. A half-dozen hippie teen-agers approach the kiosk, pause outside for a discussion. Two squad cars screech to a stop at the curb; policemen leap out, swinging batons. Most of the teen-agers disappear down the steps, and the police follow. One young boy runs past Mal, crying, "We didn't do anything! We just come from a movie!"

A struggle on the sidewalk outside the Palmer House. Mal edges close enough to watch. A big man in army clothes is beating up a youngster whose face is almost concealed by his bushy hair, mustache, and beard. The youth goes down, and the man

in khaki kicks him. "I support the guys in Vietnam!" the big
man yells. Two policemen stand to one side, watching. *Is he
really a soldier, or is he a provocateur?* Mal wonders. *It doesn't
make much difference to the kid on the ground.*

West on Madison to LaSalle, then back east on Washington.
No Helen. At Dearborn a squad car pulls up beside him, and
a cop beckons him over to the curb. Who are you? Where do
you live? What are you doing here? Were you down by the
Hilton earlier tonight? The cop's face, shadowed by his helmet,
is almost invisible. Mal answers in a voice higher than normal,
intensely conscious of his helplessness. The cop is satisfied.
"Okay, buddy, go on home. Get your ass out of the street before
somebody kicks it for you." The squad car roars away. Mal
stands swaying on the sidewalk, weak from fear and relief.

Along Washington to State, then north, beside the windows of
Marshall Field's, presenting their visions of an attainable suburban Shangri-la to an empty street. Cries and sirens to the
west, to the south. Shots somewhere in the distance, and the
scream of an el train's wheels as it rounds the curve at Lake
Street. Then, as he passes beneath the clock at the corner of
Randolph, Mal hears, incredibly:

"Mal! Mal, oh, God, is that you?"

He turns to see Helen standing against the corner of the
building. She is wearing the same white blouse and turquoise
skirt she had worn when they ate breakfast that morning under
the kooky Miró print, but the shirt is rumpled and smudged,
and the skirt shows a triangular tear over one hip. Her short,
gray-streaked hair is disheveled, and her eyes are more hollowed
than they were twelve hours before.

Mal moves to take her in his arms, but something prevents
him and he stops awkwardly a foot away from her, reaching out
to take her hand instead. "Hi, there. I was looking for you. I
saw you in front of the hotel," he says. "I know, I saw you too,"
she answers. Her hand grips his firmly, a small but positive
physical statement. "I was afraid you were hurt. They were

beating everybody." "No, they didn't lay a glove on me. How about you?" "They didn't have a chance—I ran too fast. Straight to the Palmer House. I drank two Manhattans in the Petite Café." "What brought you out on the street again?" "You," she says simply. "I kept remembering the way you looked in the crowd. I kept seeing you bleeding in a gutter somewhere." His fingers tighten and so do hers.

Before they can say more, violence explodes at the next corner, as a dozen cops try to arrest some Yippies. Two of the kids escape and sprint west on Randolph. One reaches safety down the mouth of an alley; the other stops, turns to face the police, and shouts back at them in uncontrollable defiance, "Yah, pig, your wife sucks dirty cock!"

Mal and Helen watch as a squad car starts up, covers a half block in ten seconds, and slams to a halt a few feet from the running figure. The youth is clubbed unconscious and thrown into the back of the automobile, which U-turns in the street and speeds back to Wabash Avenue.

"Those kids must be crazy," Mal says softly. "Don't they know it's all over?"

"No—because it's not," Helen answers. "Something's over—something's dead. But I think something else is only starting." She turns to him, and her eyes are wide in their shadowed sockets.

For a moment they look at one another, and then Mal takes Helen's arm, and they walk together to the subway that will take them out of the Loop's wild streets.

19

CITYSCAPE
The Lights of the Hilton

AT THE AMPHITHEATRE the Democratic Convention moved to its climax, the nomination of the presidential candidate. Traditionally, this was the time the political game should have been at its most absorbing, when delegations should caucus furiously to debate strategies, when rumors should turn despair into confidence and back to despair again in the time it took to inhale one king-sized cigarette.

Yet seats remained empty all over the auditorium as delegates crowded in lounges watching the TV films of the police attack outside the Hilton. There was a strange sort of schizophrenia in the smoky air: while the majority of the delegates behaved like Legionnaires at a stag party, vocalizing their anticipation, smacking lips, shouting slogans, pounding backs, the minority, tight-lipped with shock and dread, were riveted to the violence on the picture screens.

The majority tried to override the minority by sheer numbers and noise, but didn't succeed. A delegate from Wisconsin, a McCarthy man named Peterson, got hold of a microphone and offered a motion that the convention be postponed for two weeks and reconvened in another city to escape the intimidating violence that surrounded the hall. Mayor Daley, sitting in the middle of the Illinois delegation, signaled for the majority reaction, an avalanche of boos and catcalls.

The business of nominating the candidates began. Because

convention rules had eliminated demonstrations, it was a strangely stiff and perfunctory proceeding—until Ribicoff of Connecticut rose to nominate George McGovern. A slight, gray-haired man with a monotonous voice, speaking for a Johnny-Come-Lately candidate with no chance of success, Ribicoff began a speech that seemed valuable only because it allowed the delegates an opportunity to exchange opinions with their neighbors.

Then gradually the words of the speaker filtered into the consciousness of the crowd: "With George McGovern as President of the United States, we wouldn't have these Gestapo tactics in the streets of Chicago! With George McGovern we wouldn't have the National Guard!"

When Mayor Daley realized the meaning of the words he had just heard, his face turned as red as a first-degree burn. He rose from his chair, trembling with rage. Shaking his fist at the man on the platform, he shouted, "Fuck you, you Jew son-of-a-bitch! You mother-fucker, go home!"

Ribicoff looked down on the enraged machine boss, and his lips turned in a half smile. He leaned close to the microphone and said in a gentle voice, "How hard it is to accept the truth."

There were more speeches, and then the balloting. To no one's surprise, Hubert Humphrey received more than 1700 votes on the first ballot.

Those in the hall who felt there was something to cheer about cheered.

As most of the delegates left to go back to their hotel rooms, or get drunk, or get laid, the peace people caucused. Paul O'Dwyer of New York acted as chairman of a group that included more than 500 delegates from New York, California, Wisconsin, Minnesota, and North Dakota. Their first plan was to march to the Conrad Hilton, by way of Mayor Daley's home in the South Side white enclave of Bridgeport. When it was pointed out to them that this was a hike of five miles, much of it through some of the most dangerous streets in the black

ghetto, cooler heads prevailed and the delegates returned downtown by bus instead.

It was after 1:00 in the morning when the first peace delegates arrived at the corner of Randolph and Michigan, where
they had agreed to meet. It was nearly 3:00 before all were
present and ready to march.

Then they lighted candles, which they carried in Pepsi-Cola
cups, and began their quiet progress south to the hotel. It was
an eerie sight. They walked four abreast down the deserted
street, faces splashed by candlelight, singing protest songs from
the Depression. Theodore Bikel led them, and Arthur Miller
and Jules Feiffer, Richard Goodwin, and Donald Peterson sang
along.

Fred Moler was ready to go off duty. He was standing at the
corner of Michigan and Balbo when the delegates got there. He
had been in uniform for fourteen hours, and he had a headache,
and his eyes burned, and his mouth tasted as though his breath
smelled bad. He watched dully as the column of marchers
came to a stop across the street, each with his own tiny flame
shielded from the soft lake breeze. He heard the commander
ask politely, "What do you want to do, gentlemen?" and one of
the delegates answer, "We want to walk past the demonstrators."

What do they want to do that for? Moler asked himself
numbly. He no longer expected to find answers to the questions
that deviled him, but the questions kept coming anyway, as
though his mind were a machine with a broken off button.
*These people are big shots—are they on the same side as them
hippies? Don't they know the kind of people they are?* He
shook his head and opened and closed his big, capable hands,
as if squeezing an invisible ball in each palm.

The candlelight procession moved slowly into Grant Park,
filing between the ranks of the National Guard and the seated
demonstrators on the grass. "The delegates are here!" cried

voices deeper in the park, and there were cheers and shouts of solidarity.

Moler waited on the opposite curb, unwilling to leave the scene and unable to understand why. He watched as the delegates mixed with hippies and Yippies and SDS-ers and freaks and straights and plain ordinary people, joining them to sing "Where Have All the Flowers Gone?" and "Ain't Going To Study War No More." He was still watching when one of the demonstration leaders called through his bullhorn, "You people in the hotel—you people watching from the windows—are you with us? If you are, then blink your lights! If you support us, then blink your lights when I tell you—because the whole world's watching! Now!"

For a moment nothing happened, and then a great sigh rose from the park. Moler turned his head and looked up at the hotel behind him—the hotel that he and his fellow officers had, he believed, protected from the ravages of the mob.

Across the massive face of the building windows lit up, darkened, lit up again. Hundreds of windows. From a mile or two out in the lake, they twinkled like stars.

Why did they do that? Moler asked himself. *Don't they know all we've been through trying to help them?* He lowered his eyes from the blinking lights above him and began to walk slowly along Balbo Drive toward Wabash.

20

DEEP RIVER

WEDNESDAY NIGHT the fever broke; on Thursday and Friday the patient still groaned and shivered and sweated, but the sickness had passed its peak. By the weekend, Chicago had awakened in a welter of damp sheets to wonder what had really happened during the days of delirium.

Sheldon Schram, Sari's father, arrived from New York to accompany his daughter home. He was a good-looking man with a deeply tanned, mobile face and beautifully cut clothes. Ted met him at Michael Reese Hospital, and they had a cup of coffee together in the cafeteria.

"I think I understand something about it," Schram said, in an I-want-us-to-reach-each-other tone. "It's the Existentialist Moment of Decision, isn't it—the idea that the only way to give meaning to one's life in a meaningless world is to take action, even though the action is foredoomed to failure. Yes, I can understand that. In a sense, that's what theater is, isn't it? Or all the arts, for that matter—the attempt of the artist to take action against the meaninglessness of a chaotic cosmos. Don't you agree?"

Ted stirred his coffee a moment before he answered, tonelessly: "I think what we wanted was to stop the war."

"Yes, of course that's true in one sense—but above and beyond that, don't you feel that you kids were making a statement about your lives in a materialist society? Weren't you, in a very real way, calling for a return to humanistic cultural values, in a world where free men and women could fulfill their individual potentialities? I'm sure there was a good deal of that involved."

Ted looked at the handsome, sincere, manipulative face before him and could only nod politely and say, "Yes, sir."

Ted stayed in Chicago until Sari was released from the hospital and then drove out to the airport with her and her father. Sheldon went to a cocktail lounge to give them a few minutes together. Sari's face was more than half covered with bandages, and she moved her mouth stiffly when she talked—probably she always would, to a degree. Ted took her hand, but she didn't respond, and after a little while he released it.

"Sari," he said quietly, "what do you want to do now?"

Her eyes were free to express emotion, and they sparkled with anger. "Fight . . . them," she said. "Beat . . . them. Wipe them . . . out."

Not because he thought it would do any good, but simply because he didn't feel he had any option, Ted tried to argue with her. Violence begets violence, he said; the beginning of peace is the refusal to commit war; you can't beget life upon the body of death. Nothing he said made any difference. She stared out at the great silver jets taking off and landing outside the window, her chin raised and her hands clenched in her lap. Ted shook his head sadly. "It doesn't have to be this way," he said. "There are other ways."

Sari answered with a line from a song they both liked— Bob Dylan's "Subterranean Homesick Blues." "You . . . don't need . . . a weatherman . . ." she said stiffly, "to know which way . . . the wind blows."

They were words Ted would remember often in the months to come.

Sheldon Schram returned from the cocktail lounge, their plane began loading, and Sari rose to leave. Ted stood up to say goodbye. "Take care, Sari. See you soon." They both knew he wouldn't.

"Goodbye," Sari answered. Her eyes were suddenly blurred

with tears, and she turned and walked quickly through the loading gate. Outside, she took her father's arm, and the two tall, slim figures walked side by side to the gangway of the plane.

On Sunday and Monday and Tuesday after Convention Week, the young people left Chicago for home. Some went in their own or a friend's car, and a few by plane or bus, but the majority hitchhiked. Along the Interstates, along 66 and 80 to California, and 65 to Nashville and New Orleans, and the Indiana Tollway east, along superhighways and state blacktops and gravel county roads, they spread out from Chicago like cracks in the broken window of a police car.

Whatever the message of Convention Week was, they took it across the country with them.

Whatever the significance of what they had done, they felt pride in the way they had done it.

Thursday Mal Tolliver went back to work, smiled at everybody, fielded questions, kept his cool, and turned in a respectable amount of work. It was what he and Helen had decided he should do. After work he went home to Evanston, which was also what he and Helen had decided he should do. Marilyn looked at him with injured bitterness and hardly spoke until dinner was finished and Lisa was in bed. When she came downstairs, Mal had brought their coffee into the living room. "Sit down, Marilyn. We've got to have a talk," he said.

She picked up her cup and drank from it; her hand shook, spilling coffee into her saucer. "The only thing we have to talk about is, did you get it out of your system?" she said with an attempt at flippancy.

"Did I get what out of my system?"

"The romance—the revolution—the screwing," she said with a bright smile. "Oh, I'm not so naive as to believe you spent three nights sleeping at an old buddy's apartment. That's not what romantic figures like you do. Romantic figures like you screw their silly heads off, don't they?" Her voice began to rise, out of control: "Don't they, you selfish, immoral, irresponsible son-of-a-bitch?"

"Marilyn, shut up! I've got something important to talk to you about."

"Why don't you deny it? Why don't you say the thought never crossed your mind? Oh, no, you're not that kind of man, are you?"

"Marilyn, I want to quit the advertising business. I want to do something else."

"You're—you *what*?" She was so unprepared for his words it took her a moment to switch subjects. "What are you talking about, Mal? You mean, leave Pauncefoot Associates? Why would you want to do that? They love you there!"

"Look, Marilyn, I know we've been having a communication problem lately, so let's try to communicate better this time. Listen to me, and try to understand what I'm saying. I *want* to stay with you and Lisa." He spoke deliberately, letting the significance of his words emerge. "I *want* to keep our home together—here, if we can afford it, but, anyway, somewhere. My family is valuable to me, and I *want* to hold on to it—if I can."

"Mal, what do you mean?" she asked in a tight voice. "That you'd be willing to—"

"What I mean is what I've just said," he interrupted.

"I—see." She digested the information. "Then there really was a woman, wasn't there?" She gave a hard little laugh. "I wasn't sure—I actually thought that maybe the reason you stayed away was to call policemen dirty names in the park."

"What was important was what happened in the park—I never lied to you about that."

"Yes, well, that's something. That certainly is something. Who is the bitch—some Near North groupie you picked up at Butch McGuire's? Or some drug addict with dirty underwear who wants to change the world? Was it good? Did she really make you feel like a swinger? Was she inventive? You can tell me, Mal—we can communicate on this!"

Mal spoke carefully, with little or no emotion. He said he was willing to move out of the house that night, if Marilyn wanted him to, but that he would prefer to remain at home. If he stayed, he would work to fulfill the roles of husband and father satisfactorily, and in good faith. However, Marilyn had to accept the fact that he was leaving the agency and the advertising business. Unless she was prepared to join him in the search for a new and no doubt less remunerative career, they might just as well pack it up now.

Marilyn didn't mention other women again. She asked questions and made suggestions with crisp, impersonal competence. When did Mal want to give notice? How much did he have in company stock and profit sharing, and when would he get it? What about the two weeks' paid vacation they had coming? Did he think she should plan to get a job? What about their hospitalization?

After a few minutes Mal made them each a drink, and they talked about what he wanted to do. With his stock and profit-sharing money he might buy into a business—maybe a bookstore? or make a film, or pay the bills for a year if he wanted to write a book. They might move someplace cheaper, Maine or Montana or Tennessee. They might delay Lisa's school a year, trade the car in on a camper, and just travel a while.

Marilyn replenished their drinks, handed Mal his, and stood in the archway, clinking her ice cubes and studying the furniture in the room. *She's a good-looking woman; she should model ski clothes,* Mal thought without interest. Noticing the two little worry lines between her eyes, he added: *She better watch that frowning, though.*

"I guess this is a dumb question, Mal, but—what's so wrong with all this?" she asked. "What's so wrong with the job, and the way we live, and—me?"

He didn't answer, and after a moment she turned away and straightened a picture on the wall. "When are you going to tell them at the office?"

"I guess tomorrow. Fridays are good days for quitting or being fired."

They went to bed early. As soon as he switched the bedside lamp off, Marilyn's arms wrapped around his neck and her mouth pressed against his. Her movements were sudden and rough, and her lips were hot. When her hand told her he was ready, she mounted him, pinning his shoulders against the mattress, her head and torso silhouetted in moonlight above him. Afterward she curled up on her side of the bed, and he heard her crying quietly to herself. Finally she went to sleep.

He found quitting an exhilarating and upsetting experience. He arranged a lunch with the copywriters and art directors he liked best and made a formal announcement of his intentions. It was met with a mixture of awe, approval, and skepticism, and was debated over a number of rounds of drinks. Mal was the last to leave the table. As he watched the others make their way across the restaurant toward the door, speaking to acquaintances at other tables and talking shop to one another, he thought with an unexpected chill, *Now they're going back to work, and already they're beginning to forget me. This lunch was an amusing episode to them—to me, it was saying goodbye to something whose importance I can't begin to estimate.* He pushed back his chair and rose. *The wind of freedom has a cold edge.*

He was delighted to be able to give the news to Loren Price in the men's room. Sitting in his favorite cubicle with a copy of *The New Yorker* in his lap, he saw the familiar saddle shoes with the red rubber soles enter the room and approach the urinal. "Hey, Loren," he called, "stick your hand under here."

"What? Who's that? Is that you, Mal?"

"Wipe your hand off and stick it under the door," Mal repeated. "I want to shake it goodbye." Goodbye? Loren asked, what did he mean, goodbye? Where was he going? Mal explained that he was leaving the ad biz, and asked him again to put his hand under the door.

"Look, Mal, come by my office when you're finished, okay? I want to talk to you." The shoes began tentative steps toward the washroom door.

"I don't know if I'll be able to do that, Loren. I may have to leave without seeing you again. So put your hand under the door."

Loren giggled in embarrassment. "I don't want to shake hands goodbye in the crapper," he said. "It seems, I don't know, crude." For answer, Mal slowly extended his arm under the door of the cubicle. "Loren," he said, "this is where we've spent our finest hours. Shake, old friend." For a moment nothing happened, then Loren's hand took his in an uncertain grip. Mal immediately grasped the proffered hand firmly in both of his and drew it toward him under the door. "Loren, you've been a good friend, and I want you to know I appreciate it. I'll try to make sure you get a really good widow cutter assigned to take my place on Clutter's Candies." Loren tried to disengage his hand, but Mal held on tightly. "I mean a real widow *surgeon*, not your run-of-the-mill widow butcher that chops nouns and verbs indiscriminately. I mean a craftsman who could remove thirty-six characters from a Shakespearean sonnet without the Bard himself realizing they were gone." The washroom door opened to admit a new arrival, and Loren began tugging against Mal's two-handed grip. "I think Mr. Clutter deserves that kind of dedicated professionalism," Mal continued warmly. "After all, the old nincompoop is a Giant of American Industry."

"LEGGO MY HAND!" Loren yelped. Mal released it so suddenly the red rubber-soled shoes stumbled backward a step before their owner regained his balance. "Jesus, Mal, what are you trying to do, pull me into the damn stall with you?"

"I guess I'm just a sentimental slob," Mal said apologetically.

"Take care, Loren—I'll stop by your office if I get a chance." Watching the saddle shoes leave the washroom, he thought, *I'm even going to miss old Loren—who would have thought it?*

When he told Toby Tobin his news, the assistant account executive looked at him with shrewdly appraising eyes. "Big cweative man fa' down, go boom," he said dryly. "I thought you were digging the Big Picture a bit much when you started singing darky folk songs in the conference room."

"Well, look at it this way, Toby. Think of all the knife work I'm saving you."

"True, true. But I was counting on you for the practice. I figured you for my on-the-job training." They smiled at each other, each enjoying the feeling of naked candor that existed for the first time between them. "You know, Mal, you were never quite the right man for this business. You kept moving fast, so nobody got a long enough look at you to realize it. But you were starting to slow down. It would just have been a matter of time."

"You're right. But of course it's just a matter of time with all of us, isn't it? I slow down at thirty-six, you slow down at fifty. What do you suppose you'll find to do when they get a good look at you at fifty, Toby?"

"If you've got your name on the door by then, you don't have to worry. I intend to have my name on the door." He smiled ingenuously; his full jowls gave his otherwise thin face an unformed, boyish look. "The main thing is to want it enough, and I do."

"For your sake, I hope you keep on wanting it, because I don't think you'll ever find anything else to want." Mal glanced at his watch. "Excuse me, old buddy, but I've got a lot of other people to talk to before five." He moved toward the door without shaking hands. "See you around," he said coolly.

"You know, Mal, I'm glad you screwed yourself up," Tobin said seriously. "I'm not sure I could have done it to you by myself."

Mal grinned back at him. "Flatterer—of course you could!"

Pauncefoot was out of town, so Mal wrote him a brief letter of resignation and left it with his secretary. He threw in a couple of complimentary phrases like "the opportunity to work with one of the great advertising men in America" and "your professional leadership and personal generosity." Unlikely as it seemed now, he might have to use his ex-boss for a reference some day, and there was no point in poisoning the last well as he headed into the desert.

From Pauncefoot's office he went to the comptroller's to make arrangements for collecting his paycheck and the other monies to which he was entitled. As he had expected, the comptroller refused his demand for vacation pay. His company stock and profit-sharing amounted to better than $14,000 and would be paid to him over a thirteen-month period, the first $10,000 within thirty days, the balance twelve months later. The checks, plus his final salary check, would be mailed to his home. The comptroller explained all this with frequent wary glances at him, as if to guard against the possibility of irrational and perhaps violent behavior.

Because he planned to come into the office as often as necessary the next week to brief his successors on his accounts, he didn't bother to empty his desk. He did, however, sort through his middle drawer and remove his collection of puzzles, which consisted of three paperback books with titles like *Do You Dare to Solve This?* and a half-dozen mimeographed sheets of paper, each bearing one puzzle and its solution. The Great Triangular Duel puzzle was there, together with one about the interrelationships of nine baseball players and their families, another about a number of different nationals and their pets ("The Latvian lives next door to the yellow house and owns a zebra"), and a third bearing an abbreviated version of Euler's classic poser about the Seven Bridges of Königsberg.

If these bastards had any idea of how many hours of their time I spent on these puzzles, Mal thought fondly, *they would never trust a writer again.*

He left a little before 5:00, so he wouldn't have to share the elevator with other Pauncefoot employees bubbling over with Thank-God-it's-Friday spirit. Ignoring the temptation to stop at the Wrigley Bar, he walked along Michigan Avenue, heading for the el. The nervous energy that had sustained him during the day had evaporated. He was edgy and depressed. He either wanted to see Helen Haggarty or get drunk, or both. Instead, he headed for home. He had promised Helen he would try to hold his marriage together, and he was determined to keep his word. He didn't expect it to be possible, because he didn't think Marilyn would follow him on a course that would almost certainly lead him away from suburban affluence —but he would give it the old college try.

Nobody can expect more of me than that, he thought. What he meant was, Helen can't expect more of me than that.

The strike at the cinéma vérité was settled the Monday after Convention Week, and Mike Rogoff offered the theater for a meeting of Concerned Citizens. Dagmar Correlli worked enthusiastically generating publicity for the meeting, phoning newspaper columnists, liberal lawyers and clergymen, labor leaders and spokesmen of radical groups, administrators and faculty members of the city's colleges, and the owners of Old Town saloons. Rogoff watched her as she sat at his desk with the telephone to her ear, her unconvincing blond hair gathered in a ponytail, her dark eyes gleaming like wet black olives, her high, pointed breasts barely touching their tips to the loose-fitting Marine Corps shirt. "Listen, the only question is, are we a society of laws, or a society of police?" she snapped into the mouthpiece. "There are some of us who think the time has come to answer the question, Doctor!" Watching her, Rogoff's mouth twisted in a half smile of amusement and admiration. *My little shiksa—now all that energy is with me, instead of against me. Maybe I was better off before.*

The first meeting of the Concerned Citizens was a great success. Officers were elected, resolutions passed, committees formed, and the first signs of the inevitable struggle for control of the organization appeared. More meetings followed at weekly intervals. Ranking police officers and aldermen were interviewed. The corresponding secretary contacted other aroused groups in the city, ranging from the Independent Voters of Illinois to the street gangs of the North Side, and representatives of all the groups visited one another. The formation of a new political party was debated—necessarily referred to as the Fourth Party, since Governor Wallace had pre-empted the title of Third Party for his following. Whether or not anything of importance was happening, there was an impression of progress.

One evening in early October Mike Rogoff went to Mister Dooley's. The juke box was playing "The Rising of the Moon" as he entered, and tobacco smoke obscured the Irish-American politicians smiling down from the walls in intense and static bonhomie. He sat down on an empty stool and ordered a glass of draft beer. As he raised it to his lips, the man sitting to his left grinned and said, "Hey, the last time I saw you, the busies were climbing over benches in Grant Park to get a piece of you. I trust they didn't succeed."

Mike saw a thin-faced man with a long nose, a full and shaggy mustache, and hair that curled over his collar. The face was familiar, and in a moment Mike placed it. "Hey, yeah, Grant Park, in front of the band shell!" He extended his hand. "It's good to see you. The name's Mike Rogoff, in case you've forgotten."

"I hadn't, believe it or not. I'm Mal Tolliver." They shook hands warmly. "Say, I'm glad to run into you like this. I've wondered what happened to you after we got separated that day."

Rogoff offered a brief account of his experiences in front of the Hilton, and Mal replied with a description of some of the sights he had seen in the Loop during his search for Helen. As they listened to each other's stories, they felt the muscles in their bellies tighten again.

Mal ordered two more beers. "You know, hearing you talk about it, I feel the same outrage I felt when it was happening. I mean the *same*—not a watered-down version, like a memory that's halfway to being forgotten. And I've got a hunch that five years from now I'll still feel it the same. I don't think it's going to go away—I think it's going to sit smack in the middle of my consciousness till the day I die. You think that's possible?"

Rogoff frowned thoughtfully. "Yes, it's possible. In my life I've seen a couple of things like that, things that won't ever go away. The Depression was one. For poor people, it's like it happened last night. Afterward they may have gotten good jobs and sent their kids to college, but the sore's still there, it never scabs over; because once they were treated like they were less than human, and there wasn't a thing they could do about it." He turned to look at Mal, and his voice hardened. "Maybe the reason it stays fresh in your mind is because you can never forgive yourself for letting somebody treat you that way. Maybe the sore in your memory is a vaccination, to keep you from ever letting it happen again!"

"You think Convention Week will be like that? You think it will influence the country politically, the way the Depression did?"

"Politically?" Rogoff shrugged. "Who knows? A Fourth Party? Don't hold your breath. A takeover of the Democratic Party? I doubt it, but even if it happened, there would be more people using the exits than the entrances. Even the end of the stupid war is too much to expect." He gestured to the blowup of Mayor Curley of Boston. "Too many pols like him in both parties, with their noses in the trough."

"Then I don't get you," Mal said. "If the influence isn't political, what is it? The influence of the Depression was political, wasn't it?"

"Certainly not! It was personal! Fifty million people made a personal decision—they decided that there were certain ways people should not be treated. That no one was going to treat them that way again, and that they were not going to treat anybody else that way either. With most of them, it was a subconscious decision, which is why it wasn't political. They didn't make a judgment that capitalism had failed them, or even that the two-party system was a fake. They just went back to work as soon as they could get jobs, and voted the same way they always had. But because of what had happened to them, this country stopped believing that every American could be a success if he worked hard, that poor people were poor because they were lazy. And that, my friend, was the biggest change since Lincoln freed the slaves!"

Mal sipped his beer ruminatively. The record playing on the juke box ended and was succeeded by another that sounded much the same. "And you're saying that people may make another personal decision about what happened here, right? A decision that the Establishment shouldn't have the power to use its police to suppress dissent? And that police brutality is too high a price to pay for law and order?" Rogoff nodded, and Mal continued earnestly: "Okay—but answer me this. There were fifty million people making their decision during the Depression, and here we're talking about maybe ten thousand. That's a hell of a discrepancy."

Rogoff grinned sardonically. "Didn't you say you were in advertising? You should know that the next biggest thing to fifty million people is ten thousand people in prime time on a coast-to-coast network! Take your discrepancy and shove it at Marshall McLuhan!"

" 'The whole world's watching,' " quoted Mal softly. "That was the important thing. Nobody can ever brush it under the rug now."

"Hey, you're out of beer." Rogoff signaled for two steins and put more money on the bar. They drank companionably for the next hour, talking mostly about Convention Week and how it had affected them. The ex-Communist told anecdotes about the Concerned Citizens who met at his theater, and Mal described the film he was making with a friend, an animator. "It's about the Week, naturally—but I think we've got something really different going. It's a combination of film footage, stills, animation, and abstract art. The guy I'm working with is one of the top animators in the Midwest, and we've got a really good designer moonlighting with us, and a composer who's tired of writing jingles for Clutter's Candies. It's going to be gangbusters on the film festival circuit."

"Let me see it when you've got it cut. If it's any good, I'll book it for the cinéma vérité."

"Right." Mal glanced at his watch. "Say, man, I've got to split. It's been a blast, but I've got a lot of work to do tomorrow."

"You have an el ride out to Evanston before you can turn in? I don't envy you."

"No, just a two-block walk. I don't live in Evanston anymore. I rented a pad on Willow Street last week. Take care, Mike." He raised two fingers in the peace sign, grinned, and walked briskly out of the saloon.

A few minutes later two women came through the swinging doors. One of them was Robin Goodpasture. The other was a good-looking brunette in her early forties, a divorcée named Lois Samuels, who worked in Goody's office. They had been to the movies together, and Goody, celebrating her first day in two months without a brace on her neck, had persuaded her friend to join her for a beer at Mister Dooley's.

"Rogoff!" shouted Goody, adding her usual impolite question and pushing her way through the crowded room to join him at the bar. "This is my friend Lois, and I told her you were going to buy us a drink, thereby proving yourself to be as generous as you are handsome, so don't make a liar out of me."

Rogoff looked past Goody's impudent features to the woman beside her. He saw dark eyes that had seen much and enjoyed most of what they saw, a high-arched nose that suggested discrimination, and a full-lipped mouth that anticipated enjoyment. The dark eyes held his own so firmly it took him a moment to free his gaze to move down her full-breasted torso and slender legs to her small, graceful feet. He took a deep breath and raised his eyes to her face again. "Hello. My instinct tells me you are a brandy and soda kind of lady. May I buy you a brandy and soda?"

"I'd love one," she said. Her voice was low, and Rogoff could barely hear it over the juke box and the sudden singing in his ears.

"I'll have a beer, in case anybody gives a shit," Goody said defiantly.

Two weeks after the convention ended, Fred Moler and Charlie Horine ceased to be partners. It was Moler's idea. He found he was unable to get the image of the woman in the pink dress out of his mind; at night, before he fell asleep, he watched her somersaulting over the iron railing, and heard the wet-meat slap of her body hitting the pavement below; often, during the day, he would glance at Horine's face beside him in the squad car and remember his partner's look of hot-eyed satisfaction as he punched her backward across the sidewalk. He didn't know why this one episode of Convention Week bothered him more than any other, but it did, so much so that he often found it difficult to make conversation in the car. Horine noticed Moler's uncharacteristic reticence and tried to find out the reason. Moler wouldn't tell him, and their relationship became strained, moving from irritability toward active hostility.

"You got something eating on you, why don't you ask to be reassigned? It ain't going to break my heart, you can bet your ass on that!" Horine said harshly one day, and Moler did. Moler was teamed with a Pole named Wyzykowsky, a heavy, baldheaded man whose tongue was usually black from eating licorice candy; Horine drew a rookie named Gebhart, a randy kid who made comments about all the girls they passed and didn't like taking advice from his partner.

One evening about two weeks after Horine and Gebhart began working together, they were driving down Wilson Avenue when Horine spotted an old Buick with one taillight out. He flicked on his flasher and signaled the car to the curb, pulling up behind it. Gebhart climbed out and sauntered between the cars to the driver's window of the Buick. Inside, there were two people: the driver, a male Caucasian in his early twenties, pale, slack-lipped, and high as the top of the John Hancock building, and the driver's girl friend, an over-developed teen-ager in a peekaboo sweater with nothing under it. When he demanded the driver's license, Gebhart had both hands on the window and his eyes riveted to the girl's dark nipples. The driver reached into his pocket and produced a cheap snub-nosed .32 pistol, with which he shot Gebhart through the right eye, killing him instantly. The Buick leaped forward, and a second later Horine followed it, his wheels barely missing Gebhart's body on the pavement.

The chase was short. The Buick turned right at the first two corners and then entered an alley. Halfway to the next street the driver braked the car to a screeching halt, and he and the girl jumped out and disappeared into an open areaway between two buildings. Horine was close behind them, his pistol in his hand.

Twenty feet from the alley the areaway was blocked by a locked gate. It was seven feet tall, and the fugitives were climbing over, using a trash can for a ladder. They were barely visible against the mottled luminescense of the city night. "Stop!" shouted Horine, and fired a warning shot above their heads. The man, who was on top of the gate trying to pull his companion up beside him, released her and began firing his pistol at Horine. She sprawled backward over the trash can, and one of her arms struck Horine's pistol, deflecting his aim. In the wasted half-second before he could bring his gun to bear again, a bullet struck him in the lower abdomen. As he stumbled and began to fall, another bullet entered his chest over the heart.

He died in the ambulance twenty minutes later. The two fugitives were apprehended, and the old Buick proved to have approximately $225 worth of stolen appliances in the trunk.

Fred Moler was off duty when he heard about it. He was bowling at the Playdium, only a few blocks from the scene of the shooting. One of the other players returned from the lounge with the news. "Jesus, Fred, your old partner Charlie Horine got gunned down in an alley! Him and the new guy with him, Gebhart, some crazy junkie got them both!"

"Charlie? Charlie got killed?" Moler had been concentrating on picking up a four-ten split, and it took him a moment to grasp the meaning of the words. When he did, he stood with his bowling ball cradled in his arms, listening to the excited conversation around him. He didn't say anything until he had absorbed all the information that was available. Then he looked at Wyzykowsky and said somberly, "Maybe if I'd been with him instead of that rookie, he wouldn't have got killed." Wyzykowsky told him that was a hell of a thing to say. "No, no, Walt—we never had no trouble when we were in the car together. We always took care of things, no matter what came up. We were real good together." He put the ball down and rubbed his hands on the chalk and then on the towel. "It was me that got us split up, Walt. I asked to be reassigned. Charlie didn't want another partner—it was all my idea. Charlie would have been happy to keep on going just like we always did."

"Say, listen, Fred, you don't want to play no more, do you? Come on into the lounge and I'll buy you a drink."

"No, I don't want to play anymore." Moler didn't speak again until the two men were seated in a booth in the cocktail lounge and he had an unaccustomed double shot of whiskey in front of him. He raised the glass to his lips and drank half of it, then set it down on the table with a resolute rap. "You know what I'm going to do, Walt?"

"No, Fred, what are you going to do?"

Moler hunched his shoulders under his yellow silk bowling shirt and leaned forward purposefully. "I'm going to get out of police work. I'm going to write my stepbrother Emil and see if I can get Into Plastics."

From the bowling lanes outside the lounge, the roar of falling pins sounded like surf breaking on the beautiful beaches of Chicago.

AUTHOR'S NOTE

BECAUSE *Rivers Run Together* is a historical novel, the reader has a right to know the sources upon which it is based.

The primary source is my own experience in Lincoln and Grant parks during Convention Week. Although my attendance was spotty, and I managed to miss many of the most dramatic events, I saw enough to form the emotional and factual foundation of this book.

Published material which has proved of particular value includes *Rights In Conflict* (The Walker Report); John Schultz's *No One Was Killed*; Norman Mailer's *Miami and the Siege of Chicago*; the Illinois ACLU's *Law & Disorder*; and articles in *Time, Newsweek, Village Voice*, and the Underground Press. I'm grateful to Al Morgan's *The Whole World Is Watching* for a lip reader's translation of Mayor Daley's remarks to Senator Ribicoff.

Although *Rights In Conflict* must serve as the indispensable publication for anyone studying the subject, it has one serious flaw: its conclusion that the battle at the Conrad Hilton resulted from a "police riot"—that policemen, maddened by the provocation of the demonstrators, lost their heads and disobeyed their superiors. John Schultz is on surer ground when he says, in *No One Was Killed*, "There was no breakdown in police discipline during Convention Week . . . Police discipline, on its own terms, was superb. If the order was to club and maim, they clubbed and maimed, if the order was to keep the clubs sheathed, they kept the clubs sheathed." Few newspapermen covering the story believed the police did anything that was not expected of them by those in authority.

As I write this, five years after Convention Week, I am still unsure in my own mind how important these events are in recent American history. My instinct tells me the 1968 Democratic Convention was a watershed—that down its slope trickled the nomination of Humphrey and the election of Nixon, the madness of Weathermen and the paranoia of Watergate, the Cambodian incursion and the horror of Kent State, and the abandonment of George McGovern by the independent voters and the professionals of his own party. My instinct tells me this, even though I can't prove it.

But there must be some reason the sore won't scab over.

                                                              J. S.